THE DUKE'S WIFE

THE THREE MRS BOOK 3

JESS MICHAELS

To Elton, the best little writing companion a girl could have. And to Michael, the template for all my best romance heroes.

CHAPTER 1

Spring 1814

"We should have three matching red dresses made after what we've all been through this last year. That would be one way to thumb our noses at Society," Abigail Montgomery said with a sigh.

She caught the quick glance her two best friends exchanged behind her and she wished she had not said something so jaded. After all, Celeste and Pippa may have endured much similar humiliations over the last year, but they were both happily married now and likely not looking to make the spectacle of themselves that Abigail suddenly wished she could do.

"I think red would be beautiful with your dark hair," Pippa said carefully. "But perhaps a bit much for the first event of the Season after the end of your mourning period."

Abigail rolled her eyes. "Yes, my mourning period."

The year she had been forced to perform the public act of mourning for her husband had been...*interesting* to say the least. Filled with danger and intrigue at the beginning, what with Erasmus's secret marriages to the two very women sharing the chamber with her. There had been all kinds of danger that followed. But the year had also contained joy, for she had forged strong bonds with Celeste and Pippa. She'd watched them both find the greatest happiness in new marriages with men who adored them.

The last year of her life had been filled with loneliness, too, because she knew that a happy, romantic ending was not in the cards for her. She had loved Erasmus once...or thought she had. She'd never pictured anything but a long and successful marriage to him. Until he'd destroyed all of it, piece by tiny piece, chipping away until nothing was left. Long before she discovered he was a bigamist she had stopped feeling anything for the man but disdain. Knowing he felt the same for her.

"Are you well, dearest?" Celeste Gregory asked.

That drew Abigail from her maudlin thoughts, and she forced herself to attend. "Of course I'm well. I'm always well. So, the first event of a new Season. What a thrill. And I'm so glad you invited us to see your new gowns, Pippa. They are beautiful."

She forced a tight smile on her face for her friend. Pippa was the new Countess of Leighton and was nervous about the upcoming events of the Spring. With good reason, for her marriage came with a great deal of scandal thanks to the bigamy and the fact that she'd married their late husband's brother in a glorious, romantic rush.

Pippa was a beautiful woman. With her mop of unruly blond curls and her bright green eyes, she always looked like a slightly wicked angel. Probably why the Earl of Leighton, Rhys, adored her so much. The exterior matched the interior.

"You are certainly going to impress," Abigail mused.

Pippa had been holding up a gown with an elaborately stitched bodice that would cling to her curves just so and a fall of a slighter paler silk that made up the skirt. "I hope so," she sighed. "Appearances mean so much to the ton."

"That green matches your eyes perfectly!" Celeste cooed.

"Rhys picked the fabric," Pippa said with a blush and a happy smile. She had been married to the man just over six months and it seemed there was no dimming of the spark between them. Abigail was very happy for her friend. There were no other, less pleasant emotions that tightened her chest. Not even a one.

"Well, it's as pretty as all the rest," Celeste said, clasping her hands before her. "You will be the belle of any ball."

Pippa's smile faded slightly. "I don't know about that," she said. "I look forward to the first event of the Season. Well, the first event for Rhys and I...but I think it doesn't bode well that we haven't been invited to any others. That we must host our own fete in order to make ourselves known."

Abigail caught Pippa's hands and squeezed gently, her own troubles pushed to the background for a moment. "The way Society views your relationship to Rhys is...complicated."

"I know. Had I been legally married to Erasmus, I never even would have been allowed to marry Rhys."

"Yes," Abigail mused. "Ecclesiastic law does frown upon a woman marrying her dead husband's brother. But you were *not* legally married, so that eliminates that problem."

Pippa shrugged. "Somewhat. But the scandal of Erasmus's bigamy and the fact that I *did* marry his brother and become countess has not lessened all the burden Rhys must bear."

"You relieve his burdens, not add to them," Celeste insisted. "He's said as much to Owen many times. He has never regretted marrying you."

"Nor I him," Pippa said, tears leaping to her eyes. "But I do fear that we will not find acceptance. I am not from his world, not truly, but I can see that it matters to him. It matters how the world sees us, for our sake and for the sake of Kenley and any children we might be happy enough to have together in the future."

Abigail stiffened at the mention of Kenley Montgomery. He was the child Erasmus had sired with yet another woman in his life. The woman who had ultimately murdered him. Pippa and Rhys had taken the little boy in and were raising him as if he were their own. He was a happy, bright child, and Abigail enjoyed seeing him a great deal. Even if he did create yet another reminder of how little her late husband had given a damn about anyone but himself.

"It is very complicated," Abigail said. "And scandalous. But time will soften it. Rhys is well liked and respected by many important people. This Season and even the next may be difficult, but eventually another scandal, perhaps an even more shocking one, will happen and *they* will all shift their ire. Be strong for Rhys and for yourself and know that you are not alone. You have an army of friends and allies behind you."

"That is true." Pippa's face lit up slightly. "Of course you and Owen and Celeste will be there tomorrow. Harriet has agreed to come with Lena, and that will make an enormous splash since anyone who is anyone wants to be a member of their salon."

Abigail shifted. "Have you considered that you might wish to rescind the kind invitation to me?"

Pippa's eyes went wide. "Why would I ever do that?"

"I am the legal wife," she said softly. "If you wish to disconnect your own reputation from Erasmus's, having me there will do nothing to make that happen."

Pippa and Celeste exchanged a glance filled with meaning, and then they both stepped up to her. She was wrapped in their mutual embrace, and for a moment she felt the urge to sag into it. Collapse against them and let them be her strength. Her own, after all, had felt like it was waning for some time.

But she didn't. She had never been the kind to falter or ask for help. So she straightened her shoulders instead and shook her head. "Gracious, I don't know what I've done to deserve such affection."

"Just being you," Pippa said as they both stepped away. "And you are ridiculous if you think I don't want and need you at our party. When we rise, we will rise together. I'll hear nothing more on the subject."

"As you say," Abigail said, and was pleased her voice didn't tremble with the emotions that this unwavering support created in her.

She did adore these two women. If Erasmus had to betray her as he had, at least she was unwaveringly happy in his choices.

"Anyway, those Rhys has invited will create a lot of acceptance," Pippa continued. "I know he's mentioned Lord and Lady Goffard, the Earl of Yarrowood, the Duke of Gilmore, Sir William Livingston—"

Abigail pursed her lips and pivoted to pace to the fireplace. "You tried to gloss over Gilmore, you wicked thing. But of course Rhys is inviting him." She rolled her eyes. "Why in the world would such a good and decent man associate himself with such a...such a...cretin?"

She glanced over her shoulder to see Celeste and Pippa exchanging yet another of those loaded looks. A world of communication flowed between them, and all of it was about Abigail. Her cheeks heated and she hated herself for creating this situation. Hated the Duke of Gilmore even more for it.

Horrible man.

"Gilmore is my husband's best friend—he has been for decades," Pippa said, Abigail thought a little gently.

"He has become one of Owen's, as well," Celeste said softly. "I still don't understand why you hate him so."

Abigail let out a gasp of annoyance. "You don't? I don't understand why all of *you* don't despise him. He inserted himself into the situation with Erasmus—"

"*You* inserted him into the situation when you wrote him that anonymous letter telling him that our horrible shared husband was trying to make Gilmore's sister into wife number four," Pippa interrupted.

Abigail folded her arms. That was true. She had done that, there was no pretending otherwise.

"He...he deserved to know the truth," she said, softer this time. "He deserved a chance to save his sister if he could, and he did. I am happy that he did." She cleared her throat past the sudden lump that had formed there. "However, he doesn't know the letter writer was me, and I never want him to know. The fact remains that instead of just protecting his sister and then staying out of it, he made everything worse. He hired the investigator, he started stirring the pot, and everything came out because of it."

"Everything was going to come out regardless," Celeste said. "And I'm rather happy Gilmore hired *the investigator*, considering I married him."

Abigail bent her head. "I'm making a muck of this. Of course I'm happy Owen came and helped us all and that you two fell in love. I just...Gilmore is an arrogant, frustrating...and he's competitive..."

"You're competitive!" both of her friends said at once, and then laughed.

"I'm competitive in a *good* way," Abigail insisted.

Celeste and Pippa were smothering smiles, and that only made all this worse. Any time she talked about Gilmore, it was worse. After all, when she listed his negative qualities, whether out loud or to herself, she also couldn't help but add that he was handsome. Very handsome. Too handsome. With those broad shoulders and that defined jaw and those dark brown eyes that seemed to pierce a person to their very soul.

Why couldn't he have been less appealing? Then hating him would have somehow been easier.

Pippa shook her head. "I am sorry you feel this way, Abigail. I can only imagine how difficult it is to constantly have to cross paths with someone you dislike so strongly."

Abigail nodded. Though she and Gilmore hadn't crossed paths all that often recently. Not since the intimate gathering to celebrate Pippa and Rhys's wedding months ago. Abigail had been sequestered in her "mourning" and Gilmore had been...

Well, she knew he'd been at his estate in Cornwall over the winter. Far, far away from her.

"Perhaps the best thing you can do is to avoid him," Celeste suggested.

Abigail swallowed. "Yes. I think that will be for the best. Certainly he dislikes me as much as I dislike him, so it will be easy enough to do so."

6

With that subject resolved, at least in their estimation, Pippa and Celeste went back to examining the rest of Pippa's new gowns. But though Abigail still nodded and interjected, her mind now took her to the very unpleasant Duke of Gilmore.

Avoiding him was never easy. For some reason they always stumbled into each other's paths. But it truly was for the best. After all, returning to Society was going to be hard enough. She didn't need Gilmore's interference. She didn't need him besting her in the game they had been playing since the first moment she laid eyes on him.

～

Nathan, Duke of Gilmore, stood at the edge of the dancefloor, observing the sparsely filled ballroom of his best friend, the Earl of Leighton. His lips pressed together and he fought to keep his concern from his face in case Leighton was watching. Making his worries plain wouldn't relieve the ones of his friend.

He tried to shake off the unpleasant thoughts as he looked around at the attendees who were there. Two lower-level squires and their wives, a few untitled gentlemen. His gaze flitted to the farthest corner of the room from him, and thoughts faded.

Abigail Montgomery stood there, off by herself in the corner. She was wearing a pale blue silk gown with three-quarter sleeves done in lace. Her dark hair was pulled back in a simple low chignon and the wisps that had been artfully placed framed an oval-shaped face with high cheekbones, soft lips and brown eyes that could be sharp as a blade.

There was nothing quite so frustrating as being attracted to a woman who wholeheartedly despised you. Not that Nathan enjoyed Abigail's company either. She was beautiful and smart and could be incredibly kind...but she was also a bitter pill and he had no intention of swallowing it.

And yet he somehow found himself moving toward her, as often happened when they were in rooms together. Part of why he had begun angling not to be in those rooms anymore. But tonight he couldn't have refused Leighton even if he'd wanted to. And that left him sidling up to Abigail, her harsh sigh of annoyance ringing in his ears.

"Mrs. Montgomery," he drawled.

Her flinch was barely perceptible, but he noticed it regardless. Not that he blamed her for the reaction. Her married name was a harsh reminder of the feckless man who had given it to her. Destroyed her and a good many others in his wake.

"Gilmore," she said through clenched teeth. "What do you want?"

He choked back a laugh at her directness. Funny how a person could grate and entertain in equal measure. "Why, just your fine company, madam."

She arched a brow at him and shook her head slowly. "Try again."

He shrugged one shoulder. "You are the only person I know even slightly at this gathering beyond our hosts and the Gregorys, and they seem busy at present."

He motioned with his chin and she followed the gesture. Owen and Celeste were by the fire, heads close together. Celeste was smiling at whatever he was saying, the tiniest blush darkening her cheeks. When Nathan glanced at Abigail, her own cheeks had gone pink, as if she knew exactly the words being exchanged between the couple.

He let his glance slide to Leighton and Pippa, and she followed his eyes again. They were also close together, but unlike the Gregorys, their conversation didn't look pleasant. Pippa's cheeks were pale and Rhys frowned as they surveyed the room together.

"She's worried," Abigail said, and Nathan almost didn't recognize her voice. Normally it was sharp with barbs for him, but now it was soft, filled with concern. "And she should be. I know they hoped for better attendance."

He nodded. "Yes."

She pursed her lips. "That is all you have to say? Yes?"

He turned partially toward her. "Is there something more you think I *should* say, Mrs. Montgomery?"

She threw up her hands. "Rhys is supposed to be one of your best friends—"

"He *is* my best friend," he interrupted softly.

She ignored him and continued on as if he hadn't spoken. "—and yet you address his situation as though you are commenting on the weather or the state of the roads. But then what else is there to expect? You do not seem to have emotions, so why would you show them?"

The emotion she claimed he didn't feel rose up inside of him, but he did as he always did, always had, and shoved it down deeper, where it would not control his words or actions. "You think that me moaning about his troubles, gnashing my teeth and wailing in his parlor, will help my friend? I think you're too intelligent a person to truly believe that. You only say it to get a rise out of me, as is your sport."

They stared at each other a moment, too long a moment, and finally she folded her arms, huffed out a breath and broke the eye contact. "Of course it isn't my sport. That implies I think of you, and I assure you that I do not."

"Of course not," he said. "Nor do I think of you."

Her gaze darted to his, and he thought he sensed a hint of disappointment hidden in the deep brown depths. But it couldn't have really been there. Abigail hated him, though he wasn't entirely sure of why that was. She glanced away again, and for a moment they stood silently.

"So what is?" he asked.

She huffed out a breath. "What is what?"

"You said getting a rise out of me isn't your sport, despite your being very good at it. So what *is* your game?"

She arched a brow. "Just because you are always playing a game doesn't mean everyone else is, Your Grace."

He chuckled, and her lips pressed tighter. "Of course I don't think everyone else is. I think *you* are. You and I may not be the best of friends"—she snorted—"but we've been forced into each other's paths off and on for nearly a year now, so I've been compelled to make a study of you."

"I don't like that idea," she said.

He shrugged. "And yet here we are."

"And you think I'm playing games?"

He turned to face her a little more directly and held her gaze. "I think you like games. I think you're clever enough to get bored when you aren't playing one, even if it's only in your head. And I think...no, I *know*, you like to win."

Her gaze narrowed further. "If you think so little of me, then I wonder why you came over here. Was it only to insult me?"

"Why would what I said be an insult?" he asked. "I like to win, too."

"And you are allowed that desire. It is valued in a man. Women are not sometimes given such ability."

He wrinkled his brow and stared down at her. "That is true and, I think, ridiculous. You have the same blood as I do, the same heart as I do."

"And yet mine is supposed to pump with emotion while yours can pound with ambition." She tilted her head. "If you allow me ambition, am I to believe you actually experience emotion, Your Grace?"

He smiled despite the barb. *Because* of the barb, perhaps. "I will own it. Despite all outward appearances."

Her expression softened a moment and then she darted her gaze away, staring back out at the crowd. "I suppose I have been known to make a friendly wager now and again."

He drew back at the admission. "Have you now? Fascinating. I would not have taken you for a gambler. And what kinds of things do you wager on?"

She pursed her lips and then shrugged. "Do you see Lady Blain, Sir Richard's wife?" When Nathan scanned the small group helplessly, she glanced up at him. "The older lady in yellow. With the ridiculous feather in her hair."

He found the subject of her query easily now. An older woman with gray hair that still had streaks of black through it, adorned with the biggest peacock feather he'd ever seen. It flopped forward and back, occasionally flitting into her eyes so she had to whack it back with her hand to see. She clung to the arm of an even more ancient gentleman, who Nathan assumed was Sir Richard.

"Yes, what about her?"

"If I were to make a wager tonight, it would be during what course Lady Blain will doze off."

He blinked. "You would wager that the woman would fall asleep... at supper. At a table full of...what, fifteen guests?"

She smiled brightly up at him in response, and suddenly his heart beat a bit faster. He knew the expression wasn't exactly true, she felt no warmth toward him, but it hit him in the gut regardless.

"I would wager which course it would happen during," she corrected him. "Are you saying you do not think it would happen at all?"

"I don't see how it could," he muttered.

She folded her arms. "Very well. A pound."

"What?"

She pivoted toward him. "I bet you a pound that she falls asleep after the soup but before the cheese."

"A pound," he repeated, feeling both confused and amused.

She tilted her head. "Too rich for your blood, Your Grace?"

"You are serious."

She gave a small, thin smile. "As the grave."

He extended a hand to her. "Very well, Mrs. Montgomery, I will take that wager. One pound to the winner."

She stared at his hand a moment and then reluctantly took it. He jolted at the electric awareness that shot up his arm when he touched her. It was not something that happened often. In fact, he wasn't certain he had ever touched this woman. Normally she stayed at a fair distance from him.

But now, even through both their gloves, even in this benign way, the fact that she stirred an unexpected and unwanted desire in him was patently clear.

She tugged her hand away and shoved it behind her back. "I look forward to collecting my winnings, Your Grace. Excuse me."

She walked away without waiting for his response and glided off into the crowd toward Owen and Celeste. He watched her go, attracted and dissatisfied all at once, just as he often was when he interacted with her. But he had no time to contemplate it, nor anything else, because the bell was rung and the crowd began to file out toward the dining room and the supper where his fortune would be won...or lost on the sleepy whim of one Lady Blain.

CHAPTER 2

A bigail was seated at Pippa's right hand at one end of the table, and at the other Gilmore was on the right of Rhys. They could not have been farther apart, a situation she often requested when they were forced into the same space. She ought to have been pleased by it. And yet she found herself stealing gazes down the table at him as the party ate and chatted around her.

Gilmore was often a serious person. When she'd asked him about feeling emotions, she had expected him to brush off the very idea. He certainly didn't show them often. He was everything a good duke should be, after all, and Society did not much value anything but deep consideration and mild reaction, even to the worst situation.

And yet, when he was with Rhys, she saw fleeting glimpses of another side to the man. One she was locked out of because of their cantankerous relationship. Gilmore smiled at Rhys, he laughed at his jokes, he sat and moved with more ease. He looked like a man, not the machine she sometimes believed he must be, hard and cold. No, right now he was warm. Still hard, though. Good God, but the man was well heeled.

It was very unfair.

"Will you re-enter the marriage mart, Mrs. Montgomery?"

Abigail jolted out of her thoughts about her enemy and forced her attention to the woman across from her. The one who had just asked her an incredibly loaded question. She glanced toward Pippa, who had now focused all her attention on her plate.

The questioner was the vicar's wife, Mrs. Smith. She was older than Abigail and had a kind enough face, though it was certainly curious. She sensed that anyone within earshot was leaning a bit closer, desperate to hear her answer. Desperate to take this glimpse into her scandal back out into Society.

"I do not know," she said slowly, carefully modulating her tone so that no emotion crept in. At least she could take *that* cue from Gilmore.

"I suppose it would be difficult after—" Mrs. Smith cut herself off and her eyes dropped.

Abigail shifted in her chair slightly and wished that her cheeks didn't heat so. "Well, I hope that my friends do not judge me by the actions of another person. That we have not fallen that far yet as a society."

There were some murmurs in the affirmative, but no one would look at her. Or at Pippa, or at Celeste down the table.

Abigail suppressed a sigh. She had spoken big words, meant to shame anyone who would reject her or her friends. But the truth was, Abigail knew that society was built on exactly the kind of shunning she had described. That it was her late husband who had been wicked or cruel or foolhardy didn't really matter, *she* was judged for what he'd done as if she were party to it. And she was also judged for not being clever enough to spot his deception.

In that arena, at least, she also judged herself. Not knowing what Erasmus was the moment she saw his face all those years ago...she wondered what it *did* mean about her character.

The others around her had changed the subject and were now blessedly talking about something else. Pippa leaned closer and, beneath the table, gave Abigail's knee a squeeze.

"These are the worst days," she whispered. "It will get better, I believe that."

Abigail smiled at her friend. "You have Rhys and he adores you. What is Society's acceptance when compared to that?"

"On that score, I agree with you." Pippa stared off down the table toward her husband. "And I could be well-pleased with only that man and our family for the rest of my days. But it is important to him to rebuild what his brother destroyed. So I will do everything in my power to create that future for him."

Abigail nodded. "Well, that is true love if ever I heard it."

Pippa smiled and nudged Abigail before she whispered conspiratorially, "Look, Lady Blain has fallen asleep!"

Abigail jerked her gaze down the table and found that Lady Blain's head was lolled to the side against her shoulder, her feather flitting into the face of Reverend Smith. He tried to quietly blow air at the feather and divert it out of his eyes, to no avail.

Abigail and Pippa giggled together before Abigail murmured, "And that's how you win, Gilmore."

"What was that?" Pippa asked.

"Nothing," Abigail said with a smile as she stared down the table at the duke. He must have felt her eyes on him, for he turned toward her and their gazes met. She couldn't hold back a triumphant smile as she nudged her head slightly toward Lady Blain.

He followed her stare and saw Lady Blain's dozing. His mouth dropped open and there was no hiding or mistaking the shock that flowed over his handsome features. Nor the annoyance that followed that he had lost their little bet.

His eyes slowly returned to Abigail and he tilted his head to the side in acknowledgment of her win. The swell of pride she felt in that moment had hardly ever been equaled in her life. As if she had single-handedly slain a dragon.

A really beautiful dragon.

"Are you and Gilmore making eyes at each other?" Pippa whispered, her face lined with shock.

Before Abigail could deny that ridiculous charge, another of the women on their side of the table, Mrs. Quigley, the wife of an industrialist who was working on expanding the rail, leaned forward. "Did I hear someone say Gilmore's name?"

"You did, Mrs. Quigley," Pippa said. "The duke is an old friend of my husband's. Are you and Mr. Quigley acquainted with him?"

Mrs. Quigley waved her hand at her husband down the table. "I'm sure he's pestered the duke for investment money, but no. I am curious because he is a fine catch, isn't he? I know many mamas are interesting in landing him. Including me, truth be told."

"Isn't your daughter just sixteen?" Abigail asked with a shake of her head.

"Our Belinda won't be out for a couple of years, no," Mrs. Quigley said. "But why not plan ahead?"

Abigail pressed her lips together tightly at this ridiculous topic. The very idea that Gilmore would make his match with an eighteen-year-old child was outrageous. What in the world would he have in common with some blinking ingénue who would have no opinions of her own yet? Who had never seen or experienced anything of the world? He would bore of her in twenty seconds. No, he would be much happier with someone who would challenge him. He needed a challenge, pompous prick that he was.

"He *is* most eligible," Lady Blain said, jolting from her supper nap and right in the mix of things again. "I can think of twenty ladies who would cut off their big toe to be his."

"Money, power and looks," Mrs. Quigley sighed. "How could one not aspire to make the connection?"

Abigail somehow kept herself from rolling her eyes and forced herself to stop staring at the duke. Let the debutantes and their mamas have him if they wanted him so badly. She felt nothing about it except pity for the poor lady who would land him, only to find he was a cold fish, indeed.

A short time later, the supper concluded. Rhys had announced that the ladies would join Pippa in the sitting room and the men would go to the billiard room for port. One by one, the couples paired off, strolling together down the hallway to their respective destinations. Abigail looked for a gentleman who could take her, but was surprised, as the last couple made their way out of the room, that Gilmore was standing by, waiting for her.

She pursed her lips as she approached him and took the elbow he offered. "Shouldn't you be first in line? Your rank should make you the leader behind Rhys."

He arched a brow at her. "I am only being a good loser, Abigail. I had to believe you would want to gloat about the wager."

She glanced at him briefly and couldn't smother her smile. "I suppose you must hate that I bested you."

"No, actually," he said with a slight chuckle that made her stomach do the strangest flutter. "I am impressed, despite myself."

She blinked. He sounded...*sincere*. But that couldn't be true. Gilmore disliked her as much as she disliked him. She knew him to be utterly disagreeable when it came to her. So how could she have truly impressed him? And why did that make her chest swell a little? As if she was proud of that questionable feat!

They were almost to the sitting room where the ladies were gathering, and she sighed in relief. This was too odd an interaction and it was best to end it before it got even stranger.

"And here is where we say goodbye, Your Grace," she said, and slid her arm from his. But before she could escape him, he caught her hand and drew her back.

"I have a request," he said, his voice soft in the quiet of the hall, his gaze intent on hers.

She almost stopped breathing. "And what is that?"

"Give a man a chance to win his money back," he said with a slight smile.

She drew her hand away. She should have known this was just about his pride. He didn't like losing to her, even with such a silly wager. And if he was soft with her, it was only to make her agree to give him this second chance.

She shrugged. "How do you propose you do that?"

He shook his head. "I'm not sure yet. May I have time to ponder it and get back to you?"

"As you wish," she said, and then turned her back to him. "Good evening, Your Grace."

"Mrs. Montgomery," he drawled.

She glanced over her shoulder, but he was already heading off down the hall toward the billiard room with the other men. She pursed her lips as she fought not to shiver. The Duke of Gilmore was *not* going to make her shiver. Not tonight.

Not ever.

N athan flexed his hand over and over, shaking it out as he entered the billiard room. He could still feel the pressure of Abigail's fingers against his palm and it was most distracting. There had been a moment there when they were standing close together, when her eyes had held his, when he had only seen her as a beautiful woman, not the ice princess who viewed him at his worst, no matter what he did.

He forced his attention to his surroundings in the hope that it would quiet his stirring thoughts. The other men were already pouring port, setting up a game of billiards on the table and talking loudly. He smiled and joked with a few as he passed farther into the room and found Rhys at the sideboard.

He took the port the earl offered and clinked glasses with his friend as they surveyed the room together quietly. "Is it going as you'd like?"

He knew the answer even before Rhys frowned slightly. "I am happy for those who came tonight, but..." He trailed off and took a drink.

"You invited some of the old gang, I assume?" Nathan asked.

Rhys shrugged one shoulder. "I did. Gottard and his new viscountess, the Earl of Yarrowood, a few of the others. I got no response at all, not to decline nor to accept. The cut direct."

Nathan gripped his glass a little harder as a pulse of rage rippled through him. "Pricks."

"The message is clear, I fear," Rhys said. "And the path back to any kind of acceptance after what Erasmus did to the women...did to our family...did to—to me...it will be long and hard and perhaps not end where I'd like it to."

Nathan clapped him on the arm and squeezed gently. "Don't despair. You aren't alone in this, you know. I'm here, and I will use every bit of influence I have to help."

Rhys smiled at him. "To your detriment, perhaps."

Nathan shook his head. "I don't care."

"Hmmm," Rhys murmured, and took another drink. "I'm going to change this painful subject, if you don't mind."

"To what? The game I'm about to trounce you at?" Nathan laughed.

Rhys glared at him playfully. "No. I want to talk to you about how you and Abigail were talking intently and then you escorted her after supper. Is she no longer your nemesis?"

Nathan rolled his eyes. "If she were my nemesis, I'd have to waste a good deal of time thinking about her."

"Which you don't," Rhys said.

"No."

Rhys finished his drink with a chuckle. "So you say."

Nathan set his own half-finished glass on the sideboard and folded his arms. "I say and I mean it. The woman means nothing to me, and I nothing to her. Tonight we had a conversation and placed a wager, that's all."

"You..." Rhys blinked, confusion clear in his gaze. "You *wagered* with Abigail?"

Now that the words were repeated back to him, Nathan heard how they sounded. Wagering with a lady wasn't exactly done—it made their relationship sound intimate in some way.

"It was a foolish moment. She goaded me into it." He pursed his lips as he hoped Rhys would drop the subject. After all, there was no need to discuss it further. He certainly didn't want his friend to know that he had asked Abigail to extend the wager before he parted ways with her in the hallway.

The earl looked to have no desire to change the subject, though. He arched a brow and drew a breath to say more, but before he could, one of the men at the billiard table called out, "Gilmore ought to show us!"

Nathan turned toward the table. It was Sir Richard who spoke. and he was holding out the cue toward Nathan. "Show you what?" Nathan asked with a half-smile.

"You're the one with all the trick shots," Sir Richard clarified. "Come now, show us."

Nathan moved toward them with a laugh. What a relief to escape the subject of Abigail. Rhys was clearly reading far too much into the conversation. A break from it was best.

Besides, he did enjoy showing off his skills at billiards. He'd spent a great many hours as a young man learning all manner of tricks. He took the cue and leaned over the table to see the alignment of the balls and measure out what he would do.

And he smiled. Abigail had used her superior knowledge of the situation tonight to win their wager. Since he would name the terms for their next bet, why shouldn't he take the same opportunity?

"Are you going to shoot it or stare at it all evening?" one of the other men in the small group asked, and elicited a laugh from the others.

"Oh, don't worry," Nathan said. "I know exactly what I'm going to do."

Win. He was going to win against Abigail. And it didn't mean a damned thing, no matter how many times Rhys arched an eyebrow about it.

CHAPTER 3

Abigail smiled as her carriage pulled up to the little blue house Owen and Celeste lived in near Pettyfort Park. She was so looking forward to this afternoon. Celeste had promised a small gathering, just friends. Abigail knew Rhys and Pippa would be there. She was also excited to learn that Pippa had invited her former governess, Harriet, and her paramour, Lena Bright. The two women owned the most popular salon in London, Lady Lena's. Abigail had met them before, of course, but she hoped to get to know the pair better. Perhaps even angle to garner herself an invitation to the salon. She was so curious about it.

She went to the door and was allowed in by Owen's butler, Cookson. She was taken to the small parlor and smiled as she entered to find the party already gathered.

"I seem to be fashionably late," she said with a laugh.

Celeste and Pippa both laughed as they approached her. She was enveloped in their welcoming hugs, and for a few moment it was all giggles and catching up with these two women she hadn't even known a year ago. Couldn't have guessed when she realized their existence that she would come to love them like sisters.

Lady Lena and Harriet said their good afternoons, along with

Owen and Rhys. As everyone settled back into their cheery conversations, Abigail took a chair with a smothered smile. It seemed their party was complete—and it did not include the Duke of Gilmore.

She hadn't seen him since Rhys and Pippa's gathering a few nights before, when they'd wagered so inappropriately and he had requested a chance to win his money back. She'd waited for him to clarify how that would happen, but he'd said nothing more to her that night. He had also not reached out to her since.

And she was relieved, not disappointed. She didn't want to have some silly secret with the man. She didn't want to spend time with him. It was better just to forget the whole thing had happened and move on with her life.

Which she promptly did as she fell into a conversation with Lena Bright about Sir Walter Scott. She was perfectly comfortable and happy when Cookson stepped into the doorway and the room turned toward him with an expectant air.

"The Duke of Gilmore," he intoned.

Abigail stood with the rest of the group, but it took some effort. She would have told anyone around her that her heart sank at that announcement. She might have even tried to tell herself that it was horror and annoyance that cropped up in her chest when Cookson stepped aside and Gilmore strode into the room.

But it wasn't. To her great confusion, there was a flutter in her stomach when Gilmore scanned the room and his dark gaze settled, momentarily, on her. She shifted slightly, willing her hands to stop trembling, and then forced a scowl on her face.

"Good afternoon," he said, holding out a hand as Owen crossed the room to greet him. "Pardon my tardiness. I received a letter just as I was leaving and the answer couldn't wait."

There was something about his mouth as he said those words. A slight downturn to his lips that made Abigail wonder what the letter had been about.

It seemed Owen could sense the same, for he tilted his head. "Anything I can assist with?"

Gilmore clapped his forearm with a smile. "No. Thank you, though. I appreciate the offer."

He moved around the room, saying good afternoon to each attendee and making more personal apologies for his lateness. He was reintroduced to Lena and Harriet, and Abigail's lips thinned as he spoke to Lena in French for a moment when she brought up that she had been reading Voltaire. Showing off, of course. He couldn't seem to help himself.

Finally, though, he stepped away from the other ladies and moved to her. "Mrs. Montgomery," he drawled.

She flinched, as she always did when someone used her married name. "Your Grace."

She heard the coldness of her response, but it didn't seem to bother him, for he stepped closer as the rest of the attendees faded away from them. He smelled faintly of leather and of something sweet, perhaps lemon or orange, she wasn't certain of which. It tickled her senses and made her body react in ways she refused to name.

"I'm pleased to find you here today," he said, and had the gall to sound sincere.

"Are you?" She arched a brow. "I have a hard time believing that since you and I are well-known enemies."

He laughed, and she found herself wishing to smile in return. "That we are, yes. Mortal, it seems. No way around it. But we do have some unfinished business, don't we?"

She tensed. "And what is that?"

"Billiards."

She blinked. "Is that supposed to mean something to me?"

"I've been thinking about our wager, and I say billiards."

"That was...days ago," she said softly.

"I know. We left it with me considering what field we would meet on next." He gave her a pointed look. "Or are you backing out?"

She pursed her lips. Damnable man. "Of course not. I, sir, have honor. But I am also a lady, and billiards is a gentleman's game."

"And?"

She huffed out a breath. "It seems you would have an unfair advantage."

"Something like you did because you knew Lady Blain would fall asleep during supper?" he asked, almost sweetly but for the flash of challenge in his dark stare.

She folded her arms. "And yet I might have still been wrong. What you are suggesting requires skill. Practice."

"It requires neither," he said. "Because we won't be playing a game. And I will teach you how to do what we *will* be doing."

She froze in her spot and stared at him. There was something... wicked about what he'd just said. Something that made her think of tangled bed sheets and this man's hands on her bare skin.

She jolted backward a step. She'd dreamed of him before, hating herself when she woke, but she'd never let those wicked thoughts haunt her in her waking hours.

"Unless you are unsure of yourself," he drawled. "Then I can simply settle you with the pound you won and we can call it good."

She pressed her lips together hard. He was taunting her now. Testing her. "Fine," she said. "Billiards." His mouth twitched, and she glared even harder at him. "Stop gloating. What now?"

"Gregory?" he called out over his shoulder without breaking eye contact with her.

Owen stepped closer. "Yes?"

"I have a hankering for a game of billiards. You don't happen to have a table here, do you?"

Owen let out a snort. "It isn't that kind of house, Gilmore. We don't."

Gilmore's mouth twisted a little, as if he were disappointed not to settle the bet immediately. Before he could speak, Celeste said, "*You* have a billiard table, though, don't you, Gilmore?"

Gilmore's expression darkened a fraction and his gaze darted from Abigail. "I do. We really ought to have a gentleman's night. Play billiards, drink scotch, talk about sport."

"Excellent idea," Owen said. "I'll look at my schedule."

"And speak to Leighton," Gilmore suggested.

Owen tilted his head. "Certainly," he said slowly, and then he and Celeste moved away.

"He's right. I do have a billiard table," he said with a soft laugh. "It's a very nice billiard table, indeed."

She shook her head. "Are you suggesting that I would be entirely improper and go to your home to play billiards with you...just to win?"

That same dark expression crossed his face again. "To best me," he corrected her. "I think you'd move almost heaven and earth to do that if you thought you could."

They stared at each other for a moment, charged and heated. She wanted to deny that allegation. She wanted to tell him that she didn't care enough to want to defeat him again, this time in an arena where he reigned. But she couldn't. He was baiting her and she knew it, but she still took the bait.

"You're on, Your Grace," she said with what she hoped was a smile rather than a grimace. "When?"

"This little gathering will be over before supper," he said. "Why don't you join me after? We can eat together and then meet on the battlefield."

She caught her breath. Breaking bread with him, especially without others as a buffer, felt less adversarial than usual. But he was awaiting her response, still looking very smug.

"Fine," she said softly. "I agree to the terms. I will go to your home and allow you to teach me...some mysterious thing that has to do with billiards. And then I shall beat you at whatever it is."

"Excellent," he said. "I look forward to it, madam." He tilted his head toward her and then slipped away, leaving her staring after him.

And wishing it was the fire of competition burning in her blood rather than...something else. Something dangerous, indeed.

∼

Nathan paced the halls of his study later that evening, trying to pretend that he was thinking about work or anything else besides the woman about to join him. Asking Abigail to his house—unchaperoned no less, as she had not brought her lady's maid with her to the gathering earlier in the day—had all the potential of being perilous.

"Except that you have control over yourself," he muttered out loud. "Whatever attraction you might have toward Abigail isn't enough to turn you from being a gentleman. Even if it were, she hates you. She would never see you as anything but an adversary. Nothing untoward could ever happen, alone or not alone together."

He said the words, he tried to believe them, but he jumped when his butler stepped into the doorway and announced, "Mrs. Montgomery is here, sir. I have put her in the parlor, as you requested. Supper will be served in half an hour."

"Thank you, Gardner," he said. "I will join her directly."

The butler stepped away, and Nathan turned to the mirror above the sideboard to give himself the once-over a final time. He smoothed an errant lock of hair and straightened his frock coat. If anything was out of place, surely Abigail would mark it. He needed to be well armored to face her, in this, their latest battle.

When he was certain he would pass her judgment, he made his way down the hall. The parlor door was shut and he paused before it, trying to calm his unexpectedly racing heart. This was ridiculous. He had spent evenings with plenty of ladies before. Evenings that had ended with much more delight than this one would. He had no reason to be nervous as a green boy.

He steeled himself and entered the room.

Abigail was standing at the fireplace, staring up at the portrait that was mounted above the mantel. The picture was of his mother and father, commissioned just after their marriage. The previous duke stood stiff and straight while the duchess was in a chair in front of him. The painter had perfectly captured their expressions. He: annoyed. She: bored.

Either image could have come to life from his childhood memories.

"Good evening, Mrs. Montgomery," he said.

She pivoted from the painting and speared him with a glare. "You are most frustrating."

He blinked. "That is an inauspicious start. What have I done to offend you with only a brief greeting?"

She folded her arms, meant as a shield against him, he thought. "The way you say Montgomery. You always emphasize it. Like an accusation or a way to crow and hold it over me."

He moved forward a step, and for a moment his part in their usual sparring fell away. "That is not my intention, I assure you. I did not realize I was doing it."

"You always have," she said, her tone a little softer, more pained. "From that first moment you and Owen stormed into my house to confront Erasmus and we found him dead. I've always heard that accusation in his name."

"He nearly destroyed my sister," Nathan said softly. "I suppose I may say his name with disdain without meaning to. I will try not to do it again."

She stared at him, seemingly in shock that he would acquiesce. She cleared her throat after what seemed like a lifetime. "Last year you called me Abigail, just as Owen and Rhys do."

He nodded. "Yes. When there were three Mrs. Montgomerys to manage, it made sense to refer to each of you by your Christian names. But now that the others have taken new names, I did not wish to invoke your considerable animosity toward me by continuing to be so forward."

She shifted, and he could see the wheels turning in her mind as she tried to sort out a response. "I suppose that is a fair point. It *is* familiar to go by my first name. But I do hate the last. And since I will likely never change it as Pippa and Celeste have, I must learn to live with the disgust it engenders in me to hear it."

"Would you prefer that I call you Abigail?" he asked slowly. "At least when we are in the company of our closest friends or…" He swallowed. "Alone."

She pursed her lips. If the discussion weren't so painful, he might have laughed, for he could see how much she twisted herself both wishing for what he suggested and wanting to find a reason to cut him to shreds for doing so.

At last, she cleared her throat. "That would be agreeable."

"Then it seems only fair that you should call me by my given name, as well."

Her eyes went wide. "That would be utterly inappropriate."

"As is what you just requested of me," he said with a laugh. "But these are unusual circumstances, are they not?"

"Yes." She shook her head. "No. I call you Gilmore. Is that not familiar enough to satisfy you?"

He leaned in a little closer. "Do you not know my Christian name?"

She blinked, and the look of abject terror that crossed her face in a flash was enough to tell him what he needed to know. Still, she was bound to be contrary with him and she folded her arms. "Of course I do."

He smothered a laugh. "Then what is it?"

Her foot tapped restlessly beneath the hem of her skirt. "We all know what it is—why should I have to say it? The request is very different when it is made by you, Gilmore. The title of duke demands some respect and—"

Now he did laugh. "Please don't try to convince me that you hold any respect for me, my dear lady. We are not in mixed company—you do not have to pretend for the sake of propriety. You do not call me by my name because you do not know my name. Admit it and I will share it with you. Unless…you want to hazard a guess?"

Her gaze narrowed further. "Cain? Beelzebub? Lucifer?"

"So close. Nathan."

She was quiet for a beat. "Nathan," she said at last. "Well, that almost seems like a nice, human name. Is it a family one?"

"In fact, it is. My mother's favorite brother was named Nathan," he explained. "He died when she was very young."

She swallowed, and for a moment he saw the flash of pain across her face. He knew its source. The previous year he had done a deep dive into this woman's history when he had not been certain of her role in Montgomery's schemes and come up with a great deal about her. He did not address it now—he could not imagine she would wish him to.

"I suppose that if you are kind enough to call me Abigail in private that I cannot refuse you when you ask me to call you Nathan under the same circumstances."

"An acquiescence that deeply pains you, I know," he teased. "And I thank you for it. Would you like a drink?"

"Yes," she said, and he thought it was through clenched teeth.

"You are a fan of sherry, I think?"

"Y-Yes," she said, eyes going wide. "How did you know that?"

"We did spend quite a bit of time together last year," he said as he poured the drink and handed it over to her. "I made a study."

"Hmmm," she said as she sipped the amber liquid. "I don't know if that makes me nervous or not, based on the fact that you despise me so completely."

Nathan opened his mouth to reply when Gardner stepped into the room. "Supper is served."

"Thank you, Gardner," Nathan said, and motioned to the door. "Shall we?"

She followed him and they walked along the short corridor toward the dining room. He noted how she looked around, taking in the art on his walls, the portraits of Gilmores past. At last they reached their destination. They settled into their chairs. He at the head of the table, she off to his right so that they could continue to talk rather than shout down the long table.

Not that they spoke a great deal at the start. Soup was brought, and for a few moments they ate in what had to be called an awkward silence.

At last he said, "I don't despise you, you know. *You* have always despised me."

She arched a brow. "The first time you met me, you all but accused me of being party to Erasmus Montgomery's schemes."

He hesitated, shame flooding him. "I was...overwrought that night. I had determined that your...husband...was pursuing my sister, despite having three wives already. I was furious and ready to fight."

"And he turned out to be dead," Abigail said softly. "Or he made it look like he was dead, at any rate. That must have put you out. And so you turned on me."

"I did truly think that you might have been involved in his schemes," he explained. "You lived together when he was in London, I thought you were close. I jumped to a conclusion and lashed out."

"Yes, you did," Abigail said, worrying the napkin in her lap. "Here I'd just found my husband, seemingly dead, and been told he was a bigamist. While that wave was crashing over me, a very powerful man accused me of something vile. So yes, I did despise you."

"Deservedly so," he conceded. "My behavior that night is not something I'm proud of. The longer I came to know you, I realized that you could never have involved yourself in something so wrong. You were the ultimate victim of his crimes. I made it worse. I'm truly sorry."

CHAPTER 4

N athan's words rang in Abigail's ears, and she had no idea what to say as she stared at him in disbelief. When he'd invited her here, she'd known it was a very wrong thing to accept, given their adversarial relationship. She had pictured arguments or bitterness between them.

She had never imagined he would take responsibility for what had transpired between them a year before. That he would apologize to her with no air of dishonesty or gamesmanship. She looked into his dark eyes and saw...genuine regret.

Dropping her gaze away, she gave a nervous chuckle. "I think I like it better when you are a pompous arse."

He smiled in return. "Well, I shall never stop being that in your eyes, I don't think. I just hope I can be less a true villain."

She swallowed. "I have known a true villain, Gilmore...*Nathan.* You are not that."

He inclined his head and lifted his glass toward her. They went back to eating, and he changed the subject. For the next hour, they discussed art and music, books and politics. It was friendly, or as friendly as things could ever be between two people with often opposing views. His were, of course, the wrong ones, and she didn't hesitate to let him know it.

But at last the final course was swept from the table and Nathan rose, a slow and frustratingly graceful unfurling of muscled limbs. He held out a hand toward her, his gaze dancing with mischief she didn't want to like. Apology or not, he was still her enemy. She still didn't trust him.

"Our battlefield awaits," he said, motioning his fingers toward himself as if to beckon her to him. "Unless you want to admit defeat before we start."

She pursed her lips. "You think you softened me up at supper, but you didn't. I'm ready."

She pushed to her own feet and waved off the arm he offered. He smothered a smile, and together they walked through the long halls once more. He took her a different direction this time and she stole glances at his home as they did so. Somehow she had always pictured him in this cold, sterile environment, when she dared to picture him in his private halls at all.

But this place was not that. There was formality to it, of course. The man was a duke, whether she referred to him by his first name or not. But there was also warmth here. Personality. *His* personality, to be more specific, thanks to the masculine décor, the choice of books and paintings. It was stylish, just as the man escorting her was stylish, even if she hated to allow him even the slightest hint of something positive to his character.

He guided her into a large room with wood paneling and leather chairs. It smelled faintly of sweet cigar smoke, and there was a silver tray on the back wall with crystal glasses and a tall bottle of Scottish whisky. The middle of the room consisted of a billiard table, covered in green baize. Three balls were in the center, and a rack of cues and maces was nearby.

She glanced at him. "I still say this wager is tilted far more in your favor than the one I made a few days ago."

He smiled. "Except you aren't being expected to learn to play.

Which I would teach you, if you desired it."

She looked again at the table. Her father had loved billiards and played it all the time with his cronies. She'd sometimes watched through the crack in the door, listening to them brag about their conquests, drink their port and play. She and her sister had sometimes snuck in and rolled the balls around the table with their hands, since the cues and maces were far too big to manage.

And then their mother had caught them and that had ended that. Loudly and cruelly.

She swallowed. "Perhaps another time."

He tilted his head and looked at her as if he could see the painful thoughts in her mind. Then he shrugged. "Very well. Now, I am proficient at billiards, that is true."

She rolled her eyes but found herself laughing. "It must be nice to think so highly of oneself in every way."

"Not *every* way," he retorted with a wink that was far too cheeky. "Just the ways that I am excellent."

"A fine distinction," she said with an even stare.

"What I am better at than the game is making what we like to call trick shots."

"Trick shots?" she asked.

He didn't respond but swept up one of the cues and set out the balls on the table one behind the other. He leaned over, and her breath caught at the sudden pure focus on his face. Then he snapped the cue forward and the ball closest to him launched up and forward, hopping over the ball next to it in line and hitting the third to send it to the pocket, where it swished in.

She stared at him, knowing her eyes were wide. "That is...damned impressive."

He stood up and leaned on the cue, crossing one ankle over the other. "It must have greatly pained you to say such a thing to me."

"It did," she admitted. "I shall wash my mouth with soap when I return home to get the taste of it out."

He threw his head back and laughed, and her heart, damn it, stuttered. He was really very handsome and it was so irritating. He shouldn't be handsome. She shouldn't find him thus, not when she wanted to keep disliking him.

She sighed. "Impressive or not, I'm not sure what you want me to do now."

"Jump the ball with the other. You don't have to push the third into the pocket, just do the jump," he said. "If you can do it, then you win not one pound, but five. If you can't, I'll claim my pound back."

"Five pounds!" she repeated, eyes widening. That was not an insignificant amount of money. She wasn't hurting for funds, despite Erasmus's bad behavior. Rhys had settled her with enough for her household and a few pleasantries.

But five pounds would afford her a luxury. Like the pretty hat she'd seen at the milliner on Bond Street last week.

She licked her lips. "What are the further terms? Because you must know I couldn't do that now."

"Of course not, and I'm not unfair, despite what you think of me. I will teach you the trick for half an hour. You will get to practice another quarter hour after that. And then you'll get five tries to do it. Does that seem fair?"

"It *sounds* fair," she said slowly. "But I suppose I won't know if it is fair until I have been taught."

His eyes sparkled as he faced her. "Interesting. Well, how about this: I will teach you. If at the end of the time you think this too difficult, you may refuse the wager."

"And have you call me a coward?" she said.

"Only behind your back..." he replied.

She wrinkled her brow. A year ago this man had only been hard with her. Harsh. But now he was playful, teasing. As if their rivalry was a game, not something deeper. And in that moment, it almost felt like it could be. A playful flirtation with a handsome man for fun.

She tightened her jaw. She didn't trust him—that hadn't changed. She had to be careful how far she let him in. She'd learned that from her time with Erasmus, if nothing else.

"I'm not a coward. Very well, let us start the time to teach me."

He held her gaze a moment and then shrugged. "Let me show you the steps first."

As she watched, he slowly repeated what he'd initially done, only this time talking her through the exact spot where he'd hit the first ball, the speed and angle he'd used. She moved closer, tilting her head to watch as he repeated the shot once, twice. She crouched down to have an even view of the third time he did it.

"I see," she said.

"Now I think I should show you," he said, and motioned her toward the spot between him and the table.

She hesitated. It was a narrow space, indeed. To step there would make them...very close. Closer than they ever had been before.

"Giving up?" he asked softly.

She glared at him. He was baiting her, of course. And even knowing that, she couldn't keep herself from taking it. She stepped into the space, her back to his chest. Her heart rate increased as he wrapped one arm around the front of her to offer her the cue.

She took it, willing her hands not to shake as she leaned over the table. He stepped to the side and his hand covered hers, fingers sliding across her gloveless knuckles, adjusting the grip on the cue. He tilted the back of it higher to change the angle.

His fingers pressed into her hip next and she caught her breath. It was like dancing really, one hand on her hip, the other touching her fingers. And yet it didn't feel appropriate or as innocent as a dance might.

She felt, instead, incredibly aware of her body. No one had touched it but her in over a year. Even before Erasmus had been dead, for he hadn't touched her for months before the events leading up to his death.

Now she was hyper-aware of the scent of Nathan's skin, the slide of his rougher fingers on hers, the heat of his body at her back.

"Let me show you the pressure you'll need," he said, soft because his lips were so near her ear. He drew the cue back and then snapped it forward, and the ball did a bunny hop over the next one.

She yanked away from him and dragged the cue in front of her, though it did nothing to shield her. "I-I see what you mean," she gasped out. "I will try for myself, if you don't mind."

He lifted his hands as if in surrender and stepped away, but he didn't go far. No, he stepped to the corner of the table closest to her and removed his jacket as she leaned over the table and tried to ignore him. She aligned the balls and then drew a deep breath before she tried to find the correct position to repeat what he'd shown her.

She popped the cue forward, and the first ball bounced a little but didn't do the bunny hop he had so easily perfected like the braggadocious lout that he was. She held back a curse as she realigned everything, tried a different angle and clicked the cue against the ball again, but with less luck than before.

She lifted her head to glare at him, to declare the impossibility of what he asked, but when she did so, she could not find air to chastise him. He had rolled his shirtsleeves to the elbow as she struggled, revealing taut, muscular forearms, lined with a few intriguing veins. She stared at them, her mouth watering slightly as she licked her lips.

"Need help?" he asked.

She blinked and forced her gaze back to his face. What was she going to say to him? It was all gone now because she was apparently so wanton and lonely after the last year that she was lusting...hatefully lusting...after the Duke of Gilmore, of all people.

It was unconscionable.

"Y-Yes," she stammered. "Perhaps if you show me again."

He nodded and slipped behind her. She tried to concentrate as he aligned everything again, adjusted the angle of her body and the cue again, let his fingers drag along her hand again. He stepped away. "Now give it a pop just so," he encouraged gently. "A swift thrust of the cue."

She shut her eyes briefly and tried not to focus on the word *thrust*. When she opened them again she blocked him and these odd attractions out as best she could and rapped the cue forward. The ball jumped over the next in line, and she smiled despite herself.

"Very good." He reset the balls in the line. "Excellent. Now try to do it again by yourself swiftly so you don't forget the feeling."

She wanted to retort, despite him being correct, but fought the urge and instead did as he instructed. Once again the ball hopped. The third time she missed, the fourth she didn't clear the line, over and over she tried until finally he stepped up and took the cue.

"Excellent. But your training time, as per the parameters of our agreement, is up. Would you like a drink before you attempt the shot for the wager?"

"I think you should try it first," she said.

"Me? Oh, I see. You think I should make the shot first and then you match it?"

She nodded. "It only seems fair."

He held her stare a moment too long. "Fairness is of great importance to you."

"Fairness should be of great importance to everyone," she said, and edged past him to the sideboard. There she poured herself a whisky and stared at the liquid swirling in her glass. She sipped slowly, wincing at the burn of it.

"Now please, take your shot, Your Grace," she said.

He shrugged. "Very well."

He aligned the balls once more and then easily executed the shot she had been struggling with. She frowned. It would have been much easier if he hadn't made it look so effortless. But she had never stepped down from dragons before, even ones with perfectly constructed forearms. So she drew a shaky breath, set her drink aside and lined up her shot. She measured it carefully as he watched, eyebrow arched.

"Shoot or don't shoot, Abigail," he finally said with a chuckle.

"Don't rush me," she scolded, but she took the cue from him and then carefully leaned over the table, trying to recall the right angles. She said a brief prayer to whatever patron saint might help her make a trick shot and put a duke in his place, and then she let the cue fly forward, rapping the ball.

Everything seemed to move in slow motion as she did so. She stared as the edge of the cue hit just the right spot on the underside of the ball and it roared up and forward, only just clearing the second ball in the row.

She let out a little scream, triumph and pleasure all at once, and pivoted to face Nathan. "Ha!" she crowed as she moved toward him almost against her will. She pushed the cue against his chest gently. "There now!"

But she didn't release the cue. She meant to, but instead she left her hand there, flat against his chest. His very firm chest.

She looked up at him and he down at her in the quiet, the private of this room where no one could see them, no one would judge. And she found herself staring at full lips. He had a little scar over the top one, barely there, but she still wondered about it. Where had he gotten it? What would it feel like if he pressed it to her mouth?

"Good show," he whispered, then leaned a little closer. "Abigail," he breathed.

He was going to kiss her. She could see it in every bit of his posture, every line of his expression, every way that his breath hitched and his pupils dilated. And damn her to hell, but she wanted him to do it. She wanted to feel his horrible arms around her and his wicked mouth on hers.

Which was why she backed away, putting her back to him as she fought to regain her breath. This was not happening. She couldn't *allow* it to happen, not with this man of all men.

"While it's very satisfying to best you twice," she said. "I think that is enough stimulation for the night."

She shook her head at the innuendo of those two sentences. What was wrong with her?

But he didn't acknowledge it or argue against her pulling away. Instead, he ran a hand through his hair and nodded. "Of course. Well done, Abigail. Let me show you to the foyer and call for your carriage."

She moved to the door without waiting for him to follow, though she felt his presence behind her with every step. He was too close as they meandered down the hallway, her hands shaking at her sides as they neared the foyer. His butler met them there, and Nathan said something to the man. As Gardner hustled off, Nathan motioned her toward the front parlor.

"Just until they bring the rig," he explained.

She nodded and followed him into the room. She paced away from him, as far as possible so that the moment of weakness in the billiard room would not be repeated. To keep herself busy, she made a show of examining the portraits, just as she had in the first parlor where she had been left earlier in the evening.

She frowned at the painting she was met with. A young lady with thick blonde hair and beautiful, piercing blue eyes. The unknown woman wore modern clothing and the date of the painting was just two years before.

She glanced back and him and found he was watching her. "Is this...is this your sister?"

Nathan nodded slowly. "Yes. Ophelia."

Abigail jerked her gaze away. "I know her name."

"She...will be joining me in London in a few weeks," he said, haltingly, as if he was trying to keep himself from saying something that might hurt her.

And, of course, he had, though for once it wasn't his fault. Lady Ophelia had been one of the women Erasmus had pursued behind Abigail's back during their marriage. He had intended, it seemed, for her to be his fourth wife.

She shifted as she looked at her again. Lady Ophelia was exquisitely beautiful. "So she will be at events," she said.

"Will that be difficult for you?" he asked.

She pursed her lips. He was peeling her open with that question, revealing her vulnerability, her humiliation. She folded her arms to make it stop, but that was no barrier to his seeing stare. "No," she lied. "Why would it be? Now, I'm sure I just heard the carriage pull up. I think it's time for me to go."

She hustled toward the door, but as she began to pass him, he caught her hand. His grip was gentle but firm and she stopped, heart racing as she looked up at him.

Just like in the billiard room, his desire was unmasked. It mirrored her own, much as she tried to fight it.

"Abigail," he whispered.

"Gilmore," she returned, back to his title as another attempt at a wall between them.

He arched a brow. "Nathan. I think you must definitely call me Nathan in this moment."

"Wh-why in this moment specifically?"

"Because I'm going to kiss you," he said. "If you'll let me."

She stared at him. She had spent a great deal of time painting this man as a villain in her mind. There were reasons for it, both valid and invalid. She'd also spent far too much of that same time fantasizing about him. Dreaming of him. Of exactly what he wanted to do.

And now, in the quiet of his parlor, when she felt vulnerable and uncertain…she again wanted exactly what he requested. And she wasn't going to be strong enough to refuse him.

"Nathan," she whispered as consent.

He bent his head, slowly, like he was savoring the fraction of a second before the kiss. His lips brushed hers, gentle at first, then harder. She pivoted more fully into his chest and wound her arms around his neck. The dam broke, months of tension and sparring washed away by the rushing water of desire and need and loneliness that he erased with his touch.

She parted her lips, a silent invitation that he took hungrily. His tongue swept in, tangling with hers as his hands gripped into fists in her skirts and held her tighter against his broad chest.

She could be washed away by this. She could be saved by this. She could be destroyed by this, and it would be the most glorious demise.

But the reminder brought her back to reality. She pulled away and he immediately released her, panting as he stared down at her with as much surprise and desire as she, herself, felt.

"I've wanted to do that for a very long time," he said.

Those words wound past her heated physical reactions and settled into her mind. She wrinkled her brow at them. Until tonight, he had never expressed any interest in kissing her. Never looked at her with anything but contempt.

Her hackles lifted back into place and she glared at him. "I do not know what your game is, Your Grace, but I do not wish to play it. Good evening."

She pushed past him, and this time he let her go without argument. She flounced to her carriage and nearly tripped hurtling herself in. Her heart pounded as she settled into place and the rig trotted off. Pounded harder when she pulled the curtain back a fraction and saw that Nathan had come out to the top step and was watching her go.

She yanked the curtain shut and leaned back in her seat for the short ride home. She licked her lips and could still taste the man there. Mint, whisky, desire, a potent combination she feared would live in her mind for a long time, alongside how his hands felt on her, how alive his mouth had made her feel.

"No," she said out loud. "No. No. No."

Gilmore was handsome, yes. And tonight he had been…fun. But it didn't change the fact that he had gone out of his way to make the situation with Erasmus more difficult. That his actions had caused the public revelations that had ultimately destroyed her life.

She couldn't forget herself with him, not ever again. She would go back to avoiding him and that was that.

That was that.

CHAPTER 5

Nathan dipped his quill into the pot of ink and began to write, but within a few strokes of the pen against the parchment, the tip snapped off. He cursed beneath his breath and tossed the quill aside, leaving a line of blotted ink behind on his letter.

He pushed to his feet and paced across the room, fists gripped at his sides, barely containing a shout of frustration from his lips. He had felt out of sorts for days, to be precise. Since the night he'd kissed Abigail in the parlor. How many times had he returned to that room to stare at the place where they had stood together? How many times had he been wracked by memories of the vanilla scent of her hair, the softness of her lips as she surrendered in his arms?

Too many. Especially considering she had not been seen since.

There was a knock on the door to his study, and Nathan pivoted to face it. "Enter."

Gardner stepped inside. "The Earl of Leighton, Your Grace."

Nathan blinked. He'd all but forgotten he was expecting Rhys today, despite having told Gardner to merely bring the earl to him upon his arrival. That was what an addled mind did, it seemed.

Rhys entered the room and crossed to him, hand extended. They shook as Gardner left them and closed the door behind himself.

"You look a bit out of sorts," Rhys said as he settled into the chair across Nathan's desk. "Rough night?"

Nathan grunted his response. "Just grappling with an irritating problem. Drink?"

"Nothing for me, thank you." Rhys leaned forward as Nathan retook his place at his desk. "Anything I can help with?"

"No. And shouldn't I be asking you that? How goes the great return to Society?"

Rhys's smile fell and it was answer enough. "Eh, not well," he admitted. "I've been petitioning to have my membership in White's reinstated and...failing at it."

"I thought you liked Fitzhugh's," Nathan asked. "It's a superior establishment."

"Yes, in every way that counts," Rhys agreed. "But reputation-wise, a man of title ought to be welcome at White's. Do you disagree?"

Nathan couldn't, of course. Though Fitzhugh had more interesting membership, White's was the place to be seen and accepted. "I'll try to exert some more pressure there."

"I'm not sure it will help," Rhys sighed. "Many of our friends...your friends, I suppose now, since they aren't mine anymore, are still unwilling to be seen with me. Until more of them come back to the fold, even just in public, I feel my ship is sunk."

Nathan shook his head. "Poxy fools. I'm still shocked by their lack of faithfulness. They've known you since school, you've saved half their arses in one way or another, and they cut you?"

"Seems you are the only one fool enough to risk himself by remaining by my side." Rhys held his gaze. "Gilmore, I appreciate your fealty in this horrific set of events, but if you wish to separate yourself a little more, especially with Ophelia coming to Town for the rest of the Season—"

Nathan held up a hand. "Enough of that. We are friends, through better and worse. It is not up for debate."

Rhys's face twisted a little. It was clear he was fighting an emotional reaction to that declaration. Then he said, "Thank you."

Nathan dropped his gaze to give his friend a moment to collect himself and said, "Why don't I host a ball? I intend to do so later in the Season, as well, once my sister arrives, but nothing says I couldn't do it twice. I wager those arses we once called friends won't refuse *me*."

"That would be very helpful, yes," Rhys said.

Nathan grabbed a fresh sheet of paper to write a few notes on. "I think I could manage it within the week. Invitations can go out tomorrow. I'll ask Owen and Celeste, as well, so there will be friendly faces."

"And Abigail?" Rhys suggested. "She could likely use the help in Society, as well."

Nathan's hand froze over the list at the mention of her name. He cleared his throat and tried to keep any emotion from his voice as he said, "I do not think she'd come."

"Because of the bad blood between you?" Rhys asked.

Again, Nathan didn't know what to say. Bad blood was not how he would describe his last encounter with the woman. And she had attended a great many events where he was present before he kissed her, even as she declared over and over that she did not like him.

This, though...this felt different.

"Gilmore?" Rhys said. "What in the world is going on?"

"Nothing," Nathan said, and hated the little break to his voice. "*Gilmore.*"

Nathan lifted his gaze at last and snagged his friend's bright blue one. Rhys looked only concerned, and he knew he could trust the earl. And since keeping this inside had done him no good, perhaps it was time to try a different tactic.

"You need to promise me something."

Rhys leaned closer, concern growing on his features. "Anything."

"You will not speak to your wife about this."

Rhys's forehead wrinkled and he shook his head. "About...about what?"

"What I'm going to tell you. Pippa can't know. Because if Pippa knows, then Celeste will know and eventually Abigail will know. I don't need the problems that will cause."

Rhys sighed. "My wife and I tend to practice honesty together, though there are certainly topics she has no interest in. And since this would be your secret, not mine, perhaps it wouldn't be an issue. But I'll have to hear it first, Gilmore."

Nathan pursed his lips. While part of him envied the closeness Rhys was describing, it was also bloody inconvenient. But since this was the best answer he was likely to get, he decided to accept it.

"Abigail and I recently challenged each other to a few small wagers," he explained. "Foolish little things. She won the first, I wanted a chance to reclaim my honor. She came here a few nights ago, after tea at Owen's that day."

"She came...she came here?" Rhys repeated. "With you. On her own volition."

"The desire to best me a second time overcame her desire to burn me to a crisp, I suppose," Nathan explained. "At any rate, she came here and I was teaching her how to make a trick shot at billiards as part of the wager."

Rhys's mouth was partly agape, his eyes growing ever wider. "And?"

"I'm getting there," Nathan snapped. "*And...I...might have...kissed* her."

He had expected Rhys to respond immediately, but his friend merely stared at him. The silence stretched for what felt like a lifetime before Rhys swallowed hard and croaked out, "What now?"

Nathan huffed out a breath. "You bloody well heard me."

"You *might* have kissed her," Rhys said. "Did you kiss her or didn't you?"

"I kissed her," Nathan muttered. "In the parlor by the foyer."

"On the hand...on the cheek?"

"On the mouth, you great ridiculous arse," Nathan growled. "I kissed her on the mouth, just as you would think I might kiss a woman like that."

Rhys just kept blinking, as if he couldn't quite fathom what he'd been told. On some level, Nathan didn't blame him. He couldn't exactly fathom it himself most of the time, and so it just kept haunting him.

"What does that mean?" Rhys breathed.

Nathan pushed to his feet and paced away. "I have no bloody idea. Yes, we have been at odds since the first moment we met. Ask Owen how that first meeting went and he will attest to the fact that Abigail and I came out of the gate hot. She makes her disdain for me clear at every turn. And yet I have been…attracted to her for a very long time."

"She is pretty," Rhys said, probably to make him feel better.

"Yes, yes, she is that," Nathan said with a wave of his hand. "But she's smart as a whip. She challenges the hell out of me, she has a light in her eyes that says she knows herself and she doesn't give a damn what anyone thinks of it. Beauty is the least of her attractive qualities."

"You really do like her," Rhys said.

"Despite the fact that she is entirely maddening…yes. I'm afraid so."

Rhys sighed. "Well, I cannot say we didn't…notice the attraction."

Nathan flinched. "Yes, you and Owen both made that clear with your little comments over the last year about this. But attraction is one thing. One can wave that away like an annoying bee. I've done something about it now and that changes the situation."

"How did she react?" Rhys asked.

"I thought she might wallop me," Nathan admitted. "But she kissed me back. I felt she wanted me."

"And then?"

"And then she pulled away and walked out. She accused me of playing a game with her. She continues to despise me. I haven't seen her since. She hasn't been to any of the events where we might have encountered one another."

"Do you *want* to encounter her?" Rhys shook his head. "As you said, attraction is one thing. Even a kiss could be forgotten with a little time."

"I have no idea," Nathan said with a sigh. "That's the worst part. I don't know if I want to see her or not. I don't know if that would make it better or not."

"Very interesting."

Nathan folded his arms. "Well, you're of no help at all. Are you going to tell Pippa?"

Rhys laughed. "*That* is a complicated question. After all, this situation you find yourself in involves Pippa's friend, one of her closest friends."

Nathan held up a hand. "Leighton, please..."

Rhys nodded. "But I think, at least for now, that I can be quiet about it."

Nathan pursed his lips and then let out a long sigh. "I will invite Abigail to my ball," he said softly. "I make no promises that she'll come. Now may we change the subject?"

"Certainly," Rhys said, a twinkle in his eye as he got up. "How about a game of billiards?"

Nathan glared at him. He couldn't believe Rhys didn't recall that Nathan had been teaching Abigail some variation on the game. But he gritted his teeth. "Fine."

As they left the room, he fought to regain some modicum of control over himself. He would not be bested by Abigail Montgomery. He had to find some way to defeat this feeling inside of him...and perhaps repeated exposure to the cause was the best way.

Abigail stepped out into her herb garden and drew a long, cleansing breath. There was no better place in the world than this one, with all its beautiful plants and flowers. How she loved to step into this little corner and personally tend to her garden, planning for tinctures and salves that she could make with her carefully culti-vated plants. This was her peace, her escape. And she certainly needed it after the last few days when thoughts of her last encounter with Gilmore kept flooding her mind.

"No," she muttered to herself, and harshly thrust memories of the man away. She tugged her apron on, dug in the pocket for her gardening gloves and knelt to go to work on the plants. For a short time, it was bliss and no unwanted thoughts intruded.

"I beg your pardon, madam."

She lifted her head to find her butler standing close by. "Yes, Paisley?"

"You asked that I come to fetch you when it was ten to two."

She blinked. "Is it already? Goodness, I lost track of the time. Celeste and Pippa will be here shortly for tea."

"Yes, Mrs. Montgomery."

She looked around. It was such a beautiful day, sunny and clear and unexpectedly warm. She smiled at Paisley. "Why don't we have our tea out here? The gazebo will provide shade. Will that put the staff out too much?"

"Not at all, madam," he said with a smile. "I will bring the ladies down to you as soon as they arrive. Oh, and the post is here. Would you like it while you wait?"

She nodded and extended a hand for the letters. It was a small, rather sad stack at that and she pursed her lips as Paisley excused himself to await her visitors. She wasn't shocked at the lack of correspondence, just hurt. She had returned to Society after her proper mourning period, but like Pippa and Rhys, she was not finding the warmest welcome.

Still, there was one missive that stood out from the rest as she flipped through the pile, and she opened it with a thrill. It was from Lady Lena's Salon. An invitation to join, at last, and to the next gathering in a just a few days.

She clutched the papers to her chest with a giggle. Both Celeste and Pippa and their husbands were already members of the exclusive salon, and though Lena and Harriet were always kind to her, she hadn't been certain she would ever receive the coveted invitation. But it seemed they had been simply awaiting her official return to Society, rather than leaving her out entirely.

She'd heard so much about the intelligent conversations had there, the wonderful lectures and presentations. Rumor had it that William Blake had once attended and spoke rather shockingly about the Royal Academy.

She couldn't wait.

She was still reveling in the pleasure of the idea when she glanced down and found that another letter had fallen while she all but danced around her herb garden. She bent to pick it up and her stomach turned as she dusted it off. It was from Gilmore.

She shoved the rest into her apron pocket and, with shaking hands, broke the seal. Would he address what had happened between them a few nights before? That kiss that still haunted her dreams?

But when she unfolded the pages, it was nothing personal within at all. An invitation to a ball the next week. She didn't even think Gilmore had written it himself. It was amazing how she had been dreading whatever he'd written—now she was disappointed there wasn't some meaningful letter after all.

"Little fool," she muttered as she shoved the missive in her pocket with the rest just as Pippa and Celeste came down from the house with Paisley behind them. She waved to the butler and he smiled as he turned back on the path to allow the ladies their greetings.

There were a few moments of hugs and compliments on hair and gowns before Celeste looked around her in wonder. "Your garden is wonderful! I marvel every time I see it."

"Thank you," Abigail said, unable to contain her blush.

"And it's so helpful," Pippa added. "That mixture you made for Kenley's little cough last week did wonders. It's like he was never ill."

"I'm so pleased," Abigail said, and for a moment nothing else mattered. She adored helping others with her talent for potions. She had few opportunities to use that skill and each one made her soar. "Oh, but let's come out of the sun. The gazebo is likely ready for us."

They moved toward the little structure together, chatting about the weather. The gazebo had been hastily set for their tea, and after everyone had taken their place and Abigail had poured their cups, she sighed.

"I'm glad you are both here today," Abigail said with a smile. "I needed the distraction."

"Oh dear," Celeste said with a tilt of her head. "Is something amiss?"

"Not at all," Abigail said, darting her gaze away as the memory of Nathan kissing her roared up in her mind once again. "Just tired."

"It has been an exhausting few weeks," Pippa agreed. "And it looks to only get more complicated. Rhys was just to see Gilmore, and he told me that the duke intends to have his sister join him here in London to have a Season."

Abigail tried to pretend she didn't already know that fact. She didn't want to explain how she did for fear she would spill the rest of the facts of what had transpired between her and Gilmore.

"Lady Ophelia?" Celeste asked, almost breathlessly. "She was one of Erasmus's intended victims, wasn't she?"

"Yes," Pippa said with a frown. "Only Abigail's intervention stopped it."

"But Gilmore doesn't know it was me, nor do I wish him to," Abigail said swiftly, perhaps sharply.

There was a hesitation as her two friends stared at her, probably in shock at her harsh tone. Pippa took her hand. "Of course, my dear. We wouldn't ever tell him, though I think that might soften things between you, if he knew you were his savior."

She shook her head. "Once he knew the truth, his actions caused us to be publicly revealed. Caused the rift between us. I cannot forget that. Leave it be. I doubt he cares who told him the truth."

"I assume he does care how Ophelia fares in London, though," Pippa said. "No one else knows what happened, so her reputation is not at stake, but one would assume she might wish to talk to someone about what happened. I know she never became an official Mrs.

Montgomery, but perhaps we could welcome her as you welcomed us."

"Oh yes!" Celeste added with a smile. "Invite her to lunch with us."

Abigail swallowed. To include Ophelia in their circle clearly meant that she would be further exposed to Nathan—Gilmore. She needed to think of him as Gilmore. Becoming more intimate with his name was part of how they'd ended up kissing.

She drew a long breath to calm herself and said, "Would her brother approve, though?"

"I don't see why not," Pippa said. "Your issues aside, I think he does respect you and how you've handled yourself throughout this ordeal. And he likes Celeste and me. He makes that very clear."

Abigail nearly snorted. Gilmore had made it clear he liked her well enough when he'd breached her lips with his tongue, when he'd held her so close she could match his heartbeat.

"Unless you don't wish to welcome her for some reason," Celeste said slowly.

Abigail blinked. "Of course not, don't be silly. If she would like it and he would allow it, I will arrange it." She glanced at Pippa. "Unless you would like to?"

She almost hoped Pippa would say yes. It would give her some distance from the plan so Gilmore wouldn't read into it. And if she really didn't want to participate, she could cry off with a headache or some other false ailment.

"You welcomed us," Pippa said. "I think it makes the most sense for you to do the same for her."

Of course it did. Abigail forced a tight smile and nodded. But she could see her friends had further questions about her attitude. Ones she had no intention of answering. So instead, she dug into her pocket for the invitation to Lady Lena's Salon.

"Look at what I got," she gushed.

"Oh, so Harriet and Lena sent it!" Pippa said, clasping her hands together. "Harriet said they intended to do so. I'm so pleased, though Rhys and I will not be in attendance at that particular event."

"Nor Owen and I," Celeste said.

"Oh," Abigail said with a frown. "That is too bad. I shall not know anyone else there, beyond Lena and Harriet, of course."

"But it is a new opportunity to make friends, then," Celeste said. "Perhaps even catch the eye of some handsome intellectual who will sweep you off your feet by talking to you about poetry or science."

Abigail forced a smile, even though images of Gilmore popped into her mind once more. Damn him. "That would certainly be something."

The other two laughed, and their conversation turned to the salon and past presenters there. It gave Abigail time to breathe, time to gather herself.

She was going to have a long life ahead of her, and now that she was free of Erasmus and out of mourning, she would have to determine what that life looked like. Certainly it would not include the Duke of Gilmore.

She could not forget it.

CHAPTER 6

Nathan crossed the crowded room of Lady Lena's Salon, smiling at those in attendance as he tried to find his hosts. He found them standing together talking to another guest, but that person peeled away as he approached. He knew a little about them thanks to his relationship with Owen and Celeste Gregory.

Harriet Smith had once been Celeste's governess, but had come to London after being sacked by her parents. There she had met Lena Bright, illegitimate daughter of a duke. The two had entered into a relationship—a partnership, though anyone with eyes knew they loved each other. Ultimately they had opened the salon above Mattigan's Bookshop and built it into the most sought-after gathering place for anyone with intellect in London.

That they'd called it Lady Lena's was a spit in the face of Lena's father. Nathan knew the man, the Duke of Carrington, and he felt the man deserved whatever he got. Nasty creature.

Harriet Smith was lovely, with a round face and bright eyes. And Lena was stunning. Her curly hair was pulled away from her brown face; the result highlighted her high cheekbones and full lips. The two women smiled at Nathan as he approached and he could not help but return it.

"Your Grace." Lena extended an elegant hand. "Good evening."

"Good evening, Lady Lena," he said with a smile as he shook first her hand and then Harriet's. "And Miss Smith. A pleasure to see you both again."

"The pleasure is ours," Lena said with a smile for Harriet.

She nodded. "We are so happy you agreed to attend—we have hoped you would."

"I've meant to before, since I first received your invitation a few months ago, but the timing has never aligned. I am thrilled it did tonight." He glanced around the room. "It's quite a crush. And such a wonderful mix of people."

It was true. Men and women of all corners and walks of life mingled in the room. There was no exclusion here for race or creed or rank. The only requirement was intelligence and an interest in the wider world.

"Yes, with Jeremy Bentham here to speak about his principle of greatest happiness, we knew it would be a popular night." Harriet smiled. "But you are not alone—there is a friendly face in the crowd for you."

"Who is that?" Nathan asked.

"Mrs. Montgomery," Lena said, motioning across the room delicately.

Nathan followed the motion, and through the crowd he saw Abigail. She was standing in a small group of mostly younger men, save for one who was older. She was chatting and smiling and laughing. She looked beautiful, with her dark hair pulled back simply and then adorned with a bejeweled band. Her dress was a dark blue, the skirt also stitched with a few sparkling elements.

"Your Grace?"

Nathan blinked as he realized he was being addressed. He smiled at Harriet and Lena again. "I'm sorry, I must have become distracted," he said, letting his gaze flit back to Abigail. "Is that Mr. Bentham, himself, speaking to Abigail?"

"It is, indeed," Harriet said. "And he looks charmed, as do all in her group. Though how could one not be? I'm so glad Mrs. Montgomery's mourning period is at last at a close so we could invite her. She will be a delightful addition to the salon, I can already see."

"Yes, delightful," Nathan mused.

Harriet and Lena excused themselves then, and Nathan managed to pull his gaze away from Abigail to say his farewells so they could go speak to more of their guests. He watched Abigail a little longer, and when Mr. Bentham had shaken her hand and drifted away, along with a few of the others at her side, Nathan moved toward her.

She noticed his approach within a few steps. He knew it by the way she stiffened, even though she didn't look his way. She said something to her remaining companions and left them, moving in his direction and abandoning mooning men in her wake.

Her gaze lifted to his, at last, as they met in the middle of the room. It was not her usual disdain there to greet him. No, tonight she seemed...nervous. Her cheeks were pink, her hands gripped at her sides, her throat working as she swallowed.

"Abigail," he said softly.

She pinched her lips. "I thought we said we were only doing that in private."

He looked around. "No one is listening. But I can call you Mrs. Montgomery if it would please you."

"I don't know what would please me," he thought he heard her mutter beneath her breath, but she gazed off into the room and didn't address the question to him directly. "I didn't know you were a member."

"You don't think me an intellectual?" he teased, and her gaze came back to him sharply. He arched a brow. "Go ahead, you may sling your barbs. I am strong enough to take them."

She pursed her lips, but it seemed like she was genuinely struggling with a response. "I may not always...appreciate you, Your Grace, but I do not think you a stupid man. You very likely belong in a room like this, as much as anyone else."

He drew back a fraction. "Was that a compliment? Toward me? From you? That might be the first sign of the apocalypse."

She was trying to maintain a hard countenance, but he saw the corners of her lips twitching. He took it as a good sign, at least, and leaned a little closer. "And what would you wager on tonight, madam? If you would allow me to try to win again."

She worried her lip and the hint of a smile fell away. "I...I think we entered dangerous territory with our wagers, Your Grace. It might not be the best idea to continue them."

It wasn't a cruelly said statement, but for some reason it stung Nathan in a far deeper place than he would have imagined it could. He smoothed his hands along his jacket front and shrugged one shoulder with more nonchalance than he felt.

"As you like, Mrs. Montgomery. I can see why you would not want to break your winning streak." They were quiet a moment. Not a comfortable silence, but not an adversarial one, either. He glanced at her. "I have noted you did not yet respond to my invitation to the ball in a few days."

Once more her gaze darted to him, and she suddenly looked a little trapped. She shifted, almost as if she were planning her escape. He realized in that moment he actually wanted her at the ball. He'd acted like it was because Rhys suggested it a few days before, but that wasn't true. He wanted her there only for himself.

"Nathan," she began softly.

He pivoted to face her fully and caught her hand. Even through two layers of gloves, the act moved him. "Please," he said softly. "For Pippa and Rhys, if not for me."

Her gaze narrowed slightly, but her words contained no heat when she said, "That isn't fair."

He nodded. "No. It was badly played by me, for certain. But I think you and I both know that a lot of things aren't fair in this world."

She bent her head. "Yes."

She had hardly answered when there was a tinkle of a bell. The crowd began to take their seats, settling in for the presentation. Abigail looked up at him, holding his gaze firm for a beat.

"I-I'll be there," she said softly. "I'll come."

Nathan was shocked by his reaction. It was like someone had given him wings. He had the oddest urge to shout out with this triumph and let the world know he'd won. Instead, he kept his expression impassive and nodded. "I'm pleased. Now, would you be opposed to sitting together for the presentation?"

She rolled her eyes, and there they were, back to their usual adversarial banter. "I don't see a way to refuse you. So yes, I'll join you."

He motioned her to two of the few remaining seats in the hall, and they sat. But though she didn't look at him for the entire speech, nor during the questions afterward, he still felt like they'd moved forward tonight. Toward what, he wasn't certain, but he wasn't opposed to it.

And that was the oddest thing of all.

As those who had attended the salon began to make their way back to the street, buzzing about the gathering in small groups, Abigail felt more energized and happy than she had in years. She clasped her hands together and turned toward Nathan.

"It was wonderful, wasn't it? So fascinating to hear Mr. Bentham talk about his thoughts on happiness and improving Society. I will be thinking about it for weeks to come."

He nodded as they maneuvered through the milling crowd, down the stairs and through Mattigan's Bookshop. When the group jostled them, he placed a hand briefly on her back, and she felt the weight of every finger against her spine as he managed to keep her from being bumped by excited patrons.

They exited onto the street and found a line of attendees waiting for their carriages. Nathan waved, and she saw her driver catch his eye from the group of those waiting for their masters. The driver hustled off to fetch her rig, and that left them waiting in front of the shop.

Suddenly she felt nervous, and so she smiled up at Nathan in the hopes to diffuse those feelings he so often engendered in her. "What did you think about what he said about the reform of Poor Laws?"

Nathan's eyes lit up. "Fascinating. I think I might reach out to him to speak about it more. I sit in the House of Lords, after all. I have influence—perhaps I can sponsor some legislation on the matter."

She stared at him. "You would do so?"

He nodded.

"That would be wonderful. So many in power don't seem to think of those without it at all. And while I don't know that I believe everything the man said about the intrinsic goodness to pleasure—after all, I was married to a man who took his however he saw fit and it harmed a great many others—I do think that considering the happiness of the greater population has merits when we take actions that affect them. And I..."

She trailed off because Nathan's smile had twisted a little, almost like he found what she was saying amusing.

She folded her arms in a shield against her chest. "I am talking too much."

"Not at all," he assured her. "I just enjoy watching you exhibit such passion about something rather than despising me."

She cleared her throat. "A woman can have many facets and passions."

His smile broadened. "Indeed, that is true. Oh, here is your carriage, let me help you up."

He waved her footman to stay at the top of the rig and opened the door for her before he took her hand to assist her. She gripped his fingers, and for a moment she flashed to the last time she had touched him. In the parlor, when his lips had come down on hers and lit a fire that had no business burning through her as it had.

He was still holding her hand, and she stared down at his lean fingers, gripping hers through her thin gloves. She swallowed hard and slid her hand away. He gazed up at her, his pupils dilated much as they had been when they kissed. What would happen if she caught that hand again and drew him into the rig? What would happen if she took him back to her home and up to her bed? What would happen if she took off her gloves and touched that handsome face, traced those full lips with her thumb?

She blinked those wicked thoughts away.

"Good—goodnight," she stammered.

He inclined his head. "I'll see you at the ball in a few days. Goodnight, Abigail."

He smiled as he shut the carriage door. She heard him say something to her driver and then she was off, leaving him behind outside the bookshop. She pulled the curtain back to look, but the angle was wrong and it was too dark to see him.

She settled back into her seat, worrying her lower lip as she pondered the man she left behind. Why were these feelings coming up now? These desires...not feelings. She didn't have *feelings* for the Duke of Gilmore. That would be entirely untenable.

But desire was...something else, wasn't it? It was something biological, something natural. It didn't mean anything except that she was a woman with blood pumping through her veins. A woman who had been alone too long, watching those around her find passion and love while she was forced to wait.

Of course she would come out of mourning wanting some kind of physical attachment. And why wouldn't it be Nathan who caught her eye? They saw each other somewhat regularly thanks to their mutual friends. And he was easy to look at. There was nothing wrong with wanting him.

There, that was settled. It created pleasure and did not create pain for anyone else, so she assumed even the speaker tonight would approve. Not that she would ever speak of this to any other person.

Nor would she do anything about it. After all, she and Nathan were still enemies. Desire didn't change that. Nothing ever could.

CHAPTER 7

Abigail stood in the middle of her chamber, staring at her reflection as her maid Cora tugged and fluffed and straightened her gown.

"You do look lovely!" Celeste said from behind her. "That green is just beautiful on you."

Abigail glanced over her shoulder with a smile. Her friend had joined her tonight and would ride with her to the Gilmore ball.

"As do you," Abigail said. "Owen will not be able to take his eyes off you when he joins us. He was on a case tonight, yes?"

"Yes, finishing up a little paperwork about a minor theft," Celeste said. "I'm sure he won't be very late. He assures me Gilmore won't be cross."

Abigail turned her attention back to the mirror and tried not to react to Gilmore's name. She had been avoiding speaking to her friend about their host and she changed the subject now to keep up that avoidance.

"Are you still helping Owen with his cases?" she asked.

Celeste nodded. "Oh yes. And I enjoy it so much. I research for him and occasionally speak to witnesses, especially those who might be more nervous speaking to a man. He's also encouraged me to begin writing, which I always loved to do. Harriet was thrilled, and she and Lena offered to help me edit if I ever finish a piece."

"That's very exciting!" Abigail exclaimed. "What a thrill it would be to know a noted writer."

Celeste chuckled. "What if I were not noted?"

"How could you not be? You're brilliant. I'm sure Owen says the same."

Celeste's cheeks brightened. "I'm very lucky to have met and married a man who so supports me."

"Indeed." Abigail tried not to frown as her mind turned to the first husband they'd all shared. "Most are not so fortunate."

Cora finished with Abigail's hair and excused herself, which left Celeste and Abigail to exit her chamber. They made their way downstairs to the waiting carriage, but with every step Abigail could see Celeste had something on her mind.

"What is it, then?" she asked gently as the carriage began on its way.

"I don't want to bring up a tender subject, and I fear I already have by reminding you of how unhappy Erasmus made you," Celeste said softly.

Abigail caught her hand. "That is in the past. We are able to talk about him now, aren't we, and not have it make everything maudlin."

Celeste shrugged. "My relationship to him was not like yours and Pippa's. We were never in love. I never wanted to marry him in the first place."

Abigail sighed. "It is true that it was different for me. I went into our marriage with the highest of hopes, never dreaming what he would eventually do. But the fact is that I had stopped loving him a long time before I knew he was a bigamist fraud with dangerous intentions. My mourning period was not one of gnashing teeth or violent weeping for his loss. I reflected on my own actions during that time. My own failures. And also what I wished my future to look like...or what it *can* look like after such a scandal."

"I do not think you failed," Celeste said. "But I am curious what you hope for in your future. With Pippa and I so happy, we wish for the same for you."

"Well, you and Pippa are lucky. I do not think we can ask for that kind of beautiful lightning to strike three times for the Mrs. Montgomerys." She laughed though the subject was, indeed, painful. "Society judges me harshly because I was the only legal wife. I do not receive many invitations, except from our little circle. And I can live with that. I would rather have a few nice friends than a world of false ones."

Celeste worried her lip. "And what about...love? You cannot have truly given up on the entire concept."

Abigail took a long breath. "Right now I suppose I do miss the... comfort of a man's presence. I miss passion, to the point where it makes me very foolish."

Celeste wrinkled her brow. "What do you mean?"

"Nothing." Abigail waved her hand to dismiss the words she hadn't meant to say. "I only mean that I wouldn't mind a little attention from a gentleman. Discreetly, of course, if I could find one willing to look past my scandalous name and past."

"A...a lover?" Celeste said, her eyes widening.

Abigail didn't answer for a moment, probably because that word had hit her squarely in the chest. A lover. Yes, that was what she wanted. A man to make her feel those flutterings she had when Nathan kissed her. A man to make her feel more than that.

And since she very likely could not ask for more than a mere dalliance...why couldn't she have that?

"I wouldn't be opposed," she said softly. Then she laughed to lighten the mood. "Perhaps I will find one in the crowd tonight."

"At Gilmore's ball," Celeste said. "It is possible. There are many gentlemen attending, and you look so beautiful that they'll surely be drawn to you. I must admit, I was surprised when you agreed to come. Everyone knows how much you dislike Gilmore."

Damn, there was the subject of the duke again. And again, Abigail's heart leapt a little when he was mentioned. She really did need to find a lover if this was how she reacted.

"He can be tolerable when he chooses to be," she said, dropping her gaze away from Celeste's. Her friend was too observant to be trusted.

"Wait...you now find him tolerable?" she asked.

"No!" Abigail shook her head. "Yes. I still think he can be arrogant. I'm still angry at him for causing so much pain when he didn't have to do so. But I suppose, from time to time...he can be...*charming.*"

Celeste stared at her as if she had sprouted a second head. "Abigail?"

"I'm not saying I want to kiss the man again, I'm just saying—" She stopped and clapped a hand over her mouth as she realized the slip she had just made.

For a moment the carriage was utterly silent as Celeste stared at her, mouth agape, shaking her head slowly. At last, she seemed to gather herself and she said, "Did you say kiss him *again?*"

Abigail squirmed. "Er...yes," she whispered.

"As in you kissed him at some point before?"

"Yes." Her voice was hardly more than a squeak now. The carriage began to slow as they reached Gilmore's London home. The same one where said kiss had happened. She swallowed hard. "He kissed me. I kissed him back. We...we kissed."

A thousand questions crossed Celeste's face, but she couldn't ask them because the footman opened the door and they were helped out and guided toward the house. It was brightly lit tonight, and music and laughter drifted onto the drive.

"Please forget what I said," Abigail whispered as they entered the house and moved with the others arriving toward the ballroom in the back of the house.

"I don't think that is possible," Celeste whispered back. "This is stunning news. Amazing news."

"It's not!" Abigail hissed even as she tried to keep a smile on her face for those who were looking at her. Judging her, she knew. She caught Celeste's hand. "It means nothing. He's still Gilmore. Nothing has changed." That didn't feel true, but she said it anyway. "And I'm only here tonight for Pippa and Rhys."

She realized she was gripping Celeste's hand far too hard, as her friend peeled her fingers away. "Calm yourself," she said gently. "I won't mention it again if you don't wish to discuss it. But we are coming to the front of the line and he is right there, so bear up."

Abigail could hardly breathe as they stepped up together to Gilmore. Great God, but he was handsome in formal attire. Every piece of him was exactly where it should be, and it made her want to...muss him a little. God, she was hopeless.

"Mrs. Gregory," Gilmore said, clasping Celeste's hand. "You do look radiant tonight. I know Owen will be late—I'll keep watch for him."

"Thank you, Gilmore," Celeste said. "And for the invitation."

She moved along, though Abigail could feel her stare as she stepped up to Gilmore, herself. She couldn't make herself meet his eyes as she said, "Good evening."

"Abigail," he said softly, just so she could hear. A shiver worked up her spine. "I'm so glad you came this evening."

There was a little bit of challenge to his tone and she clung to that to find some purchase. "Why wouldn't I?" she said, a little sharper than necessary. "I said I would."

He chuckled lightly. "Yes, you did. And I'm beginning to realize that you never lie. Enjoy your evening."

She stepped away, nearly tripping over her own feet as she did so, and she hustled into the ballroom behind Celeste. Already the party was a crush, with people gathered talking and laughing as the orchestra played.

She saw Celeste talking to Pippa and Rhys a short distance away. She should go to them, of course, be with her friends. But she couldn't bear to, especially when she didn't know if Celeste was whispering her secret to them. She never should have said anything out loud.

Because now the fact that she wanted a lover and that she'd kissed Gilmore seemed all too real. And too tangled for her own good.

Nathan smiled at his guests, saying a few good evenings as he passed through the crowd. But he was not interested in stopping for deeper conversation. No, he was on a mission to find Abigail. He hadn't spoken to her since her arrival nearly an hour before, though he had caught glimpses of her. Always ducking away from him.

But now he caught sight of her, standing off along the wall, watching the dancers merrily bob by on the dancefloor. Her expression was faraway, almost sad. She didn't notice as he approached, and she jumped when he reached her and said her name.

"Your—your Grace," she stammered. "I didn't see you there."

"No, I assume not or you would have run, as you have been doing all night."

Her eyes went wide, and then the steel she so often exhibited toward him entered her face and made her back straighten. "I'm sure I don't know what you mean."

He tilted his head. "Of course you don't." The song the orchestra was playing was coming to an end, and he drew a long breath. "Is your card filled for the next, Abigail?"

She shifted. "I have not danced tonight, Your Grace, save with Owen or Rhys. So I think you know the answer."

"Then perhaps you will do me the honor?"

Her gaze flitted to his face, and he saw her trying to find a way to refuse him that would not be too rude. But then her eyes settled on his mouth, held there too long. There was the push and pull. The longing he felt mirrored back in her, forever battling with whatever her reasons were for disliking him so much.

She bent her head. "I would very much like to dance, Your Grace," she said softly.

"Excellent." The music ended, and there was a moment of bustling as the dancers from the previous song left the floor and ones for the next rushed forward to take their places.

Nathan offered his hand, and she hesitated before she took it. He led her to the floor and they waited for whatever song would be played. The first strains of the music lifted, and she briefly shut her eyes. He could have sworn she cursed beneath her breath.

"Don't know how to waltz?" he asked as he took her hand and placed his other on her hip.

She glared up at him. "Of course I know how to waltz."

"Excellent, because I am very good at it," he teased.

She continued to glare as they swept into the first steps, but her lips were twitching almost as if she wanted to laugh. "You are the most arrogant arse," she said softly.

He turned her, easily dodging a slightly drunk partygoer. "I am that. I am."

"Why did you ask me to dance?" she asked.

He lifted both brows. "Do I need a reason?"

"With you and me? I think there's always a reason, isn't there? Some underlying angle or game." She sighed. "Or is it some wager again?"

"You think I would wager about you?" he asked, good humor fading.

"I may not have as much to lose as Rhys does, but I was once a member of Society. And I see that they judge me..." She swallowed and he saw the pain in her eyes. "...laugh at me. I'm certain at least one of them is making some wretched wager at my expense."

He tightened his fingers against her hip and watched her pupils dilate in response. "You may despise me, but I hope you don't think that low of me. I would never. And if I heard someone else was, I wouldn't let it stand."

Her steps faltered slightly, but he kept her from falling, and for a few turns they were both silent. Then he drew a long breath. "Abigail, couldn't we make a truce?"

Her eyes went wide. "A—a truce?"

"Of our group of friends, we are the only ones still unattached," he said. "We see each other regularly. It will be even more regular now that you are back in Society and I will be bringing Ophelia to events once she arrives. I'd rather be your friend than your enemy." He leaned a little closer and whispered, "And I don't think you hate me as much as you pretend you do."

She jolted back at those words. It would have disrupted the couples dancing, except that the music ended at almost the same time. She executed a shaky curtsey, as if she were pulling from his arms only because of the end of the song. Then, without a word, she walked away from him.

He watched her go, weaving in and out of the groups of people, her head bent, her body curved, as if she could protect herself from attack if she made herself smaller.

He moved to follow her. He would have done so, except that as he stepped from the dancefloor, he caught a glimpse of Rhys, heading over to a small group of three men he and Nathan had called friends for decades: the Earl of Yarrowood, Viscount Goffard and Stephan Sinclair, the second son of the Duke of Featherton.

Nathan glanced around but no longer saw Abigail, so he turned his attention to his friend. This was why he'd held this ball, after all: to give Rhys a chance to renew those friendships that could help him rebuild himself.

Except that as Rhys reached the threesome, they turned up their noses and strutted away as a group. Nathan gasped. The cut direct! And half the room had seen it.

Rhys stood where he'd been left, staring after their former friends, a twisted look of pain on his face. He wiped it away soon enough and held his head up high as he walked back through the crowd to Pippa's side. She took his arm, said something to him, comforted him.

Rage shot through Nathan. Rhys had never been anything but decent to any of their friends. He had helped some of those men through difficult times of their own. And they cut him? It was enough.

Nathan marched after the group, hands clenching and unclenching at his sides. The group had exited the ballroom onto the terrace, and he followed to find them huddled together talking at the wall. No one else was out in the cool night air, and he approached them in three long steps.

"Just what the bloody hell is wrong with you?" he barked.

The men looked startled as they turned toward him.

"Gilmore," Sinclair drawled. "Nice of you to join us."

"I'm not joining you, you poxy fucks," Nathan sneered. "I asked you a question, and one of you is going to answer it."

Yarrowood straightened up from his position leaning against the terrace wall and moved forward. "There now, you can't talk to us that way."

"I can and I am," Nathan snapped. "I saw you inside. The whole damned party saw you with Leighton."

Goffard rolled his eyes. "That was the point, old boy. For everyone to see."

Nathan crossed to him and caught his jacket lapels. He shook him none too gently. "Leighton has never been anything but a friend to you. All of you. And you cut him in public? To damage him further?"

At least they had the wherewithal to look a little chagrined at Nathan's statement.

Goffard yanked away, smoothing his lapels. "What would you have us do?" he asked. "Align ourselves with him? After what his brother did? After he married one of those women taken in by Montgomery?"

"If you do, others will follow." Gilmore shook his head. "You all know what influence you have. What is the use of it if you don't use it for good? Greater good, yes, but the good of your friends?"

"Like you are," Sinclair said, his tone cool. "Inviting him and his common little wife to your party. Trying to get him back in at the club. Have you ever thought that you won't help him at all, but will only hurt yourself?"

Nathan tilted his head. "Is that a threat?"

Sinclair shrugged. "No, it simply a statement of the facts. You may wish to save the world, but we cut out the weak and the wounded for a reason. There are systems in place for a reason."

Nathan stared at him, this man he'd known since school. A person he'd called his friend. The others were not as direct in their words, but neither were they arguing against them.

"Fuck the systems," Nathan growled. "And fuck all of you. Get out of my house."

The three of them looked a little stunned at that order, but after a moment of staring and blinking, they walked away, back into the house and, Nathan assumed, out the front door. He didn't follow to be sure of it. His hands were shaking too hard, his breath was coming too short. He needed a moment to calm himself, to regain his cool.

To find a way to face Rhys and tell him what had transpired. They would have to find a better way to approach his return to Society. It seemed they could depend on no one else but each other at present.

And that wouldn't be enough.

He shook his head and stalked away down the terrace. It wrapped around the back of the house, and he found an unlocked door that led into a parlor. It was dim, for the fire had burned down, but when he added a few logs, the room brightened. He leaned against the mantel, staring into the flames, as he tried to make his wild mind settle.

"Nathan?"

He froze. In his upset, he was hearing things. Certainly that couldn't be Abigail's voice saying his name. The door to the parlor hadn't opened, no one knew he was here.

"Nathan."

He turned, and there she was standing in the same terrace doorway where he had entered a moment before. She was staring at him, dark eyes wide and hands clenched at her sides.

She drew a breath and fully entered the room, shutting the door behind her. "I-I saw you on the terrace. I heard what you said."

CHAPTER 8

Abigail watched as Nathan bent his head, his expression crumpling a fraction in the soft glow of the firelight. His hands flexed, open and shut, over and over, and finally he whispered, "So you saw."

She nodded slowly, and a sudden panic rose up in her chest. "I-I wasn't trying to eavesdrop," she tried to explain. "I had gone out onto the terrace for a moment to myself after we danced. When those men came out, I didn't want to be seen. I slipped into the shadows, hoping they'd go back inside after they smoked."

Nathan held up a hand, though he didn't look at her. "I didn't think you were eavesdropping." He let out a long sigh and ran a hand through his hair. "I came in here for a drink and a moment of my own."

"I can...I can leave you," she said, and found herself hoping he would say no. Hoping he would invite her to stay.

He looked at her, holding her stare evenly. "Would *you* like a drink?"

She knew she shouldn't. She knew she should walk away, just as she'd done after they danced, but she couldn't. Not after what she'd seen and heard on the terrace. Not when he looked so lost and forlorn.

"Yes," she whispered.

He moved to the sideboard and splashed whisky in two glasses. He handed one over to her and downed his in one gulp.

Her eyes went wide as she took a ginger sip. "I can see you are very upset."

"Yes," he ground out, and set the glass down. He paced across the room, tension coming off of him in waves. "I value loyalty in friendship. Rhys has always offered it to those he held dear. He deserves the same in return from them. To watch people we counted as friends being that feckless, being that cruel after something that wasn't even his doing or fault..."

He trailed off and his shoulders rolled forward. He looked so disappointed, so broken hearted, not for himself but for Rhys.

She moved toward him, shaking her head as she did so, even as she teased, "You do make things difficult for me."

He lifted his gaze and his forehead wrinkled with a little confusion. "Do I? How is that?"

"When we were dancing, you said I didn't hate you as much as I might pretend to." She drew a very long breath, for what she was about to say meant too much not to give it a little gravity. "And you are right."

His eyes widened and she thought she heard his breath hitch, but he didn't interrupt her, so she continued, "I want so much to see you as a villain and then you do what you did on the terrace."

"What did I do?"

"You proved that you care about more than just yourself. Heartless cad."

He did not smile, but he held her gaze evenly. "I shall try harder."

She chuckled despite herself. "Very good, I'd appreciate it." She sighed then. "You are too clever not to know that you cannot change what those other men do. Though your devastating set down of them might make them think twice about their bad behavior. But *you* are loyal, Nathan. That is admirable, and I know Rhys and Pippa both appreciate it. It means something."

"Not if I can't do anything to actually help." His voice was rough.

She reached for his hand, and they stared together as her fingers linked with his. "You do help."

His breath came a little shorter and so did hers as he looked down at her with the same expression he'd had when he last kissed her. Her world began to spin, making her forget all her good reasons for pulling away from this man. She found herself tilting her face for better access.

Except he pulled away instead of pursuing her. He dropped her hand and backed up. His voice shook a little as he said, "Not so long ago, you accused me of playing a game, Abigail, but I honestly don't understand you."

She wrinkled her brow. "What do you mean?"

"You tell me I'm an arse, then you place friendly wagers with me. I kiss you and you kiss me back, but then you hate me again. We dance, you run. I do something you perceive as kind, so you chase me into a private chamber."

Heat suffused her cheeks and she folded her arms. "I-I didn't *chase* you."

"You're here with me." He waved his arm around the empty room. "And I'm not sorry about that. But understand, I'm not the kind of man who pursues a woman who doesn't want me. Or doesn't know what she wants at all."

She stared at him, her emotions boiling inside of her and making her dizzy. What he said stung, but she could also admit, to herself if not to him, that it was true. She did reach out and then pull back when it came to him. There were a hundred reasons for that. Because she found it hard to trust anyone, even herself. Because he had hurt her and those she cared for. Because he could be arrogant and all too certain of himself...because she wanted him and it frightened her. It still frightened her, as he waited for her to say something.

He tilted his head when she gaped at him like a fish, mute with her confusion. "What do you want, Abigail?" he asked, pronouncing every word succinctly.

"I-I don't know," she snapped at last. "I *don't* know what I want. Is that what you want to hear so that you can prove to yourself that I'm nothing more than some silly woman? That I'm as foolish as you've always believed me to be?" She moved to the door. "I didn't come in here to cause strife, no matter how little you think of me."

"Then what *did* you come for?" he asked. "Say it."

She opened her mouth, shut it, and then she huffed out a breath and stormed from the room, her hands shaking as she slammed it behind her.

∼

"**F**uck."

Nathan ran both hands through his hair before he threw them in the air and paced away from the door. The woman seemed determined to push every button to make him react. She was frustrating and alluring and difficult to manage, and he hated himself for wishing she had looked him in the face and told him she wanted him.

He certainly wanted her. Down to his bones.

As he moved toward the sideboard again, ready to pour himself a second drink, the door behind him opened and he turned toward it.

Abigail stood there. All the color had gone out of her cheeks. Her hands were gripped at her sides, but they shook regardless. They held gazes, both silent as time seemed to slow to nothing. Her breath hitched as she stepped into the room and slowly shut the door behind herself.

He moved toward her, but she met him halfway. She lifted into him, groaning as their mouths met and that sound of surrender and desire was too much. He cupped her head gently, angling to deepen the kiss. His tongue was flooded with her flavor: whisky that lingered on her tongue, desire that coursed between them.

"Please," she panted against his mouth, her hands gripping harder against his jacket. "Please, please."

He backed her toward the settee and they staggered onto it in a tangled heap of arms and legs. He half covered her, half knelt on the floor. Her hands came into his hair, nails raking his scalp, tongue desperately seeking his.

It was everything and it wasn't enough. He wanted to *touch* her. He wanted to make her come right here in the parlor with a ball spinning just a few doors down, close enough that the faint echo of the music drifted into the room and provided a rhythm to their passion.

He drew back, watching her as he glided the flat of his hand down her side, her hip, her thigh. He fisted her skirt, tugging it up, waiting for her to push away again and continue that push and pull between them.

But she didn't. She slowly nodded before she caught his shoulders and yanked him into her. He kissed her while he slipped his hand beneath her skirt and felt the warmth of her body without the barrier of her dress.

He touched her calf and she sucked in a breath without breaking the kiss, he cupped her knee and she drove her tongue harder. When he stroked her thigh, her head tilted back and she gave a full-body shudder. She met his eyes as he smoothed his fingers along the flesh, finding the top of her silky stockings, then the warmth between her legs. She wasn't wearing drawers, and he lightly traced his fingers there until her thighs opened a fraction farther.

It was the invitation he'd been waiting for. She gasped as he stroked the length of her sex, massaging the outer lips, then gliding a thumb past them. She was wet and hot, and she lifted against him in silent, desperate invitation.

"Say it again," he murmured, moving his mouth to her throat.

"Say what?" she gasped, arching in a clear effort to make him touch her harder, to breach her, to give her what she wanted.

He lifted his head. "Please."

Her lips pursed, a flash of the same irritation that had always chased their relationship. Only now it was tangled with desire, and matching one fire with another felt heady and dangerous and glorious.

"Please," she murmured.

He didn't torture her anymore. He cupped her hip with the hand that wasn't under her skirt and tugged her to slouch lower on the settee. She gasped and her legs parted wider, letting his hand flatten against the warmth of her sex.

He didn't waste time, for they had very little of it. He pressed her open and stroked her sex a second time. She lifted into his palm with a tiny whimper, and he smiled. He watched her face as he did it again, again, felt her wetness increase, saw her face flush and her pupils dilate.

He began to circle her clitoris, at first slowly, then faster, harder. She gripped the side of the settee, her gasps growing faster and harder and harsher as he edged her ever closer to the point of no return. Her eyes went wide and then she fell, shattering with a heavy gasp. She writhed beneath him, tears filling her eyes. He felt her rippling against his fingers and wished he were inside of her to experience it.

He leaned in to kiss her again as he removed his hand from beneath her skirt, but before he could cover her completely, the door to the parlor opened.

He lifted his head, eyes going wide in horror as the Countess of Hartfortshire and the Duchess of Abernathe entered the chamber. They were talking, and then the duchess gasped, her cheeks going pink. The countess followed her stare and her mouth gaped.

Abigail shoved her skirts down, face flaming as she pushed Nathan off of her and flew to the other side of the room, staring at the two women. The room was silent for what felt like an eternity, and then Abigail covered her mouth and fled through the terrace door with a sob.

"Pardon *us*, Your Grace," Lady Hartfortshire said with a little smirk, and then she left the room.

The Duchess of Abernathe remained for a moment. While the

countess was known for her gossip, the duchess had always seemed to him to be a kind woman. Now she looked at him with what could only be called pity. She swallowed. "I-I will try to convince her to hold her tongue, but…"

He nodded. "I know her reputation as well as you do, Your Grace. I understand."

She turned and hustled out of the room, and Nathan could hear her calling after the countess down the hall. But it was too late. No matter what was said, he and Abigail had been seen and there would be consequences to that.

He did not follow the duchess from the room into the hall, but pivoted to the terrace door. He stepped into the cool, looking for Abigail, but she was nowhere to be found among the other guests taking a bit of air. A few of them said good evening as he passed, and it took every ounce of control in his being to say it back as if everything in his life hadn't just changed.

Not just being caught, although that was certainly part of it. But touching her. Touching her had been life changing. Powerful. Like opium, and he wanted more and more and more until all he knew was her taste and the scent of her desire and the way she felt when she arched beneath him in even more pleasure.

He shook his head. He couldn't be distracted. He reentered the ballroom and lifted on his toes to scan the room. He still didn't see Abigail, though with the crowd milling and dancing, it was entirely possible she was still here.

He moved into the masses, being bumped and jostled but barely feeling it as he looked for her. Instead, he found Rhys, Pippa, Owen and Celeste all standing together in a group. He moved toward them with what he hoped was a genuine enough smile.

"There he is! We were about to put out a search party," Owen said with a laugh as he clapped Nathan on the back.

Nathan cleared his throat. "No need for that. H-have you seen Abigail?"

Celeste and Pippa exchanged a brief look, but then Pippa shook her head. "Not for a while, actually. Why?"

Nathan held his breath as he looked around again. He saw Lady Hartfortshire on the opposite side of the room. She was gathered close with a few other ladies, talking at what seemed an impossible rate of speed. The rest of the group turned toward him, their eyes wide and their mouths dropped open. Even the Duchess of Abernathe, who was shaking her head in some obvious effort to reduce the scandal, could not help.

"Bollocks, fuck and damn," Nathan grunted.

"I beg your pardon?" Celeste asked.

"My apologies," he said. "Christ, this is a mess. I...er...did something. And now it's going to come back to haunt me."

"Did something?" Rhys repeated slowly. "What are you talking about?"

"It's complicated, let me see if I can simplify for purposes of the emergency at hand. Er...I went to one of the parlors for a moment of privacy and...and Abigail and I ended up there alone and...we...that is...we..." He glanced at Pippa and Celeste in discomfort. If not in front of ladies, he could have been more direct.

"You kissed again?" Celeste asked.

"*Again?*" Pippa burst out. "What do you mean *again?* You and Abigail kissed?"

"Please mind your tone," Nathan growled. "Yes, we kissed. But I'm afraid tonight it went a little...um...further. And we were caught by the Countess of Hartfortshire and the Duchess of Abernathe."

There was a second of stunned silence from their group of friends. Owen was the one to break it. "Oh, bollocks. Even *I* know that Lady Hartfortshire is a dreadful gossip."

"What the hell were you thinking?" Rhys asked, his blue eyes snapping with anger, and worse, with disappointment. Seeing it there was a punch in the gut, one Nathan deserved for letting himself lose control.

"I think you know what I was thinking." He arched a brow.

"Where is she?" Celeste asked, peering around the room as he had done a few moments before.

He shrugged. "I don't know. She ran out."

"God," Pippa whispered. "Come on, Celeste, let's try to find her." The women clasped hands and, with one last look at him, threaded away through the crowd to find Abigail.

Which left Nathan with Rhys and Owen, and they watched as the news of what had happened spread through the ballroom. He could actually track it as one person whispered to another and then eyes turned on him: curious, judgmental, interested.

"I suppose I should thank you for creating a stir that takes some pressure off of me," Rhys murmured. "But then again, I feel that I must protect Abigail as the closest thing to a brother that she has."

Nathan pursed his lips. "I understand that. But you don't need to tell me what I need to do or challenge me to do it. I know." He caught his breath. "I know."

And he did. He knew exactly what would happen next.

CHAPTER 9

A bigail paced her chamber, as she had been all night long. She had fled Nathan's ball in a cloud of humiliation, but also in searing sensation. Her night had been haunted by memories of staring, judging eyes...but also the feel of Nathan's hands on her, coaxing pleasure from her almost as if he had been built to do so.

She wanted more.

There was a light knock on her door, and she turned toward it to bid the person to enter. Paisley poked his head inside. "I'm sorry to disturb, madam, but you have a visitor. Several visitors, in fact."

She swallowed hard. She'd received a message from Pippa last night and another from Celeste this morning. Neither one directly addressed what had happened at the ball last night, but there was enough concern in both letters that she had to believe they knew. She didn't want to face them.

"I'll be down in a moment," she said softly.

He nodded, a flash of concern crossing his expression before he closed the door and left her alone again. She moved to her mirror. Cora had readied her an hour before, but nothing could conceal the dark circles under her eyes from lack of sleep. Her friends would see.

Still, there was no avoiding it, so she pushed her shoulders back and went downstairs. She entered the parlor, trying to force bright-ness to her face, but what she saw there stopped her short.

Celeste and Pippa were there, it was true, but alongside them were their husbands...and Nathan. He stood at the fireplace, leaning on the mantel. She might have thought him casual except for the very focused expression on his face as he stared at her.

Humiliation hit her in waves as she staggered back a step. "You... you are *all* here."

Pippa came forward to kiss her cheek and drew her gently into the room. "Paisley didn't tell you?"

"I assumed it was just you and Celeste coming to check on me," she said, her voice barely carrying. "I did not expect the entire inquisition at my door."

Pippa opened her mouth as if to respond to that statement, but Abigail held up a hand as she moved to the sideboard. "Would anyone like tea or a scone? It looks like Mrs. Smythe brought her best."

Celeste rushed forward. "Why don't you let me do that?" she asked.

Abigail shook her head, unable to meet her friend's gaze. "Let me do this normal thing, please."

Celeste pressed her lips together. "Of course," she said, squeezing her arm gently. "Of course."

No one stopped her as Abigail got tea for everyone, preparing it just as each one liked. Eventually it was only Nathan who hadn't been served. She glanced at him, as she had been avoiding doing since the first moment she entered the room.

"And what do you want, Your Grace?" Her tone was harsher than she had intended, but it was impossible to look at him now and not think of his hands on her thighs, fingers on her...

She shook her head to clear those wicked thoughts and he arched a brow as if he could read them. "Nothing for me, thank you."

She sighed. "Then sit, won't you? I can't bear you looming over me from the fireplace like you're judging the room at large."

He was quiet for what felt like a very long moment, and then he inclined his head and took a place in one of the chairs facing the two settees where Owen and Celeste and Pippa and Rhys sat. Abigail took the place beside him, though she didn't want the intimacy that image created considering the circumstances.

"Obviously you all know what happened last night," she whispered, heat filling her cheeks. "It is so entirely humiliating."

Beside her, she felt Nathan stiffen, though she wasn't sure why. He could be no more pleased about what had happened than she was. It was a nightmare for both of them.

"Lady Hartfortshire was very...insistent about telling the world she'd walked in on you and Gilmore in a delicate position," Pippa said gently. "Though I do have to say the Duchess of Abernathe did try to stop her. She apologized profusely to Celeste and me when we spoke to her."

"Oh God." Abigail covered her face with her hands. "It was bad enough before. I was barely acknowledged because of Erasmus and his bad behavior, and I was fine with that. I knew it would be that way. But now it's *my* behavior they're judging. What if it hurts you and Rhys, Pippa? What if it hurts Gilmore?"

"All of us are only concerned about *you*," Rhys said as he pushed to his feet and paced across the room.

"How can you not acknowledge that you could be damaged by this?" Abigail asked him.

"I'm damaged enough, my dear." He shrugged. "It was not your doing. And at any rate, I may not be in as poor a position as I thought. Gilmore's loyalty has an enormous impact. And, ironically, I was approached by another person last night. The Duke of Abernathe was speaking to me before the incident, and this morning Pippa and I received an invitation to some huge soiree he and the duchess are throwing. So whatever you did didn't hurt me, I assure you."

She felt a little tension leave her. "Well, at least I am happy about that. I suppose the answer to the problem is very obvious, though."

"Indeed, it is," Nathan said softly.

"I will just...go back into seclusion," she said.

Everyone in the room stared at her until she shifted beneath the weight of their gazes. Rhys was the one that moved toward her, an expression close to pity in his eyes. "I don't think that's the solution, Abigail."

She stared at him, and his words became clear. "Are you...are you talking about me marrying Gilmore?" She pivoted toward him and saw that he was not reacting with shock or anger or distress at the idea. His expression was entirely unreadable. "We despise each other!" she snapped, and then faced the room again. "He certainly doesn't want me."

"I think we've established that is decidedly untrue," Nathan said gently.

She got up and backed away, her gaze still on him. He couldn't mean that. He couldn't want this. This couldn't be happening at all.

He stood, a slow and graceful unfolding of limbs, and cleared his throat. "I appreciate the kind support from everyone, but I think Abigail and I need a moment alone."

Her hands began to shake at her sides. This was a dream, it had to be. Or a nightmare. And yet it seemed to actually be happening. Nathan really was staring at her, his dark eyes holding hers steady, no question within them...but also no affection. No emotion that she could discern at all.

"Is that really a good idea?" Rhys asked, stepping up to Abigail's side. "I stand as family to Abigail, and I think it might be best if we—"

"Please," he said, sharply and firmly. "Please."

Rhys sighed and looked at her. "Is that what you want?"

"It seems we have a great deal to discuss, and yes, perhaps that would be easier with just the two of us." A shiver worked through her and she tried to ignore it. She turned to Rhys and took his hand. "Thank you, though, for acting as my brother in this matter."

"I'll always be your brother," he said, squeezing her hand, and then motioned to the door. "Come."

"There is such a pretty view of the park from the back terrace," Pippa said as they exited as a group. "I think that would be the best place to wait."

As the door shut behind them, Abigail flinched. She turned away from Nathan, staring out at the street below and wishing she could run away down it and never return. He was silent as she did so, and finally she shook her head.

"You don't want to marry me."

He moved to stand beside her, though he didn't touch her or look at her. He cleared his throat. "I think the feeling is mutual, isn't it?"

She glanced in his direction, her mind taking her back, once more, to the moment when he'd dragged her down on the settee and pleasured her. "I...suppose."

"You suppose?" he repeated, and chuckled lightly as he faced her, arms crossed against his chest. "You've spent a year being plain about your dislike. Except every so often."

"Yes, you scolded me about my indecisiveness last night, and look where it led us."

"To the settee, Abigail." He tilted his head. "Did you dislike what I did to you there?"

"We got caught!" she burst out.

He shrugged. "Take that out of it for a moment. Did you like it when I touched you?"

"I hate you for putting me on the spot," she grumbled.

"Noted. Answer the question, please. I don't ask it to embarrass you or to win something over on you. It's important to the position we find ourselves in."

She gritted her teeth and refused to meet his gaze. "Yes, you pompous arse, I liked it. I liked it when you kissed me, I liked it when you dragged me to the end of the settee and put your hands up my skirt. I liked it when you made me...made me..."

"Come," he supplied smoothly. "I made you come. And I'd very much like to do it again, because I liked it too."

She sighed. "Well, that resolves nothing."

"It doesn't resolve *everything*," he corrected, and then he walked away. "My second question has a more difficult answer, I would imagine."

"And what is that?" she asked, watching him pace, sensing the tension increase in him. Her own heart rate increased accordingly.

He faced her. "Why do you hate me so much?"

Her eyes went wide. She hadn't expected that. Nor for his expression to be so intense. Like the answer mattered somehow.

She drew in a few breaths. What she wanted to do was set him down, be sharp, escape him and all the things that swirled between them. All the things he still didn't know.

But the time for such childish behavior was over. She had to be firm and clear and...and honest. At least as honest as she could be.

She motioned to the chairs they had abandoned a moment before. When they sat, she sighed. "We talked once about how you behaved when you first met me," she began.

He shifted. "Yes, and I apologized for being accusatory toward you when it came to your husband's bad deeds," he said.

She nodded. "That meant a great deal to me," she admitted. "But the reason I have been so contrary with you goes back to those first days and many of the days after. You see, you didn't just accuse me of something and get on my bad side...you also did things. You acted out of anger, out of a desire to protect your sister and get revenge on a man you thought dead. But because of how you acted, how you let Erasmus's actions be made public...I suffered."

He straightened up. "We were trying to determine if there were even more wives."

"You could have done that more discreetly," Abigail whispered. "In some way, you wanted Erasmus to pay, for him to be shunned. But what it resulted in was all of us wives paying instead." She leaned closer. "If someone had let it out publicly that your sister was involved with him, wouldn't you have hated him too?"

"Yes," he said softly.

She nodded. "And then there was your behavior afterward. You kept involving yourself in the situation. You kept showing up to give your opinions and share your thoughts and intrude and intrude and intrude."

To her surprise, he gave a half-smile. "A bulldog, I have always been," he admitted. "Though I hope you'll admit, sometimes I might have been right about what I said or suggested."

She hesitated, because this conversation wasn't deteriorating into the argument she had believed it would. "Occasionally. I admit that under great duress."

"I knew I had caused damage," he said slowly. "To you and the other wives, but also to Rhys, a man I consider my brother. And I was trying to help. I was heavy-handed, though, or you felt I was. And I can understand that you might not have liked me for that."

"And I was…cold to you," she said. "And argumentative. And I can see that wouldn't exactly endear me to you, either."

He smiled. "On the contrary, I find your spark very endearing a good deal of the time. Your contempt was harder. But the fact that you challenge me is actually very interesting. Most don't care."

She sighed. "I don't actually hate you, you know. I think it was a way to put my anger onto someone, because I couldn't dump it onto Erasmus. And then it became a habit. And then it became a refuge."

"A refuge?" he asked, wrinkling his brow.

She bent her head. "Because I do like touching you and kissing you and all those other things. And that is frightening. I don't want to ever be dependent on another person like I was with Erasmus. I never want anyone else to ever have the power to destroy me as he did over the years."

"I don't want that, either," he said. "I've seen what affection can do, or lack thereof. The thought of opening oneself up that way is not of interest to me anymore than it is to you. On that score, we agree."

"But?" she said. "Because I can see there is still more coming."

"You know there is only one answer here for us. We were caught doing a great deal more than kissing, and Lady Hartfortshire made it seem even worse than it was, if that is to be believed. If I leave this be, it will not only hurt you, but also my sister. And I've done one of those things once, and in the service of protecting the other. Everything we suffered in the last year will be for naught."

She sucked in a breath. "You are talking about marriage. No one will name it, but that's what you mean, isn't it?"

His expression faltered a fraction before he nodded. "Yes. Marriage."

"You don't want to marry me," she said. "You don't *want* that."

"Last night I was imprudent. I could have locked the door, I could have taken you to my bed where we wouldn't have been discovered. But I didn't. So now what I want or don't want isn't at issue."

"What about what I want or don't want?" she whispered.

He moved toward her, slowly but with purpose. His hand extended, the same hand he had used to touch her twelve hours before. He cupped her cheek, and she fought not to lean into the strength of his fingers.

"You want stability," he whispered. "You don't want to be destroyed. Marrying me will offer you that. If you don't...the talk was very bad after you departed, Abigail. And we both know that the world is an unfair place, so the consequences will fall harder on you than on me, especially since the fools already think they know something untoward about your character."

She bent her head, blinking at the tears she didn't want him to see. "Oh, God. You're right. I know you're right, I just cannot believe this is happening."

"I know. I'm sorry. So, you will marry me?" he asked.

She forced herself to look at him then. "Yes."

There was a hint of a smile on his face, but then it was gone and he was all business again. He dropped his hand away and paced from her side. "Good. Then we need a game plan on how to approach this. First, I think we simply do not allow ourselves to be destroyed. I won't be forced to race to Gretna Green or take a special license like I'm running from a consequence. We will read the banns as if this is all very normal. It will also give my sister time to arrive in a week so she can take part in the wedding, which will give it even more a sense of correctness."

He said each thing with such a cold certainty. Such a calculated air.

It certainly wasn't the great romantic gesture he was describing. Although Erasmus had been very much attached to the great romantic gesture when they courted, and look where it had landed her.

Perhaps this was better.

"You said the talk was already very bad," she said. "Are you certain we ought not to just marry with haste if that is the only solution?"

"Let them talk," he said. "And you and I will just make sure the tenor of the conversation is changed."

"How?" she asked.

"We will let it slip out, through the right parties, that you had agreed to marry me that very night, just before we were discovered. We will imply that we were swept away by our joy and great emotion for each other."

"Make it a grand love story and they'll eat it up," she murmured.

He nodded. "You were in mourning all this time, shattered by what you endured…"

"And you were there," she whispered. "Supporting me and waiting for the moment I was free to tell me how you felt."

He swallowed. "Er…yes. Something like that."

"So we'll lie."

"Not all of it is a lie, is it?" Her heart leapt a little at the thought. Then he cocked his head. "I think we *were* both swept away last night."

Heat suffused her cheeks, but she managed to squeak out, "Yes. And so we're…engaged?"

He nodded. "It seems to be so."

She stood in the middle of the room, shock flowing through her. She could hardly believe it. This time yesterday she had been pondering what to wear to Nathan's ball, and now…now she would be his duchess. What would that look like? What would it mean?

He smiled as he moved to her. He caught her hand and drew her close, close enough that her skirts brushed his boots. Close enough that she felt his breath stir her cheek before he bent his head and kissed her.

She lifted into him immediately. What else could she do when he was the only solid thing in a world that seemed determined to keep flipping on its head? She clung to him and surrendered as he deepened the kiss, slowed it, reminded her of all he could do to make her quake.

When he drew back, he steadied her on her feet before he let her go. "Don't overthink it, as I know you are wont to do."

She glared at him, though she felt no animus at his teasing. "You do know how to ruin a mood."

He smiled. "I do my best to keep you on your toes that way. We'll talk a great deal more about the marriage before the wedding comes. But now there are arrangements to make. I promise you, Abigail...I promise...it's going to be well. I will make it right for you and for me."

She blinked. For the past six years, nothing had truly been right. Erasmus was undependable even when she'd thought he cared. But this man, this man she had spent so much time actively hating...he said he would fix things. And she wanted to believe him.

Even as she watched him walk out the door without any idea what exactly they would be to each other or how he could possibly make it well.

CHAPTER 10

Nathan strode out of the parlor, fists gripped at his sides, and out the front door. His carriage was still parked on the drive and he moved toward it, but hadn't yet given his direction to the driver when he heard his name from the house behind him.

"Gilmore! Gilmore, wait!" Rhys called out.

Nathan ignored him and said a few words to his man. He got into the rig, but Rhys would not be stopped, of course. He hurtled himself in behind him and slammed the door, locking them in together as the carriage began to move.

"God's teeth," Nathan ground out. "I don't need you scolding me again, Leighton."

Rhys's brow wrinkled. "I have no intention of scolding you. Did you two work it out?"

"We're marrying." Now that he said it out loud to a third party, the truth of it hit him. "We are marrying. Abigail and I are marrying."

He rolled each word on his tongue, finding them foreign and odd...but not entirely unpleasant.

"I do understand the concept," Rhys said softly. "You needn't repeat it."

"I think I do so that I'll accept it. This time yesterday I was dealing with twenty last-minute problems with the ball and answering a letter from my sister about her arrival next week. Now...this."

"I can imagine, though I must point out you did do this to yourself."

"Thank you. Very helpful," Nathan said with a glare. "You think I don't know it? You think I don't know how complicated this all is? She dislikes me and also likes me against her will. She wants me and pushes me away. It's all push and pull with us, it always has been."

"Abigail has been through so much."

Nathan pursed his lips. Back at the beginning, when he'd first discovered what Erasmus Montgomery was trying to do to his sister, he had researched Abigail, trying to determine if she were as much of a villain as her husband. He knew a great deal about what she'd been through. More than she was aware. She hid her pains...she was rather like him in that way.

"Yes," he said softly. "I know. I can't believe I lost control like that last night."

Rhys settled back against the carriage seat with a smirk. "*I* can."

"What the hell does that mean?"

"Oh come now," Rhys said with a laugh at his indignation. "We have danced around this topic for a *year*, mate. Since all this mess began, I have watched you two. Yes, you spit and growl at each other, but I've never believed you hate each other. You defended her passionately when Owen briefly believed she might have murdered my brother—"

"Because it was a bloody stupid thing to think!" Nathan growled.

"And there you go, looking like you'll come across this carriage and throttle me to come to her aid." Rhys laughed. "And she did the same when your name came up in the investigation."

Nathan blinked. "She...did?"

"Of course. You circle each other, you play these games...but they're all foreplay."

Nathan said nothing, just sat there, staring at this man he'd called friend, called brother, for most of his life. His words did not ring false, and Nathan despised him for that.

Rhys leaned forward, draping his forearms over his knees. "Can you deny that you have wanted her for a long time?"

Nathan swallowed hard. "I hate you."

Rhys laughed again. "Just like you hate her, I know. Answer the question."

"I have...wanted her," he admitted reluctantly. "But I never planned for this."

"But it happened." Rhys shrugged. "So you'd better start planning for what's next."

"What do you think I'm doing?" Nathan snapped. "I'll need to arrange for the banns to be read, I have to write my sister and tell her the 'happy' news, I need to tap into a network to start spreading rumors about us that will change the tide—"

"That's not what I'm talking about," Rhys interrupted. "What about her? What about the marriage?"

Nathan pursed his lips. "I know she'll be a good duchess. She's clever and she can even be charming when she isn't dealing with me. After watching her handle Pippa and Celeste with grace and kindness, I know she'll be good to my sister."

"How will your sister be with her?"

Nathan flinched. Ophelia had not handled the news of Erasmus Montgomery's betrayal well. She was young and a little spoiled, but at her heart he knew she was a good person.

"I'll make sure they get along," he murmured.

"And what about you? You two, beyond the titles and the relationships outside your bedchamber door? What about when it's just you?" Rhys asked softly.

Nathan shut his eyes. He could picture sparring with her, of course. That was their natural way. And he could most definitely picture making love to her. His mouth watered with the realization that she would be his to touch and hold and have for the rest of his life. What they'd already shared gave him hope they would be very compatible in bed.

But the rest…that felt blurry to say the least. "I don't know," he said at last.

Rhys nodded. "Let me give you some advice."

"You will, whether I desire it or not."

"*Try.*" Rhys held his gaze, suddenly very serious. "Try, Gilmore. Neither of you deserve to be unhappy, not after everything you've been through."

The carriage slowed now, arriving back at Nathan's home, and he sighed. "I'll think about it. Now, will you come in with me and help me with some of the particulars?"

"Of course," Rhys said with a smile. "You're there for me, I for you. Nothing could change that."

There was relief in that statement, because he knew Rhys was protective of Abigail. But his friend was his friend, and Nathan would be able to depend upon him. He would likely need to as this strange development moved forward.

As he moved toward his impending marriage and everything that would come after.

Pippa and Celeste entered the parlor a few moments after Nathan left, and Abigail hadn't fully gathered herself. She wiped the tears from her cheeks and faked a smile she could see neither of them believed.

Celeste moved for her first and drew her in for a hug. Abigail rested her head on her friend's shoulder and let out a long, shuddering sigh.

"You'll marry?" Pippa asked.

She nodded, because she couldn't say those words. Not yet.

Celeste led her to the settee and the three of them sat together, with Abigail in the middle. They allowed her silence for a while, allowed her to sink into the truth of this.

At last, Celeste spoke. "I know you have hesitations."

"Of course I do," Abigail whispered. "Not the least of which is that neither of us want this, and it...breaks my heart. I've watched you two fall in love in the last year, marry, make lives that seem so...I'm jealous of them, of you. I can admit it. And there was some tiny, foolish part of me that wanted that same thing for myself. Wanted a man who could overlook my past and see me. Want me. *Love* me. And who I could love in return."

"And you don't think that's Gilmore," Pippa said.

"How could it be?" She sighed. "We've been adversaries for a year. This is not a marriage he desired or chose. I am certainly not the caliber of woman that a duke might have sought. He could have married someone to further his position or fortune."

Celeste laughed. "I don't think Gilmore has to worry about his fortune."

"No, certainly not," Pippa agreed. "And I have seen a lot of the man in the last year, being that he and my husband are the closest of friends. I don't think he gives much of a damn about his position."

Abigail worried her lip. That, she most definitely could see. After all, the man stood by Rhys, despite whatever damage that loyalty might do. He went to the salon and truly listened to a man speak who thought the entire system that Nathan ruled over should be dismantled for the greater happiness.

She hated to give him too much credit, but he was open-minded. And seemed to care more about right than might.

"It doesn't follow that he gives a damn about me, either," she said, more to herself than to the others.

"He obviously does or he would not have been caught doing something naughty with you," Pippa said. "What exactly was it? I don't trust gossip."

"Pippa," Celeste said softly, a warning.

"Oh, you want to know, too," Pippa said with a laugh. "Don't deny it."

"Er, he was...he touched...he..." Abigail's cheeks flamed. "With his hands. He did some things with his hands. And it was...God, it's been so long since someone touched me like that, and even when it happened, it wasn't *like that*." She shook her head. "I wanted more."

"And you'll get it," Celeste said. "Because you'll be his wife."

She shivered at that word. Wife. The duke's wife. *Gilmore's* wife.

"I'll have to determine what that means for me as we read the banns and prepare," she said. "But right now I'm in shock."

"Then we'll just have a drink," Celeste said. "May I ask poor Owen to join us? Rhys went after Gilmore, so he's pacing around the other parlor, waiting for me to say he's allowed to have some part in this."

"Yes," Abigail said with a laugh as she waved her to fetch her husband, and then moved to the sideboard to pour the drinks. But as she did so, her hands shook because the reality of what was happening was sinking in. And the reality was less terrible than she wanted it to be.

But she couldn't let her guard down. Not with Nathan, not with anyone. Pleasure or not, that was not a thing she could allow.

CHAPTER 11

A bigail was no less confused or defensive the next day than she had been the day she agreed to be Nathan's bride. She kept waiting for it to sink in, to feel real and true and normal...but it hadn't.

At least there was work to be done to fill her spinning brain. She had informed her servants of her impending marriage and discussed their future plans and who might require references if they did not come to the new home. She'd been taken aback, frankly, at the strength of their reaction to the news. Across the board, they had all been joyful and supportive, as if they'd been waiting or hoping for this. Even her choice of husband had seemed to be a delight to them.

Once that odd task was done, Abigail had written to a few remaining acquaintances, making sure to romanticize the story between them as much as possible. She had no idea if anyone would believe her poetic words about Nathan and their great "love". They'd flowed easily enough, but when she read them over, it was as if someone else had written them.

Finally, she'd begun to look around her small home and think about what she would take with her when she moved to Nathan's home here in London. She had spent a great deal of her life studying herbal remedies and healing practices, so her library was most important to her. Surely he would have room for that in that rambling house here in London, but she had to wonder if he would also have commentary about her hobby...her passion. Erasmus had certainly had a great deal of it over the years, to the point where she'd just hidden her books and never spoken to him about it.

She had just finished that inventory of her books and entered the parlor. It was laid out for tea and the furniture had been arranged for guests. The former Mrs. Montgomerys and their husbands, along with Nathan, were coming here this afternoon, but it was still half an hour until their arrival. Celeste and Pippa had suggested it and passed the invitation on to Owen, Rhys and Nathan for her. Over the last year, they had become a team, and it seemed they intended to remain so, staying at her side and guiding her.

"At least I can be grateful for that," she murmured.

Paisley stepped into the parlor and said, "The Duke of Gilmore, Mrs. Montgomery."

She wrinkled her brow. "So early? Well, I know he can never be stopped. Bring him in."

She was pleased she sounded annoyed, because her true reaction had been her heart skipping a beat and her hands starting to shake. Seeing him alone, even for just a short time, felt dangerous. In the best way.

He strode through the door, looking like he owned the room, and executed a small bow. "Abigail."

"You are abominably early," she responded, arching her brow in what she hoped looked like disapproval. "It is like you were raised in a barn."

He chuckled and that same heart rate increased now. Damn him for being so handsome. And for not rising to her bait. When he took her barbs without fighting her, it felt intimate. Playful.

"You assume I was not just because I carry *Your Grace* around on my back?" he asked with a wink. That confidence should have further irritated her, but her body got a little warmer instead. She was certainly more aware of it. Not that he noticed, thank heavens, for he continued, "And I do apologize for my early arrival, but I have a good reason. I thought you might wish to be updated on the progress of our plans without the others here, staring at us like we are fish in a bowl."

She swallowed, all desire dissipating into nerves at the mention of their future plans. "Y-yes," she stammered. "Would you like tea?"

He shook his head. "Perhaps when the others arrive. Will you sit with me?"

He motioned to the settee, and she blinked. A settee had started all this trouble, but one could remain appropriate, couldn't one?

She sat and he joined her. "The first reading of the banns will take place at St. John's in Cornwall tomorrow, which is my church. I've arranged for them to also be read here in London. I assume you attend St. Augustine, as it is of walking distance?"

"I do," she said softly.

"Excellent. Then that will dispatch that issue. An announcement of the engagement will also appear in the *Times*, the *Chronicle* and the *Post* early next week. I'm also hoping I spoke to the correct individuals so that we may see it in that hideous *Scandal Sheet* rag that comes to the Upper Ten Thousand. Many are more likely to read a blind item there than to read a paper with actual news."

"You've thought of everything," she said.

"Everything but locking the door," he replied with a tight smile.

"You keep saying that." She cocked her head and forced herself to continue, because the question she was about to ask was not a particularly safe one. She was nervous about the answer. "Is your only regret about that night that we were caught?"

He drew back slightly and nodded, almost as if the question considered no thought at all. "Yes. That surprises you?"

She worried a loose thread on the sleeve of her gown. "I just thought if you could wish something away, perhaps it would be...it would be...*all* of it?"

He held her stare for what felt like forever, and then he leaned a little closer, until she could scent that lovely clean, soapy fragrance of him. The one that sometimes haunted her dreams.

"I wanted you, Abigail. I'm not ashamed of that fact, nor of what we did, proper or not. I hope you feel the same way."

He didn't wait for her response to that statement, but cleared his throat and was back to business again. "We will marry at St. Augustine's, as well. It will be, of course, a very small affair. The Gregorys, the Earl and Countess of Leighton and my sister. Is there anyone else you wish to ask?"

She pursed her lips. "I-I don't have anyone else. My family is all gone."

The pain that accompanied that statement, even after all these years, was powerful. He seemed to sense it because he drew her hand over hers all too briefly. "I'm sorry, Abigail."

She bent her head. "So am I. It seems you have things all arranged. Not that I expected anything else from you."

"Always saw me as heavy handed, I know," he said.

"No. Organized. Driven." He arched a brow and she laughed. "And yes, heavy handed."

"Excellent. Let's not have impending nuptials end our hobby of ravaging each other. I wouldn't want life to get boring."

"With us? Impossible." She smiled, but her troubles still burned in her. "You mentioned your sister. What will Lady Ophelia think of all this?"

His mouth turned down suddenly. "Hard to say. I won't lie and tell you she's taken any of this well. When the truth came out about Montgomery, it hurt her. She thought herself in love with him, I suppose."

Abigail flinched. She knew that feeling. Knew how easily Erasmus could manipulate a situation, a longing. And Ophelia was so young. "I'm sorry she endured so much."

"Certainly she endured less than you or Pippa or Celeste. She might be difficult when she comes to London, when she meets you. Or she might decide she likes you just to spite me."

"I hope that's true," Abigail said softly. She got up and walked away, feeling his gaze on her back with every step. "The others will be here shortly."

"How about a wager, Abigail?"

She pivoted to face him, eyebrows lifting in confusion. "A wager? Is that wise?"

"We aren't exactly wise when it comes to each other, are we?"

She caught her breath because he was suddenly looking at her like he wanted to devour her. And she felt no fear in that idea. "I suppose not. What would we wager on?"

He pushed to his feet and smoothed his jacket. "Hmmm. Well, why not make the best of a bad situation? Who will bring up the wedding, or the scandal surrounding it, first?"

She smothered a laugh despite herself. "That is easy. Celeste will say it first. But then she'll take it back. Try to play it off."

"Fascinating theory," he said. "But you are, as usual, wrong."

"Cad!" she burst out, now unable to keep herself from laughing out loud. "Then who do you say, since you are so clever?"

"Rhys will be the one," he said, all certainty in the way he held himself and the tone of his voice. "He's bound and determined to play the role of your judgmental brother to the rogue who ruined you. I'm surprised he hasn't called me to the dueling ground."

At that her smile fell. "Please tell me your friendship is not truly threatened."

"You are worried, Abigail? For me?" He winked again. "You needn't be. Nothing will end our friendship, I assure you."

"Good," she said, real relief pulsing through her. She pushed it aside with further teasing. "After all, you have so few friends, don't you?"

"Through the heart, my lady," he said, clutching his chest with one hand in dramatic flair. "Now, do you accept the wager?"

"What do I win?" she asked. His brows went up again and she held up her hands. "I've bested you twice, Your Grace, I will surely win. I want to know my prize."

"Minx," he growled and then tapped his chin with his forefinger. "Let me see...terms...terms...terms... What is it you want?"

She couldn't help it. Her gaze slipped to his lips for the briefest moment, and her mind jerked her back to his mouth on hers as he dragged her down the settee. His hands bringing her such expert pleasure. She swallowed hard and his pupils dilated.

"What about a kiss?" he asked, taunting her with what she clearly couldn't hide. Damn him for seeing her so clearly.

"A kiss?" she repeated, trying to make her voice sound like that hadn't been on her mind. Like she didn't even remember they'd kissed before. That she didn't even know what a kiss was.

He nodded slowly, never breaking eye contact. "We're going to be married in a few weeks, aren't we? It's all practice now."

"And what would you win?" she asked, wishing her voice wasn't so rough in response.

"I thought you were so certain of your impending victory, Abigail. Why even prepare for losing?"

"You might cheat," she said.

He snorted out a laugh. "She impugns my honor yet again. My lady, I am at your feet, what would you be willing to give me if I should be so lucky, or so cunning, as to win?"

She really only wanted that damned kiss, but she couldn't say that. The words wouldn't come for one, but she also didn't want to admit it to him. She didn't want to let him win and have this desire to hold over her. She didn't want to change their relationship and risk any more of herself than she already had.

"You'll win your pound back," she said with a smile.

He choked out a laugh and then nodded. "That, my dear, is a bargain."

She extended a hand for them to shake on the deal. He took it, but tugged her close instead. Close enough that her chest brushed his, that his breath warmed her skin. He bent his head and his mouth was on hers again.

Despite the fact that they had kissed before, that they would be married soon, that she wanted his mouth on hers, it was still a surprise whenever he did it. As shocking as the first time it had happened; as potent, too.

He was gentle this time, his mouth almost feather-light against hers. She wanted more and lifted into him, parting her lips to welcome him. He took slowly, too slowly, almost tortuously slowly. He tasted her, savoring, teasing and her knees went weak with it. With him.

But before things could go too far, before she could lose herself in him, he pulled away and smiled at her.

"I-I thought that's what I'd win," she gasped, breathless and shaky. "Are you conceding already?"

He shook his head. "Not at all," he said. "I was thinking you'd win a very different kind of kiss."

He released her then, with her mouth gaping in surprise, and stepped away just as Paisley appeared in the doorway to announce the arrival of the rest of their group. But even as she pulled herself back together and managed to properly greet her friends, she knew she would only be thinking of that wicked suggestion the rest of the day.

It had been a long afternoon, but a pleasant one. It was impossible not to enjoy spending time with Abigail, Rhys, Pippa, Owen and Celeste. And watching the three women interact, their strong friendship on display every time they exchanged a look or laughed at a joke, was wonderful. Their bond was that of sisters, and Nathan was glad Abigail had such a support system in her life.

No one, as of yet, had mentioned the upcoming wedding. But the tension of it had hung in the room all day. Along with tension of a different kind. Since their kiss, Abigail had sent quite a few side glances his way. Sometimes her gaze dropped to his mouth, sometimes she seemed to jerk herself out of thought and force herself back into conversation.

He had distracted her...and he liked it far too much for his own good. Not that he had any intention of stopping. He had no idea what a marriage to this woman would look like, but it was happening. If they had desire between them, that was better than animus, it was better than fear or mistrust.

At least it was a start.

"With all that is going on, is there anything we can do to help with the wedding?" Celeste asked. She blushed. "Not that you are over-whelmed. You're both capable people. And perhaps since you haven't brought it up, you don't want to talk about it, which is also fine."

Abigail's face lost all color and she jerked her gaze toward Nathan. He smothered a laugh at her expression, a mix of triumph, a hint of terror and a heavy dose or anticipation. After all, she knew what she'd won. He'd tried to make it very clear. And he liked that she licked her lips in response. He liked that she gripped her hands into fists in her lap. He liked that he moved her in some way.

"I...we..." Abigail stammered.

Nathan interrupted, smoothly giving their friends the same infor-mation he had shared with her a short time before. When he was finished, Pippa leaned forward. "Then we'll see your sister very soon."

He nodded. "She is due to arrive here in four or five days, depending on the roads. She will stay for the remainder of the Season."

Abigail worried her lip, but said nothing. He felt her anxiety about the arrival of his sister, but there was little he could do to ease it.

The gazes of their friends shifted between them, and Rhys pushed to his feet. "It is getting late," he said. "And I suppose we should be moving along and let Abigail get back to whatever plans she's working on."

They all stood and moved as a chattering group into the foyer. Paisley called for carriages, and it was a jolly group as Celeste and Owen got into their rig first, followed by Pippa and Rhys. Nathan stood on Abigail's landing, waving to their friends. He rested his opposite hand on the small of her back and felt her reaction ripple through her.

He glanced down at her, their eyes met. "Should I go?" he asked, softly enough that only she could hear. "Or do you want your kiss?"

She held his gaze a moment. A very long moment, indeed, and then she glanced at the footman who was still standing on the drive, waiting for instruction. "The duke will be staying a while longer. We will call for you when he is ready."

She glanced at Nathan again, brief and nervous, and then she stepped back into the house, leaving him to follow behind, hands shaking and mouth watering with anticipation.

CHAPTER 12

A bigail led Nathan down the hall, past the parlor where they had spent time with their friends, past the dining room, past the library, and stepped into the last room on the right, motioning him to enter first.

He drew in a breath as he did so. "This was Montgomery's study."

She followed him inside and slowly shut the door with shaking hands. "Yes. I think you've been here before."

He nodded. "When Owen brought me so we could confront Montgomery, this is where we found his…his body."

"Only he had faked his death," she said. "To frame me and start a new life with whatever settlement his poor brother would pay to the mother of his illegitimate child." She shook her head. "God, just saying it out loud makes my stomach turn. It's like something out of a book, not something that happens to a real person."

"But the room looks different now," Nathan said, turning to look at the chamber from all angles. "It looks like…you."

She smiled at the observation and glanced around the room, herself. "After Erasmus was truly dead, after Rhys gifted this house to me as fully my own, I decided I would reclaim it for myself. This room was the first place I did it. I cleaned it out of anything that reminded me of him and made it mine. I replaced or refinished the furniture, I made it lighter and brighter as best I could."

"You took it back," he said.

"Yes, I suppose that's true. I needed to take something back after all he'd done." She swallowed hard at the admission. It felt so intimate to reveal so much to this man she'd been wary of since almost the first moment she met him. "Now I use it as a study, a place for my books."

He moved to the shelves, sliding his finger across the books about plant types, poisons, remedies and medicines. "You are remarkable," he said softly as he faced her.

She felt the heat in her cheeks and turned away from him. "Not truly. I am a woman who married a very foolish man. I believed in him for too long. And once I didn't...well, I was trapped, wasn't I?"

He opened his mouth but shut it before he spoke. Still, she could see what he wanted to say. He wanted to tell her she wasn't trapped anymore. Except she was. So was he. Their imprudence had ensured that.

He cleared his throat. "I hope we can create something similar to this space for you in my home."

She drew in a long breath. "That would be nice. I'll miss this place. There are many happy memories here, not just the unhappy ones."

He nodded. "What do you intend to do with this house?"

She shrugged. "Gift it back to Rhys, I suppose. He can sell it which might help a bit with the financial burden his brother left him."

Nathan stared at her a long, charged moment. Then he moved toward her, slowly but steadily. When he stopped, he cupped her cheek. "I'm going to repeat my earlier assertion. *You* are remarkable."

He leaned in and his lips touched hers. The kiss earlier had been gentle, restrained, but this one wasn't. He cupped the back of her head, holding her close as he plundered her mouth. He was driven now, just as he had been the night they were caught at the ball. She trembled just thinking about it as he backed her toward the pretty velvet settee she had placed before her fire for reading or studying.

But before he could lower her there, he broke the kiss. A strange expression crossed his face and he backed up, holding up a finger. "Don't move."

She wrinkled her brow and stared as he crossed back to the door. For a brief moment, she thought he might leave, but instead he turned the key in the lock and pivoted back to her with a smile.

"There. Now there will be no regrets."

A nervous laugh escaped her lips as she watched him stalk back across the floor to her. He removed his jacket as he did so and tossed it aside. He loosened his cufflinks and set them on the table beside her settee before he rolled his sleeves up to the elbow.

The thrill she got when she looked at his bare forearms was unreal. She wasn't prepared for it, because arms seemed such an innocuous thing. His weren't, though. Corded with muscle, lightly peppered with dark hair...they flexed as he pressed a hand into the cushion next to her backside and leaned in.

She met his kiss halfway, digging her fingers into his biceps as if she could retain some kind of control over what was happening. She couldn't. He lowered her against the settee, just as he had at his house a few nights before.

He half-covered her, and it wasn't enough weight. She wanted more. She wanted it all. She wanted naked bodies, slick with sweat, grinding against each other. She wanted the smooth slide of him deep inside of her. She wanted to know his taste and the expression on his face when he found pleasure thanks to her.

She wanted all those wicked, intimate things with this man she had called her enemy for almost a year. Now he didn't feel like an enemy anymore. But as he parted his mouth from hers and held her stare, he also wasn't a friend.

He was something else. Something she couldn't yet define, or was perhaps too afraid to. He was her future, for better or for worse.

"I want you to know something," he said softly.

She swallowed. What he was saying required her to think. She didn't know if she remembered how to think. Her head was spinning from him touching her and kissing her.

"What is that?" she choked out.

"We wager and we play, and that's fine," he said. "But I only want to do this if you want me to."

She blinked as she stared up at him. She had loved Erasmus Montgomery. She would have, before the lies upon lies came out, called him a good man. And yet he had never given her such quarter in their marriage. Once she took his name, he had made it very clear that she would do what he liked, when he liked it. Mostly that had been fine. When it hadn't been, she had drifted away and thought of other things.

But this man, this man she bantered with and sparred with and occasionally despised, told her that what *she* wanted was what mattered. That he was at her service, not the other way around.

And it made her want him more than she had ever wanted any person in her life.

She drew in a long breath to calm her racing heart, and then she said, "Your Grace, if you renege on this bargain, I will call you out for pistols at dawn."

His mouth twitched. "Are you a good shot?"

She leaned a little closer, almost touching her lips to his. "Excellent."

"Better not risk it then," he said. She waited for him to kiss her, but instead he dropped his mouth to her throat, nudging the side of it with his nose, licking and kissing a trail to the edge of her gown.

"May I take this off?" he asked. She glanced over the back of the settee toward the door. "It's locked," he reminded her. "It will be easier that way. And I admit, I very much want to see you without it."

She let out a long breath. "No one has seen me…like that in a very long time."

He nodded. "I can make it worth the wait."

She squeezed her eyes shut. They would be married shortly and he would see her without her clothes then at any rate. And right now she so wanted what he had promised her. She so wanted what he'd already given in those stolen moments at the ball. She wanted pleasure. She wanted his focused attention on her. She wanted him.

She opened her eyes and found him watching her, silent and seemingly patient. "Yes."

He smiled and tugged her into a seated position. Her gown's buttons were along the back, and he wrapped his arms around her and began to unfasten them. She turned her cheek into his shoulder as he did so, drawing in a deep whiff of his scent, memorizing the feel of his linen shirt against her skin.

His breath hitched, his fingers fumbled for a moment, but he managed to unfasten and draw her dress down, away from her shoulders, down her arms. It bunched at her waist, and for a moment he leaned back to look at her in her chemise.

The intensity of his gaze heated her cheeks and she forced a nervous laugh. "Already disappointed?"

His brow wrinkled. "On the contrary. I'm just trying to pace myself so my eagerness doesn't make me look like a green boy."

"Are you so very eager, Your Grace?" she whispered.

He slipped a finger beneath one chemise strap and lowered it to her elbow. He followed the path of it with his lips. "So. Very. Eager."

He repeated the action on the other side, and suddenly she was naked from the waist up. They leaned back together on the cushions again, and his mouth moved from her shoulder to her collarbone. He traced the line of it with his lips, then lower. When he nudged his cheek against her nipple, she gasped at the faint hint of stubble stroking against the ultrasensitive skin. With a chuckle, he turned his face and blew a gust of warm air there.

She arched, shamelessly seeking more sensation, and he didn't deny her. He darted out his tongue and touched it to her nipple, the tiniest lick, then harder, harder. And then he sucked her and she shut her eyes. She dug her fingers into his hair, not caring if she mussed him as she held him to her breast and reveled in sensation. He was an expert at pleasure, teasing her with his tongue, with his teeth, sending a pulse of pleasure through her body to settle between her legs.

When she was shaking, when she was a puddle on the settee, only then did he move to her opposite breast, starting all over there as she writhed.

At last, he hooked his hands around her bunched dress and chemise and tugged them lower. She lifted her backside to free herself, and as he pulled the fabric over her hips, she kicked it away.

She was naked, spread out on her settee in front of a roaring fire that cast a glow over her skin. There was no hiding from him now, though she strangely didn't feel a desire to do so. He looked at her, and it felt...right. Not uncomfortable. If anything, watching his pupils dilate made her arch her back a little further, give him a better view.

"Perfect," he breathed as he shifted his position.

In the parlor at his home, the last time he'd touched her, he'd knelt on the floor before her, like he wanted to worship at her altar. He did the same now as he dragged his mouth down the slight swell of her belly, across the curve of her hip. The light touch of his lips was like lightning, and it ricocheted through her, sparking every nerve and fiber of her being. She felt like she was floating, like she was glowing.

And then he placed a hand on each thigh and urged her legs apart. Time stopped. She stared down at him, watching as he looked at her sex. He licked his lips and she almost came undone right then and there.

"To the victor go the spoils," he murmured. "Though I think *I* might have actually won the prize."

He lowered his mouth as he said it, and pressed it to her inner thigh. His rough cheek stroked again, this time between her legs, and she let out a sound from her throat that was like nothing she'd ever heard before from her own body. It was like someone had bottled her need and her loneliness and her desire and then uncorked it after all this time.

Nathan drank it like it was fine wine. He peeled her open, massaging gently as she lifted to him. She forced her eyes open and watched, breathless as he finally put his mouth against her sex. His tongue traced her slit, gently at the first swipe, harder with the second. She dug her hands into his hair again and ground against him helplessly as he chuckled against her flesh.

"Oh yes," he murmured. "This is going to be fun."

He didn't speak again. He simply dove into pleasuring her with the enthusiasm of a man who truly loved what he was doing. Back and forth, he stroked his tongue across her length, swiping her clean of the evidence of her desire, renewing it with every touch. He held her hips steady as he began to focus more on her clitoris, sucking then retreating, sucking longer and then he was gone again.

She rolled her head against the settee cushion, fingers clenching and releasing against his scalp. He sucked in earnest now, rolling his tongue around her clitoris, every tiny groan vibrating through her and making her vision blur.

She felt the orgasm coming. She ground against him to find it faster, to make it harder. They had one shared goal now, her pleasure, and he seemed determined to take her there. The cliff edged neared and she reached for it, reached for it.

And then she fell. Waves of pleasure ripped through her, and her hips flailed out of control, even as he held her steady with one hand. With the other, he breached her with a finger, and she gripped it with every pulsating surge. He never stopped tormenting her, sucking and licking as tears streamed down her face and her body went limp, at last, against the settee.

He lifted his head, and for a moment all was still and quiet. She flopped a forearm over her face. She'd touched herself, of course. She knew how to give herself pleasure with her own hand, but she had forgotten how powerful it was to have another person do it. To have someone *want* to make her shake, to make her cry out. And certainly her husband had never done it so well as Nathan just had.

There was a light tap against her arm, and then he lifted it gently and peeked beneath.

His chin was slick with her release, his lips red from pleasuring her. She lowered her arm and cupped the back of his neck, drawing him to her so she could kiss him deeply. She tasted herself on his mouth, sweet and salty, earthy.

When they parted, she shook her head. "My God."

He gave a half-smile, arrogant and proud. "Happy to oblige, my dear."

She giggled despite herself and swatted him on the arm. "Please tell me that you're not going to be even more insufferable than usual."

"I absolutely intend to be," he said. "Now that I know how beautiful you are when you fall over the edge of pleasure, I'm going to congratulate myself about it five times a day."

She smiled again as she reached out and traced the line of his forearm, her palm tickled by the faint smattering of hair there. She bit her lip. "It seems only fair to even the score, doesn't it?" She glanced at his trousers, where the bulge of his erection pressed against the fabric.

He followed the line of her stare and smiled. "You won a prize today for a wager and I always pay promptly and fully. This..." He caught her hand and pressed it to his cock through his trousers. It twitched, and she sucked in a breath. "...will keep."

He leaned in, bracing his hands on the pillow behind her head. He kissed her once more and then shoved to his feet. She stared, utterly confused by his...was it a rejection? Not exactly; after all, he had just rocked her entire being to its core. And she could see he wanted her, so it wasn't that.

But he was just going to...walk away?

She stood on unsteady legs, tugging her chemise free of her gown as she did so. She slid it over her head and watched as he moved to the mirror over her fireplace. He fixed himself, smoothing hair made wild by her fingertips. He looked almost a proper duke again when he was finished. Only she knew the truth.

"Here, let me help you," he said.

She stepped into her dress, and he motioned her to turn around. He fastened her with the same efficiency he had made her come undone. She might have thought him completely unmoved but that he leaned in and pressed a warm kiss to the side of her neck. He sucked gently, and she found herself leaning back against his chest, ready to start all over again.

"You are a temptation," he grunted, his voice thick. He stepped away and began to unroll his sleeves, refastening his cufflinks before he put his jacket back on. "But one I must resist just a while longer."

She nodded and hoped she looked as nonchalant as he did. "What are your plans this evening?"

He unlocked the door and they walked out together, back down the hall toward the foyer where he signaled for his carriage. As they waited, he said, "I've a supper meeting with a friend, someone I hope can help Rhys in his predicament. And, of course, I will be waxing poetic about our great romance." He leaned in a bit closer. "It will be much easier to do with your taste still on my tongue."

Her cheeks flamed and he laughed as he stepped away toward the carriage that had just pulled up to her door. "Goodnight, Abigail."

"Goodnight," she managed to croak out. She watched as he drove off into the growing dark, and shivered.

What had happened here today was...very confusing. She had no idea where they stood and less of an idea of what their marriage would be like. But there would be passion. It seemed he would make that happen.

And if he wouldn't, she would.

CHAPTER 13

Nathan paced the parlor that faced the street, pausing occasionally to glance out the window toward the drive. His sister would be arriving any moment. He hadn't seen Ophelia in over a month, since his last trip to Cornwall. He missed her, troublesome though she sometimes was.

He would have been excited except that he still didn't know how she would react to Abigail. Her letter after he'd told her of the engagement and asked her to come to London early had been...well, it wasn't exactly supportive. She'd had a thousand questions and concerns.

That wasn't the only trouble on his mind, though. Abigail, herself, was to join them for tea later, after his sister had settled in. He hadn't seen *her* for almost a week, since he left her after he pleasured her in her study.

He had dreamed of her every night since. Her taste, her scent, the sounds she made as she arched beneath him were all burned into his mind. He wanted more. Wanted it so much that the power of it frightened him a bit. Which was why he had been avoiding her and telling himself he was just busy with preparations for Ophelia's arrival and his wedding to Abigail.

Abigail had been no better, of course. She had not sought him out, either. And when he wrote to her, to ask her questions or invite her as he had today, she wrote only short, one-word answers.

Blue.

Thursday.

Yes.

He didn't think she was upset with him. Certainly, she hadn't seemed that way when he left her, and Rhys and Owen assured him she was simply swamped with the work of shutting down her house and her last preparations for the wedding.

Perhaps he could speak to her about it today. Try to connect on a level beyond their usual sparring or the surprising and all-consuming passion that pulsed between them beneath the surface.

"Your Grace?" his butler said from the foyer, and Nathan jolted back to reality.

His sister's carriage had arrived while he was daydreaming of Abigail. He rushed to the foyer and outside just as a footman helped Ophelia down from the rig. She looked up at him from the bottom of the stairs, and then her face broke into the wicked grin he knew and loved so well.

"Nathan!" she squealed as she rushed up to greet him while the footman helped her companion, Miss Cross, down behind her.

They embraced, and Nathan welcomed the warmth that spread through him at her presence. Though Ophelia was eleven years his junior, they had always been close. Even closer after the death of their parents when she was eleven and he twenty-two. He had been thrown into the position of duke and of father figure. Once past the initial terror, he had thrived in both roles in the near-decade that followed.

Ophelia was the person he adored most and who frustrated him most—until he met Abigail, that is. She broke their hug and looked up into his face. "You look tired."

He shook his head as he tucked her hand into the crook of his elbow and drew her into the house. She greeted the butler, Gardner, and then followed Nathan into the parlor he had recently deserted.

"I suppose I *am* tired," he admitted. "Would you sit?"

"After the last few days of travel?" she said with a laugh. "No, I will pace ceaselessly and drive you mad instead."

He smiled as she began to do so. "I'm so happy you're home. I've missed you."

"Of course you have," she teased. "And I admit, I'm happy to be back in London. After...everything that happened last year, hiding away felt right. But I've been bored of late and I know I cannot avoid the Season forever."

"I hope you won't want to after a while. I hope you'll reconnect with friends and make some new ones and actually enjoy the parties and balls."

She arched a brow. "You mean you hope I'll swiftly find a husband so that we will both be leg shackled."

He rolled his eyes. "Yes, that's why I've indulged you hiding away in Cornwall...because I'm determined to see you wed by Michaelmas."

She snorted a laugh. "Well, I suppose I could try. Though the last time I rushed a courtship, you didn't quite like the results."

He could not laugh with her about the close call they had endured with Erasmus Montgomery. When his face fell, so did hers. She moved toward him to take his hand and stared up into his face. "I'm sorry. I ought not to tease. Even after a year, I know this still affects you. And now it is all tangled up in your own impending marriage."

He swallowed. That was, he supposed, true. Abigail was Montgomery's widow...the bastard's only legal wife. But Nathan had stopped considering her in that way months and months ago. When he thought of her, it was always about her intelligence, her wit, her sharp tongue, or more recently, how she felt in his arms.

"Nathan?"

He jolted. "I'm sorry. Woolgathering, I suppose."

"Are we going to talk about *her*?" Ophelia asked, and this time her tone was much more serious.

"Abigail?" he asked.

She nodded, her face becoming even more serious. "Yes. *Her*. Am I going to meet her before I'm forced to call her sister?"

He let out his breath in a long sigh and released her hand. He paced away. "She is coming for tea later," he said. "So yes, you will meet her. And we can talk about her all you like. What do you wish to know?"

"It isn't what I wish to know so much as my concerns about what I already do."

"Ophelia—"

She raised a hand. "Don't say my name that way. Don't try to pretend I'm being ridiculous. I have a right to my feelings and to be protective of you when it comes to a woman you will be tied to for the rest of your life."

He pursed his lips, forcing himself to tamp down a sudden urge to defend his fiancée. "Yes, you were clear in your letter that you had questions. I guessed you also had concerns. But you have not yet met Abigail, so I hope you haven't prejudged her."

"How can I not?" She paced across the room just as she'd promised to earlier. "Consider who she was linked to, married to! Consider that she only just escaped the scandal of her husband's death and now she has stepped into another one with you."

He shook his head. "I never said—"

"That your hasty plan to marry this woman was because of a scandal?" his sister asked. She arched a brow. "Come now, Nathan. You had to know I'd find out either by my own ways or from the fact that so many in my acquaintance were champing at the bit to tell me."

He ran a hand through his hair. "They are talking. Even all the way in Cornwall."

"Of course they are." She gave him a much gentler look. "They always are."

"Neither scandal is her fault."

She drew back. "How can you say that?"

"Do you think it was *your* fault that Erasmus Montgomery lied to and attempted to seduce you?" he asked, holding her gaze evenly.

She shifted. "Sometimes."

It was as if someone had punched him in the stomach. He took a long step toward her. "Ophelia..."

"I am an intelligent person," she said softly. "And yet I missed the signs that Montgomery was a liar and a charlatan. When I feel that way, when I torment myself over it, I remind myself that I only had limited contact with him. Just a few stolen moments where he convinced me I wanted whatever lie he was selling."

"That is true," he said. "I'm glad you can see it."

"Then why can't you see the opposite facts about Abigail? She was married to the man for five years. How could she have not known his true character? How could she not have been complicit in his bad deeds?"

He flinched because he, too, had those thoughts when he first met Abigail. His harsh words about those thoughts were part of why she had been so determined to hate him over the past year. And he had come to realize, quite quickly, that he was wrong. So was his sister.

"If you have an open mind when you meet her, you will see her character, her mind, her heart. You will see that she is not the villain you have created in your mind."

"You want to protect me," Ophelia said. "You must grant me the permission to feel the same desire when it comes to you."

He sighed, then caught her hand and tugged her in for a brief hug. "I appreciate you riding to my defense. In this case, I don't require it."

She tilted her head. "Do you care for this woman?"

He blinked. There was a question he hadn't allowed himself to consider overly much during the last year. But *did* he care?

"I won't tell you that Abigail and I have not butted heads. It seems our pastime. But I have come to...like her."

He said it and realized it was true. He did like the woman he had once called a menace. She was still a menace, of course...but that was no longer said in seriousness. Perhaps it never had been.

Ophelia pulled a face. "High praise for the woman you shall spend your life with. Nathan—"

He held up a hand. "The banns have already been read for the first time, Ophelia. The second is but a few days away. The marriage *is* happening, so there is no use in talking 'round and 'round in circles about it. You'll meet her and you'll see who she is."

His sister pinched her lips. "Fine. I suppose I will. Now, it has been a long trip and I think I'll go to my chamber and freshen up before she arrives."

She leaned up to kiss his cheek, then turned to go. He caught her arm before she could. "Ophelia," he said softly. "Just promise me you'll be...nice."

She shifted. "Ugh. Very well, I will try. For you."

She slipped away, leaving him to watch her go. And to grapple with the fact that he wanted Ophelia to *like* Abigail. Which meant he was far more invested in what their lives would look like intertwined than he had originally allowed himself to believe.

∾

Abigail's hands were shaking as she followed Gardner to the parlor. He announced her and then stepped aside to allow her entry.

She found Nathan first, standing by the window. Their eyes locked and her heart made the funniest flutter. She hadn't seen him in nearly a week, and she realized in that moment that she'd truly missed him. It was unconscionable.

He began to cross to her and she let her gaze flit around the room, looking for his sister. A young lady stood at the sideboard, setting down the teapot in her hand. She was pretty, with blond hair and a lovely pink dress that was fitted to perfection. She had to be Ophelia. Her eyes looked too much like Nathan's not to be. Eyes that bored into her, though her expression was neutral as she flicked her gaze over Abigail from head to toe.

"Good afternoon," Nathan said as he reached her. "I'm so glad you've arrived. May I present to you my sister, Lady Ophelia. Ophelia, this is Abigail. Mrs. Montgomery."

Abigail flinched at the use of her married name. So did Ophelia, so at least they had that in common. She extended a hand toward the young woman and tried to make her smile bright. "My lady."

Ophelia looked at her outstretched fingers for what felt like a few seconds too long and then shook her hand. "Mrs. *Montgomery.*"

Had Ophelia emphasized the name? Abigail couldn't tell if she was being paranoid or observant. Nathan didn't seem to react as he motioned them both to sit. Ophelia took one of the chairs and Nathan the other, leaving Abigail to take a place on the settee, staring at them as if they were a firing squad.

For a little while, it was only small talk between them. They spoke of the weather and the roads during Ophelia's journey from Cornwall. It was a strange thing. Abigail had always seen Nathan as so certain of himself, and yet he seemed nervous as he managed the conversation. She could see how much he wanted them to like each other.

And she couldn't help but smile, despite the fact that she had no idea if his acrobatics were working. Ophelia was still entirely unreadable no matter where the conversation moved. She did watch Abigail, though. Reading her, she thought. Just as Nathan had done back at the beginning.

Abigail smiled at Ophelia. "You've been away from London a while, I think. Do you have any plans for your time here?"

"Just a wedding," Ophelia said with a light laugh. When she smiled, it did soften her considerably. "I think you have lived mostly in London, though, haven't you? At least since your marriage to Erasmus Montgomery."

Nathan stiffened. He leaned forward. "You know, there's really no need to discuss—"

Abigail kept her gaze on his sister and interrupted. "I don't agree, Your Grace. I think it's very important we address this subject. It is the elephant in every room I enter, and your sister has a special interest in the topic because of her own past with the man."

There was a slight flutter of emotion of Ophelia's face, but she wiped it away almost immediately. Still, that brief glimpse of pain was one Abigail recognized. She'd certainly felt it, herself. That was their common ground, after all. At least some of it.

"I can understand why you would want to know more about my past with Montgomery," Abigail continued. "So did the others."

"The other wives," Ophelia said softly.

"Yes. You will surely meet Pippa and Celeste, as they are great friends to me and to your brother. Their husbands are the best of men."

Ophelia wrinkled her brow. "How could you all become friends, I wonder?"

Abigail smiled. "It is a unique sisterhood that we entered thanks to my feckless husband and his wicked actions. We bonded over our anger and our loss at first, and came to truly care about each other later. There are things I can say to those two women that no one else in the world would understand because we've been through a common ordeal. As have you. So I hope you know you are welcome in our circle."

Ophelia seemed to consider that offer. Then she leaned forward. "I suppose you and I will also share a different kind of *sisterhood*. Since you are to marry Nathan."

There was an edge to her voice that carried a warning. It was one Abigail didn't ignore, nor would she avoid this confrontation if that was what Ophelia desired. They might as well get it out into the open.

Though judging from the way Nathan had leaned back in his chair, covering half his mouth with his knuckles as if he was physically trying to keep himself from intervening, he was less comfortable.

"Yes," Abigail said slowly. "It is true that you and I will share a different bond because of my marriage."

"Was that by design?"

Abigail blinked. "By design? You mean…I would marry him to get to know you?"

"No." Ophelia arched a brow. "That you would marry him to benefit yourself. To save yourself."

"Ophelia!" Nathan snapped.

Ophelia turned toward him with a scowl. "You asked me to be nice. I am asking nicely."

Abigail straightened slightly. "You are as protective of His Grace— of Nathan—as he is of you. You two are very lucky to have each other."

Ophelia's attention shifted back to her. "You don't have brothers?"

She managed to keep from flinching. "No. Only a sister."

"And where is she?"

Abigail cleared her throat, fighting against the pain that answer still caused in her. "She died."

The hardness on Ophelia's face fell away in an instant, revealing nothing but empathy and sadness, a touch of guilt. In that moment, Abigail saw the potential to be friends with this woman. If she could get past her trust barriers, a woman like Lady Ophelia would likely be a very good friend.

"I am sorry," Ophelia said softly.

"Thank you. I am as well." Abigail leaned forward. "My engagement to your brother was sudden, and yes, it was born out of a scandal caused by imprudence. However, it was never by design. And since I have endured a very unhappy marriage, I am compelled to do everything in my power to make sure I don't repeat that. Despite the fact that I think your brother is occasionally an overbearing arse..."

Nathan barked out a laugh at that, and Ophelia's eyes grew wide as she smothered a smile.

"...that does not mean I wish to torture him." Abigail glanced at him. "Much. We will have to find a way to come to terms and not hurt each other. That is all that I have in mind when I think of a marriage to him."

Nathan's expression softened at that statement and her heart lurched a little. They had avoided discussing the definition of what this marriage would look like in the whirlwind of what had caused it to come to be. This was the first time either of them had dared hint about it.

But she felt the truth of her own words with every beat of her heart. She didn't want to be unhappy, and she certainly didn't want to cause unhappiness in another person. So she would have to do her best, try her best and hope that Nathan would do the same over the years to come.

She realized that Ophelia was now staring between her and Nathan, a contemplative expression on her face. She smoothed her hands against her skirt before she stood up. "You have been very honest, Abigail, and I deeply appreciate it. But I find myself a little tired after travel. I think I shall excuse myself if you don't mind."

Abigail followed her to her feet. "Of course not. There will be plenty of time for us to get to know each other better over the next few weeks. I very much look forward to it."

Ophelia nodded, then squeezed her brother's hand and slipped from the room. Nathan stared after her for a moment and then let out a long sigh. "I'm sorry she turned the conversation to such delicate topics."

Abigail shrugged. "I'm not. I'd rather have her be direct like that than to have her secretly hate me and never say a word so I might correct any misconceptions she might have."

"Well, that's very kind of you, but that isn't what I meant."

She swallowed because his gaze had suddenly become very focused. "What did you mean then?"

He moved to the door and slowly closed it. Her heart began to throb, because a closed door had come to mean a great deal for them. But he stayed there, as if he were trying to respect the distance between them.

"I meant she mentioned your sister. She mentioned Ella."

She recoiled at the mention of Ella's name. She knew she'd never given it to him. She rarely spoke of her at all. But he was looking at her like he knew, like he understood. Her hands shook as she clutched them together before her.

"How do you know her name?"

CHAPTER 14

Nathan could feel the waves of pain coming off of Abigail, and he wanted to rush to her side. To hold her close. To comfort her. But he also felt something else coming from her, something angry and accusatory, something defensive. So he honored that and stayed at the door so as not to crowd her.

"Don't just stare at me," she hissed. "Answer me. How do you know about Ella?"

He cleared his throat. Honesty was best here, no matter what it would cause. "I…looked into your past."

Her nostrils flared, and for a moment he was torn back in time to the first time they'd met. To how she had looked at him with disdain and dislike and it had been genuine. Seeing it again made him realize how far they'd come…and how far they could fall if they weren't careful with the delicate relationship they were developing.

"Of course you did," she said, turning away and going to the window. "I'm sure you were trying to find some information you could use to prove I was the villain you wanted me to be."

He drew in a shaky breath and took a step toward her. "You don't know how much I want to give you some flippant answer instead of the truth."

She caught her breath as she faced him again. "I think I understand that, actually. We have never been open with each other, never trusted each other enough to be. But...as uncomfortable as it is, we must now, or we shall both be miserable. I wasn't lying to your sister when I said I didn't want that. So please, just tell me everything."

She was so earnest in those words. He didn't think he'd ever seen her so open when she looked at him and it was intoxicating. He never wanted it to go away. He wanted to earn that look for the rest of their lives.

He cleared his throat. "I was so angry with Montgomery," he said. "And I...I couldn't believe you didn't know his true nature."

He watched how those words hit her. Felt the pain of them, felt the wrongness now that he knew her better.

"Just like everyone else," she said at last, so softly she almost couldn't be heard.

"Yes," he admitted. "I was as wrong and foolish as everyone else back then. But I want you to know that the more I grew acquainted with you, both through my intrusive and wrongheaded actions and from the time I spent from you, the more I understood you were not the kind of person who could ever support that man's actions. The more I knew that you were a decent person, with a warrior's heart."

Her eyes went wide at that response, and he couldn't blame her. A year ago he wouldn't have admitted to such a thing. But the world had changed since then. *They* had changed.

"I thought I was a menace," she said with the faint hint of a smile. And that faint hint gave him hope. If she could tease with him, that meant she didn't hate him. At least no more than usual.

"You're both," he teased back. Then he drew a ragged breath and reached for her, praying she would allow him to touch her. She did, shivering when he traced his fingers along the line of her jaw, across the curve of her cheek. "But the fact remains, I *do* know about your past."

She shut her eyes and leaned into his hand. Her face was lined with more of that pain. "About Ella."

He nodded. "And once I did know it, so much made sense. How protective you were of Celeste and Pippa, how welcoming you were under the worst of circumstances. I liked you a little more."

A hint of a smile tilted her lips. "Oh, that must have burned you down to your very core."

"It was horrible," he teased, but then he got more serious. "Can you forgive me for what I did?"

She drew a ragged breath. "Once upon a time, not so very long ago, I would have slapped your face for what you just admitted. But I can see now, because I know you better too, that you were doing what you could to defend and protect your sister. I know how much that duty, that privilege means to you. And *that*, I understand. So yes, I forgive you."

He let out a shuddering sigh and telling relief coursed through him. "Thank you."

She stared up at him, searching his face, searching his soul, he thought. Then she said, "Would you...would you like to know more about her?"

He drew back a fraction. "Y-Yes. I would, if you want to tell me. Now or some other time."

"I think the time is now," she said on another ragged sigh. "Because the future is coming, isn't it? And it's one where we will need to trust each other, at least a little. So I'll tell you about Ella, Nathan. I'll tell you everything."

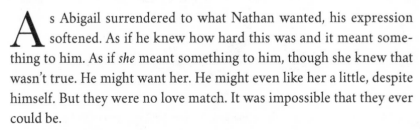

As Abigail surrendered to what Nathan wanted, his expression softened. As if he knew how hard this was and it meant something to him. As if *she* meant something to him, though she knew that wasn't true. He might want her. He might even like her a little, despite himself. But they were no love match. It was impossible that they ever could be.

And yet his approval, his support, meant something.

She sighed, and suddenly she felt so very tired. Like the weight of the last year, of the last few weeks, had finally buckled her knees. "May we sit, though?"

He nodded immediately and led her back to the settee. Only this time he didn't take a place in the chair across from her, but on the cushions beside her. He took her hand and held it against his knee while he waited, unspeaking, not pushing, for her to tell him about the most devastating pain she had ever endured.

"She was five years younger than I was, but Ella and I were very close. We had to be. Our father was very strict, stern. He was the second son of the Earl of Middleton, and I realize now he was driven to prove himself. He was not loving. And our mother was flighty as a nervous hen. She spent money and bought ridiculous hats and could be fun and play. But she wasn't very focused on us, and we both knew we couldn't really depend on her."

"So you depended on each other," Nathan said.

"Yes. I think you know a little about that."

He nodded, but didn't elaborate or try to take anything from her story. So she continued, "She was eight when the fever took hold. At first no one took it very seriously, but within a day or two, it was obvious she was in danger. My father brought in the best doctors from London."

She pressed her lips together, squeezed the hand Nathan wasn't holding until her knuckles went white.

"Take your time," he said softly.

She nodded. "They were butchers. So many of those men are butchers, with medieval torture practices masquerading as cures. I stood in that room and watched as they tormented her. They bled her, they burned her, they soaked her in freezing water, they forced her to walk, they—" She squeezed her eyes shut and repeated, "They tormented her."

His hand tightened on hers. "I'm so sorry."

"I watched them killing her, and I begged my parents to fetch the healer the villagers sometimes spoke about. A woman who lived just outside the grounds of our estate. They refused and refused. Finally the doctors gave up. They packed up and shrugged and said there was nothing they could do. They told us to prepare ourselves."

She bent her head, her breath labored as she tried so hard not to go back to that night. "I ran from the house. I ran and screamed and cried all the way to the healer's cottage. Two miles through the woods without a coat, only in my slippers. I must have looked a fright when I got there."

"What did she do?"

"Put me on her horse and we rode back together. I had such high hopes that she could save the day. But when she looked at Ella, she could see it was too late. But she gave my sister comfort and stayed with her until the end."

Abigail felt the tears streaming down her face as she spoke. Told this story she had kept silent for years.

Nathan gently wiped some of those tears from her cheeks with his thumb. "You did everything you could."

"Yes," she agreed. "But my parents hadn't. Those doctors hadn't. I became obsessed with the healer. Her name was Francine Boyd. I was deep in grief, furious that no one had listened to me. And furious that my parents seemed to get over what had happened fairly quickly, even as I drowned in it. Francie took pity on me, I suppose. She knew if I had something to study, I would go less mad in my grief. She taught me."

"What did the second son of an earl and his flighty, silly wife think of that?" he asked, and he sounded impressed, which was more important to her than it should have been.

"They were livid, of course," Abigail said, and smiled for the first time since beginning this story. "But something had broken between us the night my sister drew her last breath. And I didn't give a damn if they were angry. If they forbade me, I snuck out. If they punished me, I took it with a smile. Eventually they gave up."

"You are a stubborn thing," he said softly.

"Yes." She shifted a little. "Erasmus hated my interest as much as they did. He used to rail at me, threaten to burn all my books to make me respectable. He wouldn't let me go to Francie's funeral when she died a year after we married." She lifted her chin. "When he died, I immediately tore out the garden and replaced it with herbs...to spite him. But I suppose you also wouldn't want your duchess to do something so...common."

His brow wrinkled, and he looked confused by her statement. "Why would I stop you?" She blinked, and he continued, "I think it's healthy to have a passion. Especially one that could be of great help to others. I encourage you to continue your study. There are experts to consult—we can find them. You will have your own private study at my home here in London. We can transform it into a library with space for experimentation if you'd like. There is plenty of room in my garden here to plant whatever you like. And there is a greenhouse at my estate in Cornwall. It is yours, as well. Grow anything you would find useful."

She stared at him, her heart rate increasing with every effortless support of her dreams. Without thinking, she wrapped her arms around his neck and lifted into him for a kiss.

He was still for a moment, as if the action shocked him. But then he angled her across his lap so he could deepen the kiss. She relaxed against him, the pain of her confession melting away at his touch.

Eventually, he pulled back a little, and she stared up into his eyes. She shook her head. "You are very confusing."

He burst out a laugh. "Am I?"

She nodded as she tugged from his arms and righted herself on the settee once more. "But I appreciate the support. I don't fully trust it... but I appreciate it."

"Good. I like keeping you on your toes," he said.

"I'd wager you do," she said with her own laugh.

"Oh, a wager! What do you have in mind?"

She rolled her eyes, the tension and connection of the last few moments tempered now. She thought perhaps he did that on purpose, for both their comfort. "You are a cad, Your Grace."

"Proudly so."

"But do you think it's wise to make these bets? They tend to lead us into temptation."

He tilted his head. "Well, we are to be married in just a little more than a week, once the third set of banns are read on Sunday. So temptation is on the table, as far as I'm concerned, as long as you agree."

She nodded slowly. "I...do." When his eyes lit up, she got to her feet and moved away from him. Mostly so that she didn't do something too foolish. "And I would *wager* that there will be some nasty blind item about us before our wedding, probably the morning of."

He shook his head. "Well, that is no wager. I've done my best to make sure a few blind items appear about us."

"No, those are nice things. That we're truly in..." She cleared her throat. "...in love. I'm talking about something cruel. Something horrible."

His face twisted. "Like what? You must have a little more specificity, Abigail."

She glared at him playfully. "Someone will say that I have a secret fortune and you are angling for it."

"Interesting." He stroked his fingers over his chin. "*Do* you have a secret fortune I should be angling for?"

"No." She smiled. "Nothing to my name, I'm afraid, except for a pile of dusty books and a few pretty gowns."

"I've been known to put a high value on a pretty gown," he said. "Very well. Then I think the blind item will contain a strong implication that I have gotten you with child."

She froze and stared at him. A child. With him. He would want children, of course. Heirs and spares were required for a man of his station.

What kind of father would he be? Harsh like her own? Distant like so many? Or would he be kind and loving and unfashionably involved in the raising of his sons and daughters?

"Abigail?" he said, tilting his head. "Are you well?"

"Yes." She shook her thoughts away. "I was just thinking what a good guess that is. Better than mine, considering the way we were caught together and your reminder that we've been spreading the word that we are *desperately* in love."

He got to his feet and smoothed his jacket. "Yes. That seems to be taking, too. A few women positively cooed with congratulations when I was at Mattigan's Bookshop the other day."

She smiled, because that was the bookshop below Lady Lena's Salon. That he had returned there, that it was a place *she* could return to even after she wed because he supported her ability to do so, was very exciting.

"Then is it a wager?" she asked.

"We have not determined what we are wagering for," he said. "You have now revealed you have no massive fortune, so I think we should not bet with money."

She let her gaze move over him. He did cut a fine figure—he always had. And if he had admitted out loud that he'd always wanted her, she could admit to herself that those desires had always been returned. Even more so now that she knew the warmth of his touch, the ease with which he could make her come undone.

She wanted to do the same to him. She wanted to feel him squirm for her. Cry out for her. Shake for her.

"I agree." She stepped closer. "If you win, I will give you a kiss."

He stared at her a moment, his expression going just a fraction wild as he realized what she was saying. "A kiss like…"

"Yes, like the one you gave me," she said softly. "Unless you don't want that."

"Sometimes ladies don't want to do that," he said.

"This lady does."

His pupils dilated and he cleared his throat. "You're going to kill me," he muttered, and she thought it was more to himself than to her. "I'll be dead within a month of being wed. Happily dead, it seems."

"Nathan," she said.

He shook his head. "Yes. Of course. I agree to your terms. But what do you want if you win?"

She folded her arms. She did want something, but there wasn't anything playful or sensual about it. It was a risk to ask, but here they were and this was the perfect opportunity.

"I have told you something very painful from my past," she said slowly. "If I win, I want to know something about you."

"Some dark secret," he said. She nodded. He held her gaze firmly. "You assume I have one."

"You became a duke and what amounted to a father when you were in your very early twenties. You hide this playful side I'm now seeing under very serious layers. And you protect those you love as if you are afraid to lose them. I *know* there is a dark secret."

She saw a flicker of pain cross his face. Just for a moment, but then it was gone. He reached out to catch her hand and lifted it to his lips. "Very well. Your kiss, my secret. May the best person win."

She smiled. "I already have, Your Grace. Three times."

His laughter echoed in the room and continued to do so until he caught her waist and drew her in for a kiss that sealed the bargain. And she feared it would one day seal much more. Seal her to him, seal her heart.

And she still wasn't certain she could allow that to happen.

CHAPTER 15

Nathan stood on the terrace overlooking his garden with Owen and Rhys flanking him on either side. They were talking, but he wasn't paying attention to the words. He was staring down below where Pippa, Celeste, Abigail and Ophelia were walking together. Ophelia was smiling, seemingly welcomed fully into the group. That was thanks to Abigail, he knew. Abigail, who had pushed away her own pain to make a place for all the women Erasmus Montgomery had betrayed.

"They seem to be getting along," Owen said, interrupting Nathan's thoughts. "That was a concern, wasn't it? That Lady Ophelia wouldn't let Abigail close thanks to their mutual connection to Montgomery?"

Nathan frowned. "There are still...challenges. Every chance she gets, Ophelia says she doesn't like that my future is forced. And she's standoffish to Abigail. Even now, look at her."

They all looked toward the women again and watched as Ophelia stepped away so she wouldn't have to stand next to Abigail. He saw his future wife frown. She was trying and Ophelia was *being* trying.

"I see. But that's understandable," Rhys said. "You two have always been close. You rush to her defense, she to yours."

"Yes. I just hope one day she will soften to Abigail. Her defenses must be worn down eventually. Abigail has that way about her."

Rhys turned to face him slowly. "Are you still only talking about Ophelia, Gilmore? Or does that statement also apply to you?"

Nathan shook his head. He didn't want to talk about that, not even with his two closest friends. "Don't start."

Rhys rolled his eyes and Owen laughed. "No one has to start, but you must know that the connection growing between you two is obvious, especially to us."

"So you will not let it go. Why did I expect it? You two are so very intrusive."

Owen shrugged. "Intrusive is my occupation."

"It's more of a hobby for me," Rhys said.

Nathan couldn't control his laughter at that. "Perhaps there *is* a softening between Abigail and me. I suppose there must be, given what is coming in just a few days. A wedding. More to the point, a marriage. I will be honest that I have no idea what that will look like."

Owen clasped Nathan's bicep. "Talk to her. I'm sure she has the same hesitations and uncertainty. Neither of you planned this and it's happened so fast—talking to her is the first step toward avoiding misunderstanding and hopefully heartache."

Nathan glanced down again. It seemed Abigail had recovered from her disappointment at Ophelia's rejection, for she had her arm linked with Celeste, and the two were talking and laughing as the foursome meandered up the pathway to the house. Soften though she might, she was never as relaxed with him. Never as lit up.

He had to wonder if she ever would be. If they could ever overcome a bad start and make a future worth fighting for.

Abigail walked up the garden path, her arm through Celeste's, and glanced up at the terrace above. Nathan and the other two men were still there, and he was still watching her. Always watching her. That focused attention sent a shiver of awareness through her that settled in most inconvenient places.

Damn him for having that power. And damn herself for giving it to him.

"It has been such a lovely day," Celeste said, but Abigail caught her glance at Pippa.

"But?" Abigail said.

To her surprise, it was Ophelia who responded. "How do you know there is a but?"

Abigail fought the urge to crow at even this small bend in her hesitant future sister-in-law. Ophelia was a tough nut to crack, though Abigail understood the reasons and had no intention of giving up on her attempts to win the young woman over.

Abigail squeezed Celeste's arm. "I've known these two long enough to know the little lilt of concern in their voices. Plus they just gave each other the most meaningful look. Oh, there it is again!"

Ophelia's eyes went wide. "I *did* see it. They glanced at each other so seriously. Should I step away and let you three talk alone?"

"No," Abigail insisted, and held her stare evenly. "You are part of our little circle now. There is no escaping."

Ophelia's lips parted a fraction, and for a brief moment Abigail saw how much that statement meant to her. But then she straightened her spine and glanced away. Still, Abigail had won a little ground, it seemed. She would celebrate it.

"Go ahead, you two, I have nothing to hide from Ophelia," she said. "Give me whatever bad news you've been hiding all day. I'm ready for it." She sounded so brave, though her heart had started to race. She was so tired of waiting for another shoe to drop. A year of it was too much.

Celeste sighed. "Did you...did you happen to see the *Scandal Sheet* paper this morning?"

Abigail caught her breath. "You know, I didn't. Paisley must have hidden it from me. Which means there was something about me in it. Oh God, what now?"

Pippa took a step toward her. "There was a blind item and it implied...it implied that Gilmore might be marrying you so hastily because he wanted to make sure your child was legitimate."

Abigail dropped Celeste's arm and stared. "They implied I was pregnant?"

Celeste nodded. "I'm so sorry to upset you."

Abigail glanced up at the terrace again and her mouth twitched with a smile as she found Nathan. After three tries, the man had finally won one of their wagers. "Oh, he is going to be *insufferable*," she muttered.

"What was that?" Ophelia asked.

Abigail shook her head, trying not to think about what they had agreed he would win if the rumor about them was this. She wasn't sure she could keep the wickedness from her expression.

"Nothing," she said. "And I'm not upset. Gilmore and I already discussed that this was a possibility. I assume he knows?" That he hadn't come crowing to her the moment she arrived showed restraint.

Ophelia shrugged. "I don't know. He never said anything. But we also didn't get the paper. I wonder if Gardner hid it, as well."

"Well, I will tell him," Abigail said, and tried to think of the best way to reveal it. She had an idea. A very sinful idea. "We will be married soon, though. And when no child is produced in less than nine months, I suppose everyone will know the rumors weren't true."

Celeste sighed, as if pleased she hadn't upset her friend. "Speaking of the wedding, are you excited? We are just days away."

There was no mistaking the light of interest that brightened Ophelia's gaze. Abigail would have to tread carefully in her answer if she wanted to continue to chip away at the young lady's defenses.

"I will be glad to be done with the waiting. It's only been a few weeks, but it has felt interminable. I am a little...nervous. The future still seems uncertain, I don't know what my life will be like."

Up above, Rhys waved to them and Pippa smiled. "I think they're saying we should join them."

Abigail nodded and followed as Pippa and Celeste started up the stone stairs that led up to the terrace on the second floor. Ophelia stayed behind the others and fell into step beside Abigail.

"Comfortable," she said, staring straight ahead as they reached the top of the stairs.

Abigail stopped there and shook her head. "I'm sorry?"

Ophelia faced her. "You said you cannot picture your life. It will be comfortable. My brother will ensure it."

"I'm sure you are right."

Ophelia held her gaze a moment. "He is a good man. Don't let him down," she said softly, and then turned to join the others.

Abigail blinked at the edict. Don't let him down? She didn't intend to do so. She didn't want to. But how to do that remained to be seen.

The group of friends stood in the foyer together hours later, servants rushing coats and gloves to them, carriages being brought around. It was a scene of laughter and fun, but Abigail felt very much on edge.

She knew what was about to happen. And she was practically jumping out of her skin in anticipation. Into the carriages the couples went, and as Ophelia went back into the house, Abigail and Nathan stood on the step, waving to their friends together.

"That was a lovely night," she said with a contented smile.

"It was," he agreed as they came back into the foyer. "Did you have a nice time?" he asked Ophelia.

She smiled. "It was lovely. I've always liked Leighton, the former Mrs. Montgomerys are both lovely and Mr. Gregory is fascinating. I enjoy all their company very much."

"And you shall have a great deal of it, and I hope come to count us *all* as friends," Abigail said softly.

Ophelia inclined her head. Her lips tightened a little, her hesitation plain. She sighed. "You know, I am tired. Perhaps I shall excuse myself and read for a while. I'm sure you two wouldn't mind a little time alone."

Abigail tried not to look at Nathan. Surely he would see her intentions in her eyes, and she wasn't ready for that yet. "Goodnight, Ophelia," she said.

Ophelia looked at her a long moment. "Goodnight, Abigail." Then she kissed her brother's cheek and left them.

Now they were alone in the foyer, and Abigail glanced up at him. "I do have something to speak to you about," she said, trying not to bounce with nervous excitement.

His brow wrinkled. "Do you? Well, then that will give me an opportunity to show you something. Come."

He took her arm and they moved up the hall together past parlors and other rooms. He led her into one and she looked around. She'd thought it was another parlor, but it wasn't. It was a small study with tall, empty bookshelves and a cherrywood desk.

"It's lovely," she said.

"I thought it should be your study, and had the desk brought in and the shelves emptied in anticipation. Does it suit you?"

She stared at him a moment, emotions welling in her chest. Then she walked away and truly looked at the room. It wasn't large, but it was the perfect size for her. And the desk faced the window, which looked down over the gardens below. "I love it," she breathed. "Thank you."

The thanks seemed to make him uncomfortable, for he was shifting when she looked back at him. He cleared his throat. "We can speak about the decorations."

She worried her lip a moment, then refocused and meandered around the room further, always heading toward the door. She stopped there and closed it. His eyes widened a fraction.

"What you have to say must be very serious," he said.

She nodded. "It is. But first, what can you tell me about the desk?"

He looked confused as he glanced toward the escritoire. "It's...

wood? It's been in the attic for ages. I think it might have belonged to my grandmother. She loved to write."

"I see. And is it sturdy?"

He blinked. "Sturdy?"

"Yes."

He moved to it and pressed down on the top. The wood didn't tremble or shake. "It seems to be. Why? Do you intend to put something heavy on it?"

"Perhaps." She was practically bouncing now. He was so flummoxed, and it was just too much fun to cause it. "Will you lean on it?"

"Lean on it," he repeated. "Certainly."

He cocked his hip onto the tabletop and held out his hands as if to say *there*.

She nodded slowly. "Stay there, please."

She pivoted back to the door and turned the key. When she faced him again, his pupils had dilated and his gaze was much more focused. She drew in a shaky breath.

"I am going to say this once to you, Nathan." She moved toward him. "Just once."

He arched a brow. "Say whatever you would like to say."

She crossed the rest of the distance to him. With him half-seated on the desk, they were now of equal height. She licked her lips as she leaned toward him.

"You."

She brushed her lips to his and placed a hand on his chest before gliding it down. Together they watched her fingers slide lower and lower until she pressed her palm into his muscular thigh, then cupped it between his legs. She slid it across the fall front of his trousers and he sucked in a hard breath.

"Were."

She unfastened one button, then another, and then dropped the fall front down. His cock was half-hard already and bounced free. She glanced down at him and shivered. It was a very nice cock, and it hardened further as she stared, curling toward his belly.

It was filthy to have him fully clothed, his jacket open, his cock naked before her. She traced a finger over the head of him, reveling in the silky skin there. It had been so long since she touched a man this way, and when his breath kept catching it drove her mad.

She shifted down, onto her knees, and looked up at him.

"Right."

Then she fisted him in her palm and licked him.

Normally Nathan could find a response to any situation. He prided himself on being quick on his feet. But having Abigail drop to her knees and take his cock into her mouth erased any reasonable response he might have had. She'd said he was right, but he couldn't fathom what she meant because she sucked him and stars exploded before his eyes.

He gripped the desk edge with both hands, surrendering to what she was doing because he had no other choice. She had conquered him, and he was hers to do with as she wished. And oh, what she did. She rubbed her tongue hard against the underside of his cock as she took him deeper and deeper into her throat. When she reached her limit, she reversed the slide. She steadied herself with a hand on his thigh, while with the other she pumped the root of his cock, lubricating it with her spit.

Pleasure so sharp it bordered right on the edge of pain ripped through him. He had held back with Abigail for weeks, taking pleasure only in her pleasure and using his hand to relieve himself of the tension later. But now this was all about him, and it buckled his knees.

She swirled her tongue around him in a slow circle as she pumped, and he found himself tilting his hips on every thrust. Taking a little more of her mouth. She didn't retreat. She took him, every inch.

He forced his eyes open to look down at her and found her gazing up at him as she worked him. Their eyes met, and she smiled around his cock.

He nearly came undone right then and there. She was reveling in this. In unmanning him, in putting him on the edge, in giving him pleasure. Reveling in their connection just as he did when he made her quake.

She took him deeper again, right to the edge of what he had to believe was her limit, and let out the tiniest groan. It vibrated through his cock, and he grunted her name, pushing his fingers into her hair. Her strokes became faster, her tongue more active against him, and the pleasure notched up accordingly. He was racing at lightning speed toward release, his heated blood pounding in his ears as his legs began to shake.

"Abigail," he grunted. "Abigail, I'm going to spend. You can...please just..."

She held his gaze. He knew she understood him, but she kept him in her mouth, driving him, pushing him, stealing his control with every suck and thrust and swirl. He could take it no longer, and with a guttural cry, he came.

She took it. All of it, sucking him until he had nothing left to give and it was only then that she released him from her mouth with a pop and looked up at him with a smile. Her mouth was pink, her lips slick with his essence, and she looked entirely proud of herself. Not that she shouldn't.

"Well," he said when he could find the wherewithal to speak. "*That* was remarkable."

She laughed as she pushed back to her feet. "Yes," she agreed. "Very much so."

She leaned in and kissed him. He tasted the faint hint of himself on her lips and caught her arms to kiss her harder. They were both panting when they parted, his desire mirrored perfectly in her dark eyes.

But she didn't ask for anything. She didn't demand pleasure returned. She simply backed away and smoothed her skirts and hair. "You must be very proud. You finally won one of our wagers."

He was trying to get his mind to work as he tucked his cock back into his trousers and refastened himself. "Yes, you said I was right just before you...you..."

"Made your eyes cross with pleasure?" she said sweetly. Too sweetly.

He chuckled. "Yes. That. Does that mean there was a blind item about us in a gossip rag as we expected there would be?"

"In the *Scandal Sheet* this morning," she said. "You might want to ask your butler where he hid it. I intend to ask Paisley the same thing. Apparently I might very well be with child."

He shook his head. "A miracle."

"Indeed." Her smile faded a fraction. "But on the whole, our ruse seems to have worked. The hostility about the scandal seems to have been at least partly replaced with some acceptance of our impending union. So we won't hurt Ophelia's chances, it seems. We might have even raised Pippa and Rhys's standing a bit."

He nodded. "At the very least we've distracted the worst of the gossips."

She shifted a little, as if she were uncomfortable. "Well, I've dispatched with your prize, so I suppose it's time for me to go."

She pivoted as if she would lead the way out of the room, but he caught her arm and held her steady. "Wait, Abigail."

She stared up at him, her bottom lip trembling just the slightest bit. He felt her tension, her worry, her uncertainty in a way he'd never felt it before. And he wanted, so desperately, to fix it.

"Let's talk about the future," he said softly. "We've avoided that topic, perhaps because we were both shocked by the way we were pushed down this hill by scandal. But we need to face it, don't we?"

"So say all our friends," she said. "But I hardly know where to begin."

He drew in a long breath. "You were trapped once in a marriage that turned unhappy. I don't want that to be your life with me. What do you *want* the future to look like?"

Her eyes widened a bit, as if shocked that he would care about her needs. He supposed she must be. Not only had few people in her life given her that consideration, but the two of them had been enemies of a sort for a long time. She could lean into him all she liked, but that didn't mean she fully trusted him. Would she ever?

She sighed and pulled away from him. "You are not as horrible as I once believed you to be," she began.

He smiled. "Thank you. I think."

"You ought to thank me—it's quite a capitulation on my part to admit it," she teased, though her face retained some of its concern, its fear. "Do you know why I stopped loving Erasmus Montgomery?"

He blinked. "Because he turned out to be a bigamist with two other wives, faked his own death and then tried to frame you for it? Also, he held you hostage briefly before he was shot and *actually* died."

She winced at the quick recitation of everything she'd endured a year ago. "That wasn't it. The marriage failed a long time before all of that. Erasmus lied. Little lies, bigger ones. Things meant to embarrass me. Sometimes they weren't about me at all, but it was like he had a compulsion to tell untruths. *That's* what broke our trust and our love and our bond. By the time we got to the end, to all the biggest lies, I was already numb to it."

She looked small standing there by the window, the moonlight from outside framing her. She looked pained, not just on the surface as she sometimes allowed him to see, but deep down to her bones. For the first time, he truly understood how she had been worn down by years as Montgomery's bride. How deeply each moment had hurt and changed her.

He understood why trust did not come easy. Why she had so many walls up. And he also saw that it wouldn't be easy, perhaps it would even be impossible, to dismantle those walls.

"You and I are not in love," she continued. "No matter what Society believes. So you can't break my heart like he once did. But if I were to look into the future and see exactly what I'd wish, I would ask that you not lie to me."

"That is a simple request," he said softly.

"Is it?"

He bent his head and thought of all the tiny ways people hurt each other in the world. "I suppose it isn't."

She sighed. "What about you? What do you need to be happy with this arrangement?"

"I want you, Abigail." He moved to her now as he said those words, and was pleased that she straightened up, tracking him with interest in those dark eyes. "I want you far more than is rational or prudent. I burn to touch you, and all this waiting only makes it more powerful. I want to be lovers. Enthusiastic lovers. I want to learn everything there is to know about your pleasure and use it."

She swallowed, her pupils dilating and her breath catching with each wicked word.

"I...I could agree to that. I obviously want you, as well." She reached out and traced her fingers along the top of his hand. A feather-light touch that soothed more than it enflamed. "Can we agree to that connection and not reach for more? I don't want us to push for something else or complicate what is already complicated. I might..." She rolled her eyes. "I might actually *like* you, Your Grace. And I might want you. And that sounds like it could be a happy union. Let's not get tangled up in the pressure from our friends to call it love or act like this is something either of us would have chosen."

Being friends and lovers sounded like a good thing. Her proposal should have made him happy and yet, as he stared down into those warm brown eyes, he felt a little...empty at the suggestion. He pushed that reaction away and caught her by the waist. He drew her close and kissed her.

She returned the kiss enthusiastically, her hands coming up to grip his lapels as she let out the prettiest little moan he'd ever heard. When they parted, he smiled down at her without releasing her. "I think friends, however begrudgingly, and lovers, extremely passionately, will be very good."

She smiled back, a broad and very real expression that softened her face. Made her even more lovely, difficult as that was to imagine.

"I'm not going to see you until the wedding," she said before she leaned up to kiss him again.

He pulled away. "No? Why?"

"Because I want to find out if you'll miss me," she teased as she tugged from his arms and crossed away from him to the door.

But as she unlocked it and flitted her way into the hall with only a cheeky glance over her shoulder, one thing became perfectly clear: he was definitely going to miss her.

And considering what they had just agreed to in their marriage, that could be a very bad thing.

CHAPTER 16

When the carriage pulled up to the little church near Abigail's house, her heart leapt. St. Augustine's was not the biggest or brightest chapel in all of London, but today it was the center of her world. The place where she would become the Duchess of Gilmore. Nathan's wife. And despite weeks of planning and their conversation about the marriage days before, she didn't feel ready.

The footman opened the door, and Rhys, who was standing up for her, stepped out first. He helped her down and smiled toward the small crowd that had gathered. The marriage was one with such a stir around it that some had come just to catch a glimpse. Abigail waved weakly and smiled as best she could so that no one would later say she had been forced down the aisle. There was no use in undoing all the good they'd done with the gossips.

She took Rhys's arm and they stepped into the vestibule of the church. The doors to the main hall were closed, and two men stood by to open them. Once they had, this moment would be truly happening.

Rhys began to guide her in that direction, but she held him back. "Wait," she said.

She glanced up at him and found him staring down at her with warmth and kindness. Her fears subsided a moment, replaced with gratitude and affection toward this man. He was Erasmus Montgomery's brother, but he was nothing like him.

"Thank you," she said softly, so no one else could hear the words. "You have been like a brother to me, and a far kinder one than perhaps I deserved. I wanted you to know how much I appreciate that."

His expression softened further and he squeezed her hand gently. "I will always be your brother if you need one. And I hope with all my heart that you and Gilmore will be happy together. You both deserve it."

She thought briefly of the limits she had asked Nathan to put on their union. The ones he had immediately agreed to. She doubted Rhys, who loved Pippa with all his heart, who had sacrificed everything to be with her, would consider what she and Nathan had come to terms about was *happiness*.

But she nodded. "We shouldn't keep them waiting," she said.

He patted her hand before the doors opened, revealing the small church interior. Nathan stood at the altar, and he turned as she entered. Her breath caught. He was dressed in full formal attire, every part of him perfection. He was outrageously handsome, looked every inch the stern duke.

He smiled at her, and something in her relaxed. The fears melted, the worries gone. She moved toward him, toward her future and their life together. For the first time since they'd been caught in his parlor, she didn't question herself. Whatever happened, it would work itself out.

The party, which had begun in the morning after the wedding was completed and ran far into the afternoon, was at last beginning to wind down. It had been a rousing success. Many influential people with titles had attended, offering congratulations to Nathan and Abigail. The Duke and Duchess of Abernathe had been chief among them, and Nathan had been warmed that the popular duke had also made a point to connect with Rhys and Pippa.

Somehow everything had seemed to work out. But now people were saying their goodbyes, tipsily making their way to their carriages to go home or to the next party. That left only Rhys and Pippa and Celeste and Owen, along with Ophelia. And, of course, Abigail.

It had been marvelous to watch her during this, her first day at his duchess. She had been remarkable. Welcoming and warm, easy with the staff, the center of the room and not just because she was the bride. There was just something about her that made people want to be near her. She saw the essence of those around her, she made them comfortable.

Except for him, of course. She never made him comfortable. Only he liked that. He liked sparring with her, especially when it wasn't too serious. He liked that she challenged him.

She moved toward him with an expression of confusion. "You are staring at me so intently, I must wonder if I've something on my face," she said as she reached him.

He shook his head. "Nothing at all. I was just thinking how well it went today."

"Yes," she breathed. "I couldn't believe it. People were…joyful for us. Your whisper campaign worked. They all believe we have some love story for the ages. It will ease everything."

He nodded. "Good. I want things to be easy for you, Abigail. I know they haven't often been."

She stiffened slightly. He felt her drawing away with that statement. "I suppose I meant more for Ophelia."

"What about me?"

They turned to find Ophelia had slipped behind them, her expression unreadable. He'd watched his sister throughout the day, as well. She'd been observing Abigail closely and every once in a while he'd seen just a hint that she was impressed with his new wife.

"We were just discussing how well the party went," Abigail said.

"You were such a help today and I wanted to tell you how much I appreciate it."

Ophelia blinked. "I...thank you, Abigail. You did wonderfully, I must say, under what I know were trying circumstances."

Abigail's blush said how much the hard-won compliment meant to her. "Thank you. Er, you looked like you had a nice time."

Ophelia nodded slowly. "I did, actually. I reconnected with some old friends and got to spend some time with a few new ones." She glanced at Rhys, Pippa, Celeste and Owen with a wink. "In fact, Rhys and Pippa have been kind enough to invite me to stay with them for two days, and I've accepted that lovely offer."

"Stay with them?" Nathan said, glancing at the pair. "Why?"

"We thought you might want some time alone as newlyweds," Rhys said.

Once again, Abigail shifted, as if the topic made her uncomfortable. She was forever looking for material to build a wall. And he shouldn't have cared so much about that fact.

"That is kind," Abigail said at last, her cheeks brightening to pink.

"Well, consider it my wedding gift," Ophelia said as she leaned up to kiss Nathan's cheek. She pivoted to Abigail and for a moment the two women simply looked at each other. Then Ophelia reached out and squeezed her hand briefly. "Congratulations, Your Grace."

Abigail laughed. "I'm still getting accustomed to that."

"And now we should leave the happy couple to their peace," Celeste said. "Why don't the rest of you join Owen and me for supper tonight?"

"That sounds delightful," Pippa said as she caught Rhys's arm. The crowd of them moved toward the door, talking and laughing.

The final goodbyes were said and the carriages loaded and then they were off. Nathan and Abigail stood beside each other on the step, waving them into the increasing darkness of the late afternoon. When they were gone, Nathan turned toward his wife. His *wife*. She looked up at him, eyes wide with uncertainty, but also anticipation. He saw the desire in her, felt it echoed in himself.

He held out his arm. "Are you ready, Your Grace?"

She blinked, and it was clear she took his meaning. Then she slipped her hand into the crook of his arm. "Yes, *Nathan*."

⁓

Abigail could barely breathe as Nathan led her through the massive carved double doors at the end of the hallway and into the antechamber of his chamber. Their chamber. This set of connected rooms were their chambers now. He released her and she moved forward into the big sitting space. A private parlor with comfortable-looking furniture.

Behind her, he cleared his throat and she turned to face him. He arched a brow and then very deliberately locked the door. She laughed at what had become one of their little in-jokes.

"Not that I think anyone would dare try to intrude on our wedding night," he said. "But better to be safe than sorry."

"It's a pretty room," she said.

He nodded. "I agree. I've always liked this little private space. I often read here in the evenings."

She smiled. "Well, perhaps we will read here together."

Something in his expression softened at that suggestion, but then the corner of his mouth lifted in a wicked half-smile. "But not tonight."

Her breath caught, and she glanced past him toward the closed chamber door. There was another behind her, and she wasn't sure which was the duke's bedroom and which the duchess's. But they would enter one of those two and then...well, they would finally get to purge all the unfinished business between them.

It was a powerful thought. Almost too powerful, and she struggled to reduce the meaning of that moment. "You don't want to read tonight?"

"No," he said softly.

She lifted her gaze to him. "What would you like to do?"

He tilted his head. "What I would like to do, wife, is to take you into that room—" He jerked a thumb behind him toward the door. "—my room, strip you out of that very pretty gown, lick your entire body until you are shaking and then finally do the thing I've been dreaming of for far too long."

She swallowed hard. "And what is that?"

"Take you," he said softly as he moved toward her a long step. "Fit myself inside of you and claim you." He moved again. "Make you scream this house down and scandalize the servants and the neighbors."

They were mere inches apart now, and he reached for her hand, tracing his fingers along the top, then in the cup of her palm. He lifted it to his lips and pressed a warm kiss there.

"You've a very high opinion of yourself," she choked out, her voice trembling far too much to pretend she wasn't moved by him. He turned her hand over and kissed her palm, kissed the place where her thumb and forefinger met. "What if we aren't good at this?"

He barked out a laugh. "We've been very, very good at everything that came before," he said. "I have great faith in our abilities. But I suppose we shall see, won't we? Come on."

He tugged her toward his door and opened it without releasing her hand. They moved forward together, him backing her in, his mesmerizing gaze never leaving hers. Finally he released her hand and she realized they had moved into the middle of his chamber.

As he went back to shut the door, she took in the space. She should have been admiring every detail of the room, but all she could look at was his bed. His very big bed with the tall posters and gauzy curtains drawn back.

"Big enough?" he whispered, close to her ear suddenly.

She jumped. "That remains to be seen," she teased.

He laughed as he wrapped an arm around her waist and turned her into his chest. "Minx," he whispered just before his mouth met hers.

It might have started as a gentle kiss, but it quickly escalated. She opened to him and he took, claimed, plundered. She gripped the lapels of his jacket and lifted into him, wanting to be closer as his hands tightened on her hips. When they broke apart, they were both panting, and seeing that she affected him the same way he did her was powerful.

"I know it's been a long time," he said softly, his fingers tightening and loosening against her body in a rhythmic way. "So if you want me to stop at any point, you only have to tell me."

Her brow wrinkled. "This is...this is your husbandly right, Nathan."

He recoiled slightly. "Is that what he told you? This is my deepest pleasure, Abigail, but only if it's also yours. If you want to stop, we stop. No recriminations, no questions. We stop."

Tears stung her eyes, and she stared up at this man she had once despised and now continually surprised her. It would be very easy to care for him deeply. To risk herself far more than she wanted to do. She would have to tread very carefully here and always strive to keep what her body wanted separate from her heart.

"Please touch me," she whispered. "That's what I know I want."

His pupils dilated as he cupped her jawline gently, tilting her face for better access, and then kissed her again. There was something about it, something that shifted and told her that they wouldn't stop again until they'd shared each other completely. Until she was truly his bride, until she had shattered in pleasure the way she craved to do.

As he kissed her, his hands roved over her body, bunching her dress into his fists, using it as leverage to drag her ever closer. Her heart was racing and her breath came short as anticipation mounted. Just when she thought she could take no more, he glided his fingers up the long line of buttons along her spine and began to unfasten them one by one.

She drew back and watched his expression as he did so. His gaze was hooded and intense as he locked it to hers, holding her steady with just that look.

"Nathan," she whispered.

His fingers slowed. "What do you need?"

Her breath hitched. In her life, she could almost count the number of times someone had asked her that on just one hand. When he asked it, it seemed like he meant it. Her hands shook as she reached up to trace his cheek with her fingertip, across his bottom lip.

"Too much?" he whispered.

She nodded. "But also not enough. I want to please you. I want to be pleased and yet I'm shaking like a leaf."

He smiled against her fingertip. "If you surrender, just a little, I promise you I will make this good for you. You don't have to hold on with both hands." His own hands gripped against her back. "I have you."

She blinked. Surrender. She'd done that once and it hadn't worked out in the slightest. But she wanted so badly what he offered.

"Yes."

His mouth found hers again, this time with less desperation. He stripped open her buttons down to her waist with what felt like only a flick of his wrist and then his fingers slid beneath the fabric of her gown. Though she was wearing a chemise beneath, the pressure still made her shiver, and she turned from his mouth to bury her face in his shoulder. Sensation hit her in waves, waves that built as he pushed her dress off her shoulders, down her arms.

He'd seen her naked before, of course. That dizzying day on the settee was something she'd dreamed about many times since. But now he was going to look at her and she was his wife. That changed things somehow. Made them mean something more. Because he had to be pleased with her for the rest of his life. If he wasn't...well, she already knew how that would turn out.

She stepped away from him and lifted her chin as she pushed out of her dress. It pooled at her feet, and she stepped out and kicked it aside. Her undergarments were pretty but the fabric was thin, and with the firelight behind her, she was fairly certain there was very little to be left to the imagination.

"My God, you are something," he said as he looped a finger around the thin chemise strap and tugged so it drooped against her shoulder.

"I could look at you like this all day. All week. And your scent." He leaned in and brushed his lips to the spot where her neck and shoulder met. "It's been driving me wild for months. What is it?"

She blinked. Months. How could that be? They'd been enemies months ago. Not playful, but truly at odds. He had to be exaggerating or caught up in the moment.

"Cinnamon," she whispered, digging her fingers into his hair as he moved his mouth along her neck toward her ear. "Vanilla," she gasped because when he nipped her earlobe her entire body reacted with a lurch of electric pleasure. "I don't know what else, I can't think of anything but what you're doing."

He chuckled against her skin. "You. The rest of it is you."

He backed her toward the bed as he continued kissing her throat, sucking hard enough that there was a tiny hint of pain, laving with his tongue to soothe. When her backside hit the high edge of the mattress, she bit back a cry.

He pulled away from her and tugged the chemise the rest of the way down her body. Slowly. Slow enough that she felt the silken slide on every inch of her. When it puddled at her feet, he caught her bare hips and lifted her onto the edge of the bed. They were face to face now, and he took advantage. He kissed her, deeper than before, longer than before, with far more purpose.

It was amazing. She'd been kissed before. Well-kissed by this very man. And yet every time he did it, it gave her the same thrill as a first kiss. It pulled her under soft waves, it made her forget everything around her. All there was was him. All there ever would be was this.

"This seems unfair," she said after they'd kissed for what felt like a lifetime.

He smiled against her mouth. "Ah, a complaint to be lodged. Excellent. What is unfair?"

"I am all but naked and you are fully clothed," she said.

He nodded. "That's true. It does seem unfair. How about this? I will remove all of this if you take off your stocking and slippers?"

She shrugged. "That is acceptable."

"I do love our negotiations," he said, and pressed a quick kiss to her lips.

He backed away and she scurried to roll her stockings down her legs and unbuckle her slippers. It was quick work and by the time she had done it, he had removed his boots and jacket.

"I'm realizing I haven't actually seen you with your clothing off," she mused. "Your..." She motioned toward his crotch.

"My cock," he said.

Her eyes went wide. "Well, if you want to be vulgar about it."

"You've had it in your mouth, Your Grace," he said. "I very much want to be vulgar about it with you in this room when you're naked."

She laughed despite herself. "Fine. I've seen your cock. It's a very nice cock. Did I tell you that at the time?"

"You did not," he said, and his lips twitched. "I'm flattered."

"But I haven't seen the rest." She waved her hand. "So if you could hurry it along, I would like to remedy that situation."

He gave a lazy mock salute but did not rush in the slightest as he unwound his cravat, unbuttoned his shirt and then pulled it over his head.

She lunged forward so quickly she nearly threw herself off the bed as she stared at the half-naked form of the Duke of Gilmore. She'd felt the strength of him when he pulled her close, but seeing the evidence of it was another thing entirely.

He had well defined, muscular shoulders and arms, and a broad chest that tapered into a narrow waist. His chest hair was a shade lighter than the dark hair on his head and made the most fascinating v that pointed into the waist of his trousers.

"Your mouth is open, Abigail," he said softly.

She glanced at his face. "I-I didn't expect you to be so... so...perfect."

"I can't hear that enough. Though I am not, I assure you."

She shook her head. "How do you look like that under all those layers of propriety?"

"I box," he said. "And I'm not opposed to work on my estate when I go there."

She nodded. "I'll take your word for it. I approve, by the way." She bit her lip. "I very much approve."

He gave a slow grin, but said nothing more as he unfastened his trousers. Carefully he lowered the fall front and his cock, which was fully hard, bounced free. She hardly noticed as he stepped from the trousers because all she could do was look at him.

"Still approve?" he asked softly as he moved toward the bed.

Her breath hitched. "Oh yes," she whispered. "I more than approve."

"Good," he said. "And I think it's obvious I approve." He motioned to that same hard cock. "So we are in accord, perhaps for the first time in our relationship. And I have a very specific way to celebrate that fact."

She smiled at him as she wrapped her arms around his neck and leaned in to kiss him. "So do I. So let's celebrate."

CHAPTER 17

Nathan kissed her briefly, but Abigail was surprised when he pulled back almost immediately. He placed a hand on her shoulder and urged her onto her back. She followed that silent order and rested back her elbows to watch him. He placed a hand on each thigh and she shivered at that intimate touch. When he gently pressed, she opened to him and he let out a great, almost relieved sigh.

"So pretty," he murmured before he extended a trembling finger and stroked it across her sex.

She sucked in a breath at the jolt of sensation the press of flesh on flesh created. It was a remarkable thing, for he had touched her like this before but it still felt new and exciting and wonderful. She wanted more and at last she was going to get it.

But he seemed in no hurry to possess her. He stroked that same finger back and forth across her entrance, smiling as she arched against him. And when she thought she might go mad from the teasing, he bent his head and licked her.

The garbled cry that escaped her lips was hardly human. She gripped the coverlet in her fists, turning her face into her shoulder as he pleasured her. And oh, he did pleasure her. He sucked her clitoris, he swirled the tip of his tongue around it, he groaned against her wet sex like this was as much a pleasure for him as it was for her. Her hips rose to meet him. He cupped them in both hands, his fingers digging against her flesh as they spiraled together toward shattering climax.

When she reached it, she cried out his name, no longer caring if the household heard it. He continued to suck and tease her through the ceaseless waves of pleasure, and it was only when she flopped back against the bed, panting with pleasure, that he lifted his head from between her legs and smiled. His lips were slick with her release, his eyes bright with triumph and desire.

She stared at him in wonder. So often he looked every inch the proper duke. Certainly he had looked so today when she entered the church and looked down the aisle to him. He was serious and pulled together and sometimes even stern. She had seen a glimpse in the last few weeks of something beyond that external presentation.

He teased, he wagered, he laughed. He drew her in with all those things, no matter how hard she fought the tide. And when he touched her, it was like she dropped yet another level deeper. Now, in the privacy of their bedchamber, he looked like a wicked rake, celebrating a conquest. He looked like a man whose body she wanted to learn over weeks and months and years to come. A man who would make her pleasure a study, like it was the most important subject in the world.

"You look at me like you've never seen me before." He chuckled as he moved up her body.

She scooted fully onto the bed, resting her head on the pillows and shivering as he took a place beside her. He lay on his side, his head propped up on his hand, watching her.

"I can hardly see at all thanks to that display," she said with a laugh of her own.

"That was the goal. But now I have another." His smile faded and the rake turned into a rogue, a pirate bent on claiming.

She touched his chest, dragged her hands lower across his stomach, across his bare hip. He shuddered as she took him in hand and stroked his cock once, twice.

"Christ, you'll unman me before we've even begun," he grunted, but he didn't pull away from her. He surged against her palm, seeking what she could give.

"I wouldn't want that," she whispered.

He loomed over her, kissing her so she could taste her release, pinning her back on the bed as he covered her. She opened her legs to him willingly, her heart racing as they aligned for the next part in this dance they'd been playing at for weeks.

He stared down at her, his gaze holding her captive as he nudged her entrance. And then he was sliding home, slowly and gently, but ever forward. His eyes never left hers, and she caught her breath at the intensity of it all. The sensation mixed with the expression, joined to their fact that their breath had settled into the same rhythm. She was stretched by him, but there was no pain, only pleasure.

He held still when he was buried to the hilt. He leaned in to kiss her, this time gently. "My God, you feel good," he murmured.

She flexed around him. "So do you."

He squeezed his eyes shut and groaned in pleasure, and she flexed again. This time when he opened his eyes, there was danger there. Beautiful, captivating danger.

"You and your games," he whispered. Then he drew back, almost all the way from her body, and thrust. She lifted into him, gasping in pleasure.

Animal was the only way she could describe what happened next. She dug her hands into his shoulders, he crushed his mouth to hers and they moved together. A war of their bodies, a race to release. His hips ground against hers with every thrust and she reached for him at the same time. Her body, still tingling from the last release, found its way easier the second time. She climbed the mountain as he pounded into her mercilessly, and at the top she arched her back, clawing at him for purchase as wave after wave of pleasure stole her control. He pressed his mouth to her throat, scraping his teeth there, whispering lurid, dirty encouragement as she came and came. And when she felt she could take no more, when she was weak from him, only then did he drive into her, faster and harder, his neck flexing and his breath short.

He roared in pleasure, pouring himself deep within her, and then collapsed against her, their sweat slicked bodies still trembling from what had just happened. She clung to him, changed by this, changed by him—there was no denying it.

But she knew she would have to control it, just as she controlled everything in her life. Even if it broke her.

 ∿

Nathan lay on his side, facing Abigail. She held his gaze, but he could see the little shifts in her body, feel the tension in her. He smiled in the hopes it would soothe her.

"So...were we good at it?" he asked.

For a moment she looked confused, and then he saw the memory of what she'd worried over earlier return. "Yes." She laughed. "I'd say we were."

"Excellent," he whispered as he traced his fingers up the line of her naked side. "I like being good at this with you."

Her smile softened, and for a moment all the tension fled. He saw a glimpse of something he had never expected, hadn't thought to want in the whirlwind of the past few weeks. He saw a future, with playful sparring and passionate nights. He saw Abigail at his side in the good and bad times. He saw children with her smile, his eyes. He saw a life where there was no wall between them.

And it was beautiful.

She cleared her throat and rolled onto her back, and the vision faded as she pulled away.

"Abigail—" he began.

She slid to the opposite side of the bed and got up, searching around the floor for her dress. "Yes?" Her tone was falsely bright.

"Abigail, look at me."

She did so, though it seemed reluctant. "Yes?" she repeated.

"Talk to me," he said softly. "What just happened?"

She shrugged. "Nothing. We made love and this marriage is now legal."

He arched a brow. She huffed out a breath. "And it was very good. I enjoyed myself. But it's not that late, and we'll have supper soon. I think I'll go explore my chamber, perhaps take a hot bath. We'll see each other in a few hours."

He wrinkled his brow, but didn't get up or try to stop her as she gathered her things in a pile in her arms. She didn't even try to dress as she hustled to the door and fought to open it with her hands full.

"Bollocks," she muttered under her breath.

He could have gotten up and helped her, but she didn't even look at him. It was obvious she wanted to flee, so he let her flail until she finally got the door unlocked and opened, then stepped into the antechamber. He heard the door to the duchess's chamber open then shut, and she was gone.

He stared at the now-open door in utter confusion and disappointment. Here he'd thought there was a connection. No, he *knew* there was. And she ran from it. From him.

The walls he'd hoped to ease down were most definitely still up. The question was, could they ever be brought down? The larger question, the one that haunted him as he stared at the place in his bed that still smelled of her skin, was...did he want them to be?

Abigail sat in the tub, water steaming around her and she should have felt relaxed by the soothing heat. Only she didn't because her errant mind took her to places it shouldn't go. Places it had been going far too often as of late, she could admit that to herself.

She kept thinking of Nathan. Of the passion that had flared between them only an hour before. Only if it had just been passion, that wouldn't have been a problem. Passion was what they had agreed to not that many days ago when negotiating the terms of their marriage.

The problem was that more than just passion had lifted its head that day. She had felt a connection to Nathan when he touched her, when he shattered her...and when he lay beside her, his dark brown gaze locked with hers. She had melted a fraction, felt herself sliding toward him in spirit, as well as body.

Only one other time in her life had she done that. Erasmus Montgomery had made her heart flutter too. She couldn't trust that feeling. It was the way to heartache. She knew it in her head.

But her heart was the problem. Even now she felt the swell of it as she pictured Nathan. Her mind spun up a dozen beautiful scenarios where they didn't merely share passion, but shared their lives and their souls and their futures in every way.

"Foolish, overly romantic—" she muttered, then drew in a huge breath of air and slid beneath the water. She lay in the silence, her eyes closed, and tried to get herself together.

The Duke of Gilmore was her husband, thanks to a set of foolish mistakes that had set them on this path. She could accept that because there was no other choice. She could even accept that she might like him a little. That he might not be the ogre she had once made him out to be.

But she would not...she shuddered to even think the word...love him. She didn't love him. She couldn't. She had no faith in the emotion, nor the foolish decisions it almost always led to. At least for her.

Her lungs burned, and she slowly surfaced for a gulp of air. When she did, she found Nathan standing in the doorway, clad only in a dressing gown, his pupils dilated as he watched her. She swallowed and fought the urge to cover herself. It was a little late for that now. And her body wasn't the problem, at any rate.

"I didn't see you there."

He smiled. "No, you were busy playing mermaid at the bottom of the tub."

The words were playful, the tone was too, but there was tension around his mouth. Her getting out of their bed and practically running into her chamber had clearly left him with...questions. Ones she had no answers to.

"It's a big tub."

He took a long step into the room. "Abigail, did I do something to upset you?"

"Not at all. I had fun." She tried to make her tone light, as if what had happened earlier had no meaning. "I'm looking forward to having fun again."

He swallowed. There it was, the way she could maintain power and break connection. If she made the sex between them pleasurable but meaningless, it kept his mind on something she could control.

"Come here," she said softly, crooking her finger.

He hesitated but only for a fraction of a second before he moved toward her. He sank down on his knees next to the tub. She pulled her hand out from in the waves and traced a wet fingertip along his jaw. His eyes fluttered shut, and she smiled.

When she felt a flutter in her stomach, it was just because she wanted him. Because having even a small amount of power over him was intoxicating. She was reading too much into it when she thought it was something deeper.

He lifted a hand into her hair slowly, then wrapped the length of her wet locks around and around his hand. The tug against her scalp made her sex tingle, and she let out a low sigh.

"Mine," he murmured before he kissed her, hard and unyielding.

She nodded against his mouth, pushing those fluttering feelings away when they resurfaced. "Whatever you want," she murmured back, and gently caught his lower lip between her teeth.

He drew back, his eyes wide, and released her hair. "Stand up."

She did so, taking her time so that when she rose out of the water, rivulets of water running over her curves, he could truly appreciate the show. "Now what?" she asked.

He grabbed one of the towels her maid had left for her and

dropped it on the floor in front of the tub. "Step out," he said, his voice hoarse and rough.

She held out a hand, lifting her chin like a queen. He shook his head as he took it and steadied her. But the moment she was flat on her feet on the towel, he pivoted her around so her naked, wet back was against his front.

"Nathan!" she squealed. "I'm soaking you."

He sucked the side of her throat and slid a hand down the center of her body. When he reached her sex, he parted her lips and stroked her gently. "Seems like I'm soaking you."

He pushed his robe open. She felt the tickle of his hair against her back, her thighs as he pulled her harder against him. His cock was hard against her backside, and she pulsed back against it with a whimper.

"Minx," he whispered, and bent her over. She wrapped her hands around the edge of the tub and gasped as he speared her in one long thrust.

He took her, hard and fast. She felt the desperation in his strokes, the need to have her and to find that same connection they'd made earlier. She shut her eyes, focusing on the pleasure and not the emotions. And oh, there was pleasure. This new angle found spots in her she had never known existed, a new flavor of the pleasure. She reached between her legs and touched herself as he thrust harder and faster.

Water sloshed on the ground around them as she ground back into him. Her fingers were coated with wetness that was from far more than her bath. He caught her hair again, tugging gently, and it pushed her over the edge where she had been dancing.

She came, grinding hard against him. Harder when he cried out and she felt the hot flood of him deep within her. For a moment they remained that way, bent over the tub, water pooling at their feet. He withdrew at last, shaking his head as he stood.

"Good God, woman, you will be the death of me."

She laughed as she grabbed another towel from a nearby chair and wrapped it around herself. She leaned up to kiss him briefly before she stepped away. "What a way to go, though, Your Grace."

"Indeed," he agreed, and huffed out a long breath. He was watching her, his gaze intent and focused, so she turned away. He frowned as she did so—she caught the expression from the corner of her eye.

"I'm famished," she said, hoping to keep her tone light.

He cleared his throat. "We could dress and have supper? I'm sure Mrs. Wheaton has a spread worthy of a king left over from the wedding luncheon."

"Perfect," she said, and moved toward the bell to call her maid back.

He stayed in the room a moment, then sighed when she didn't turn back and padded out toward his own chamber. She breathed a sigh of relief that they hadn't treaded into more dangerous waters, and pushed away disappointment at the same.

She could control the relationship with this man. She had to and she would.

CHAPTER 18

Nathan paced the parlor at Rhys and Pippa's house two days after the wedding, waiting for his friends to arrive to greet him, his sister in tow. He was not in a good humor and feared it would be difficult to keep that to himself.

He should have been in a wonderful mood. He'd spent the last two days alone with Abigail, exploring every delicious inch of her body. They were perfectly matched in the bedroom, and his hunger for her only grew every time they touched. The problem was that the moment they were finished making love, off she went to the adjoining bedroom. She never slept with him in his bed. She never allowed deeper connection in any way. Sex, playful surface banter, food. That was all they shared.

Why that wasn't enough, he wasn't certain. It was within the parameters they had set for their marriage weeks before.

Pippa and Rhys entered the room, their toddler, Kenley, clinging to Pippa's hand. In that moment, they looked like such a happy family, despite all they'd been through. Despite the fact the boy was Montgomery's child with yet another woman, the pair loved him as their own. Nothing would ever change that, or make them pull away from each other.

Jealousy gripped him and he forced a smile as he greeted them. "Good afternoon."

They responded in kind, but Pippa tilted her head. "Where is Abigail? I thought she would join you today. Kenley wanted to see her."

The little boy turned into her skirts with a shy look for Nathan.

Nathan pursed his lips. "She is working on her study, I believe, and on making herself an herbal garden. She was busy."

Pippa and Rhys exchanged a brief look before Rhys waved to the chair near the fire. As Pippa got them all tea, Nathan sat. Rhys took a place at the settee across from him, Kenley perched on his knee, and Nathan could see his old friend had a great deal on his mind to say.

To avoid it, he said, "Where is my sister?"

Pippa smiled as she handed him over a cup, prepared just as he liked it. She took her own place beside Rhys. "Ophelia was still preparing. She should be ready momentarily."

Nathan shook his head. "She's always marched to her own drum and kept her own time. I hope she was a good house guest."

Pippa's eyes lit up with genuine pleasure. "Most definitely. She is so lively and amusing."

Rhys nodded. "Indeed, she has grown into a charming companion. A firebrand, but charming."

Nathan shook his head. "Her firebrand side is sometimes my trouble. But then again, what would I be if the ladies in my life didn't keep me on my toes?"

Pippa wrinkled her brow. "I assume you are also referring to Abigail."

He caught his breath. "I should have known you would swing the conversation back to her as soon as possible."

"It's difficult not to be curious as to how things have gone between you since your marriage," Rhys said. "Without getting too detailed."

Nathan ran a hand through his hair. He'd been frustrated and now his friends were offering him a sounding board.

"We're fine," he began slowly. "When we're together...*together*..."

Rhys rolled his eyes. "Yes, we understand."

"...it's very good. She just pushes me away any other time, keeps me at arm's length."

Pippa let out a long sigh. "Celeste and I worried about that. Please don't judge her, Gilmore. She's been through so much."

"I know," he said swiftly. "I don't judge her, nor do I wish to force her into a situation she doesn't desire. And I shouldn't be upset. We already agreed this isn't going to be a love match. I suppose I must be patient as we determine what kind of friends we can be."

"Friends," Pippa repeated, arching a brow.

Nathan was uncertain of her tone. She almost sounded...annoyed. "Yes?"

She set her teacup down with a clatter, and now there was no doubt she was annoyed, given her expression. "You two are the most stubborn arses."

"In front of the child?" Rhys said with a playful glare for her as he covered the little boy's ears.

She laughed. "They deserve the label, I cannot sugarcoat it."

Nathan blinked, for he had never seen Pippa so animated. "I...that is not the response I was expecting."

"Well, it is the one I have." She got up and paced away. When she pivoted back, she crossed her arms. "There is clearly a connection between you two, whether you want to acknowledge it or not. We've all seen it, and not just in the last month, but in the last year. I saw it the first time you two were in a room together."

He flinched. "You imagined things then, Pippa. I guarantee you there was no connection between us a year ago. As for now, I don't wish to be indelicate, but I don't deny there is a bond between myself and Abigail. But it is physical. There is little more."

"Fine. Ruin your life." She glared at him before she took Kenley from Rhys and then stomped to the doorway. "I'll check on Ophelia."

Nathan gaped at where she'd gone and then turned his stare on Rhys. The earl had not moved and arched a brow in his direction. "My wife is a little...*passionate* about this."

"Apparently so," Nathan said. "And I appreciate she is a romantic."

"She is that." Rhys laughed.

"But certainly she's no fool. She...and all the rest of you...must understand that not every person can have some great love."

"Don't you want it?" Rhys asked.

Nathan stared at him. Want it. A great love. "I..."

"I mean, a year or two ago, you and I might have waxed on about how it didn't exist. Based on our pasts, we would have believed it. But things are different now. You've seen Celeste and Owen together. You've seen Pippa and me. You know that kind of true connection, that kind of deep love exists."

"I have seen it," Nathan said softly. "I'm grateful that my best friend, my brother, has found it, and that Owen and Celeste could also be so lucky. But I've also seen the ugly side of such an emotion. I've seen what happens when people want something they can't get."

"So because of your mother or your sister or your friend of a friend's bad experience, you won't even try?" Rhys held up both hands. "Seems a bit cowardly."

Nathan flinched. He knew Rhys was trying to get a rise out of him. And damn if it wasn't working, because he felt a very strong desire to have a screaming match. Luckily, there was no chance to do so. Pippa returned to the room, this time without Kenley, but with Ophelia at her side.

"Nathan," Ophelia said with a bright smile.

He pushed to his feet with one final glare for Rhys and then embraced his sister. "I hope you had a marvelous time."

She smiled at Pippa and Rhys. "Truly marvelous. Thank you both for hosting me and for letting me indulge myself as a token aunt to Kenley. I adore him."

"It was our pleasure," Rhys said. "We would love to do it again, perhaps at my country estate later in the summer."

"I would love it," Ophelia said.

Any annoyance Nathan had been feeling toward his friends and their prying faded away at the pleasure on his sister's face. Ophelia had shied away from London after last year's events. She'd pretended she was fine, but he'd felt her big personality shrink and hadn't liked it. But the fire was back in her now. The brightness and boldness that he both loved and which drove him mad.

"Look at your schedules," he said with a nod to his friends. "And we will do the same."

"We'll talk about it next time we see you," Pippa said as she put an arm around Ophelia. "Which must be soon. All of us must have supper together."

They began to walk toward the foyer together, their heads together as they schemed. Rhys and Nathan followed, but as Ophelia and Pippa continued to talk at the carriage door, Rhys stopped him. "I know we push," he said. "Everyone just wants you both to be happy."

Nathan stared at his friend. "But all of you have the same definition of what happy is. And Abigail might not ever allow for it. Even if I did want it. So we'll have to find our own way."

Rhys nodded, but there was no mistaking the disappointment in his eyes as he shook Nathan's hand. It stung, almost like he'd done something wrong that he couldn't take back.

So he got into the carriage feeling very out of sorts, humming with even more tension than he'd felt when he arrived.

"You look cross," Ophelia said as the carriage began to move.

Nathan huffed out a breath. "Yes, that seems to be the consensus amongst those who feel they can comment on my life."

"I'm your sister—it is my prerogative," Ophelia said. "And shouldn't you be blissful in these first few days of your marriage? The fact that you are harrumphing like a bear does not bode well."

She looked truly concerned, and Nathan did his best to relax a little. Loosen his shoulders. "I'm very well, I promise you. I am happy."

She didn't look convinced. He didn't feel convinced either, but that was beside the point.

"I wish I could have prevented you from being forced into this union," she said softly. "You saved me last year and I could not save you."

He tilted his head. "The material difference being that I caused my own troubles whereas you did not, and that Abigail is not the black-guard Erasmus Montgomery was."

Ophelia shrugged and turned her attention out the window. "I suppose we'll see. She is spoken of very highly by Pippa and Leighton, and that does recommend her. But I will not fully trust her until I see some further proof that your happiness means something to her. You deserve that."

She was quiet the rest of the ride home. He probably should have filled the silence, tried harder to convince her that she was being too dour about the situation.

Only he wasn't certain that was true. Rhys and Pippa had also brought up the topic of happiness. And that had been the subject of the talk at the salon weeks and weeks earlier. It was something he had rarely considered in his life. Happiness was a luxury, and one he wasn't certain he could afford.

But now he found himself wanting it. Though he didn't know what the definition would be, or if he could find it with a woman who seemed determined to keep him at arm's length.

Exactly as they had agreed to do.

Abigail paced her new study, distracted and discombobulated. It wasn't that she didn't have anything to do. The boxes of books from her former home had all arrived that morning. She needed to catalogue and shelve them. And there was the matter of overseeing the herb garden. Though Nathan had agreed to allow her most of the greenhouse in his country estate, he had also had a corner of his garden in London cleared. There were directives to be given about building boxes for certain herbs and creating extra shade for others.

She was doing none of it. Instead she wandered from one side of the room to the other feeling...well, icky was the only way she could describe it.

She rolled her eyes at the childish word, but it was most apt. She didn't feel right and she had been trying to avoid the reason for that. But it was impossible.

It had been three days since Ophelia had returned to Nathan's home. *Abigail's* home. She was trying very hard to recall that it was her home, too. Sometimes it felt like it. Nights where she and Nathan sat quietly in the library, each reading. Occasionally he looked up and she saw the bright spark of interest.

Hours in his bed felt very much like home, too.

The man was magical. That was all there was to it, and her body sang to his music in a way it had never done before.

It didn't change the fact that her days were spent alone. By design. She found things to keep her busy and separate from Nathan. And once they'd made love, she always went back to her room.

It was the only sanctuary she had to the feelings that sometimes accompanied his touch. Feelings she didn't want. Feelings he didn't reciprocate, no matter how disappointed he looked when she left him.

And so today she thought of all those things. All those confusing, tangled things, and *icky* it was.

There was a light knock on her door, and she turned, expecting to see a footman with more boxes. Instead it was Nathan himself, holding a small trunk.

"This is the last of it, I'm told," he said as he came into the room.

She blinked. "And so you carried it yourself?"

"I was coming to see you either way." He glanced toward the pile of crates and trunks. "Should I stack it with the others?"

She nodded and watched him do so. He was not wearing a jacket so his shoulder muscles flexed in a very distracting fashion against the linen of his shirt.

"You said you were coming to see me," she said. "Did you need something?"

He didn't respond, but looked around the room slowly. "It's coming together. All that hard work is paying off."

She looked with him. The room did look more like her now.

Flowers were on the mantel, as well as a miniature of her late sister. Her desk was neatly stacked with a few papers and letters. The curtains had been changed and were perpetually open, as was the window when the weather was fair.

"Once I unpack the books, I think it will feel more like it is mine," she said.

He inched toward her, and she stiffened. If he touched her, especially here in this room where they had shared such a powerful encounter before their marriage, she wasn't sure she could take it. She already sometimes found herself staring at the desk, thinking of the way Nathan's neck had flexed as she sucked him. If he did more than that, the room would always be *theirs*, not hers.

And she needed a space in this house that didn't make her think of him all the time.

She ducked behind the desk and sat down. He frowned but didn't pursue further. "Did you need something?" she repeated.

"I don't know if *need*, but I did have a few topics to discuss," he said slowly. "Firstly, Rhys and Pippa have extended a very kind invitation for my sister to join them at their country estate at the end of the summer. We're invited to join them, as Celeste and Owen will also be there, at least for a short time."

She blinked. Go to a country estate? Together? Where they would be surrounded by loving couples who would certainly be planning tricks to make them closer? It sounded both a dream and a nightmare.

"I will likely have a great deal to do here, Nathan," she said. "Organizing this library will take weeks, even months, if I'm to do it right. But you should go. Ophelia will love it, and you'll enjoy spending time with our friends."

He stared at her a long moment. Too long. And she realized there was frustration in his eyes. But he didn't express it as he continued, "Very well. The second item to discuss is that I'd like to host a ball for Ophelia. And to celebrate our marriage."

She stiffened. "I...didn't we celebrate it enough at the reception after the wedding?"

He arched a brow. "People will assume a ball so soon after will at least partly be for that purpose. Will it be so difficult for you to pretend you are attached to me to continue our ruse?"

Her lips parted. "I..."

"We should only have to do that a few more times this Season, if it helps," he continued, and the sharpness of his tone was like a knife to her heart. "After all, if we seem to have drifted apart next year, I suppose everyone will assume it is just the nature of love. It ends."

"Is that what we're doing—drifting apart?" she asked, wishing panic didn't grip her chest when she said it. "Last night we seemed to be very much together."

"And yet you back away from me today," he said with a shrug. "So it remains to be seen."

"Nathan, this is what we agreed to," she said softly.

"Yes," he said. "And I can see it's vitally important to you that you stick to the letter of that agreement. Even whatever friendship we seemed to be forming before the marriage seems to be too far for you."

She flinched, because it was a fair assessment. She *had* withdrawn from their playful games, because when they flirted it made her want more. More than sex, more than a marriage of convenience. She sometimes wanted bright flashes of something else. Of everything.

"I'm sorry to disappoint you."

He stared at her. "That is all you have to say?"

She refused to look at him, instead looking at the inkwell in front of her. She fiddled with it absently. "I don't know what else to say."

He huffed out a breath and went to the door. There he ran a hand through his hair. "I don't want this to be miserable, Abigail. Not for you, not for me."

With that, he left her study. She gazed after him, heart burning. There was some small part of her that hoped he would come back, as she had done that night they quarreled in this very house. The night that had changed everything between them and led to this marriage.

But he didn't.

She flinched. Erasmus had often stormed out during arguments. Sometimes he hadn't come back for days. Those little fights had begun the ultimate fracture of their union. And her eyes stung at the thought that she was traveling the same road. With a very different man, of course.

But the destination, loneliness, was very much the same.

She yanked a piece of vellum closer and uncorked the ink so she could write a note. And then she was going to have to figure some things out, but not here.

CHAPTER 19

Nathan stormed across the width of the garden, hands fisted at his sides. Emotions bubbled up in him, the kind he had long ago trained to push down deep inside. But Abigail unleashed them all, the good and the bad. She was uniquely frustrating that way.

But if he had some air, he would calm down and he could be more rational. That was what he needed to do, after all. Be rational.

Except before he could calm himself, one of the gardeners came scurrying across the garden toward him, tugging muddy gloves from his hands as he went.

"I'm sorry to disturb, Your Grace," he puffed. "But Her Grace mentioned she would come to see the plot you asked us to set aside for her?"

Nathan glanced past the man and saw that, indeed, a section of flowers and bushes had been ripped out in the corner of his garden. The dark, rich earth was ready for Abigail's direction. Ready for her to plant something there and make it better. Make it more hers than it had been before, just as she had done to her study, to the duchess chamber, to every place she touched. The garden would be yet one more corner of his life she would alter.

But she hesitated to do so, it seemed. Just like she did with him.

"Your Grace?" the man said, tilting his head.

"I don't know what Her Grace's plans are," Nathan said, his tone a little harsher than he had intended. He drew in a deep breath and softened it. "I will inquire if I see her. For now, cover the ground so it doesn't turn to mud and...assume she will join you later."

"Yes, Your Grace," the man said with an incline of his head before he rushed back to continue his work.

"Haven't heard you bark like that in a long time, *Your Grace.*"

Nathan turned back toward the house and found Ophelia coming across the garden toward him. He sighed. It seemed there would be no respite from questions today. No chance to catch his breath.

"I was sharp with him, I know."

"You sounded a little like—"

"Don't say Father," he choked out. "Please."

She pursed her lips as she reached out to take his hand. She squeezed gently. "You're not him."

He sighed. Sometimes he wasn't entirely certain of that. "I will apologize later."

Ophelia explored his face. "You are frustrated."

He wanted to deny it. After all, Ophelia already had complicated emotions when it came to Abigail—he didn't want to make them worse. And his marital problems, whatever they were, were certainly none of her business anyway. But since he could not seem to hide his exasperation from her, he grunted, "Yes."

"About her," Ophelia said gently.

He nodded slowly. "Yes."

"Are you in love with her?"

He froze at the question and stared down into his sister's face, but he didn't see her anymore. He only saw the truth, one he had been trying to avoid for weeks, but no...it was longer than that. The truth he had been trying to avoid for months. Close to a year.

"Yes," he said softly, almost compelled to do so. "I am in love with her."

When he said it out loud, it almost buckled him. And it shamed him because it felt so true, despite all the times he'd denied it.

"Nathan," Ophelia breathed, her expression lined with surprise and soft kindness.

"I don't know if it matters, though."

"Of course it matters!" Ophelia cried out, then tempered her tone when the servants glanced at them from across the garden. "Come, talk to me about it."

He arched a brow in her direction. "When I know you have mixed feelings about her at best?"

Ophelia let out her breath slowly. "I *have* hesitated when it comes to her. I don't think I've made that a secret to either of you. And I had my reasons. But I've also watched you two together. Watched her by herself. I've tried to be open and to be honest, she is very difficult to dislike."

He felt a surge of relief despite his upset. "I'm happy to hear it."

"So won't you talk to me about your troubles?" Ophelia pressed.

He ran a hand through his hair. "Abigail *never* wanted this," he said. "And my feelings won't change that fact."

Ophelia folded her arms. "That's ridiculous. No, this marriage didn't come about under the best of circumstances. If you'd had more time before to resolve these issues, it couldn't have hurt. But I see how she watches you, Nathan! I *see* the connection between you because it is impossible not to see it."

He swallowed hard. Could that be true? "Then what do you think I should do?"

"What you need is a good talking to."

He stared at her a moment. "You are enjoying playing parent to me, aren't you?"

She smiled and it was almost giddy. "Turnabout is fair play after all these years, yes."

"A talking to," he repeated. "And you think you are the one to give it?"

She glared at him. "Don't underestimate me, Nathan."

"I would never," he said softly.

"Let me fetch her," Ophelia said. "I'll talk to her briefly, and then we'll come out here where it's warm and sunny and we will work this out."

He sighed. He so very much wanted to work it out. And perhaps Ophelia was correct that with a mediator they could speak more honestly. It was worth a try, at any rate.

"Fine, but please don't push."

"I am a member of the House of Gilmore. We are made to push." When he glared at her, she laughed. "But I will be delicate. Try to calm yourself. I will be back with her shortly."

She disappeared into the house and left Nathan to wander around the garden. He did so, examining flowers like he cared when all he really cared about was Abigail. What would Ophelia say to her? More to the point, what would *he* say to her? Did one just come out and say that one loved one's wife? In the garden, of all places? In front of others? Was that done? Would it work or would it push Abigail even further into her shell?

Ophelia appeared from the house again after a few moments, and his heart sank. She was alone. Abigail had refused to join them. He felt sick at that realization.

"She wasn't in her study," Ophelia said, her face lined with worry. "But this was."

She held out a folded sheet of paper with Nathan's name written across it. He drew a long breath before he took it and began to read:

I'm sorry we quarreled. I am not trying to hurt you. I'm going to visit Celeste in the hopes I can clear my head. Abigail.

He stared at the words, but also the hand they were written in. Abigail had not written to him during the course of their relationship. Or when she did, it was never more than a word or two in response to a question. Now he examined the swirls of her handwriting and it felt...familiar.

"What does it say?"

He handed the note over because he couldn't bear to read it

aloud. But as he paced away, something niggled in the back of his head. Like a word he couldn't remember but was just on the tip of his tongue.

"Nathan..." Ophelia's voice sounded tense—it trembled—and he turned back to find her holding out the note, her hand shaking. "I... this hand looks like...it looks like the note you received that told you about Erasmus Montgomery's duplicity." She sucked in a harsh breath. "The one that brought you to my rescue and revealed the truth of his bigamy."

He snatched the note and read it again, not for the content, but just to see the swirl and curve of each letter. "How do you know that?" he asked.

Ophelia shivered. "I looked at that letter so many times a year ago, I could tell you everything about it, from the ink blot in the corner of the page to the way the hand shook a little at the end. I am almost certain it is true."

Nathan swallowed hard as the ramifications of that became clear. He held out a hand to his sister. "Come. We'll become fully certain together."

She wrinkled her brow in concern, but let him lead her into the house and down the halls until they came to his study. He released her as he crossed to his desk and opened his top drawer. He dug around for a moment and then found the letter, the original letter. He set it on the table with Abigail's note beside it.

Ophelia stared. "You kept it?" she whispered.

He nodded. "I did." He leaned over it and she came around the desk to do the same.

"Look, the way she writes her *E*. It leans just a little to the left, just like the original note," Ophelia said softly.

"The same with the capital *I*."

He looked from one note to the other. She had signed her note today as *Abigail*. The other note was signed *An anonymous friend*. And looking at the capital *A* was what brought everything into sharp relief and kept him from doubting the truth any further. She had a unique way of writing the letter, a confidence from writing it over and over her entire life.

"She wrote it," he whispered. "She wrote the letter that brought all of us together." He stared at it again and then ran a hand through his hair. "Fuck."

~

When Nathan burst into the parlor, Rhys and Pippa were sitting by the fireplace, each reading a book. Kenley was at their feet, building a tower from blocks.

"I am sorry, my lord," their butler said with a frustrated glare for Nathan. "I tried to stop him, but—"

"Did you know?" Nathan snapped over him.

Rhys lifted a hand as he slowly rose from the chair. "It's all right, Coleman." He swept Kenley up from the floor and crossed to the servant. "Do you think you could take this young man to see his governess?"

The butler nodded and took the child as if he were accustomed to doing so, then left the room, shutting the door behind himself quietly.

"Did you know?" Nathan repeated, his heart pounding so loudly in his ears he could scarcely hear anything else.

Pippa got up, her pretty face lined with deep concern. "Know what, Gilmore? What is going on?"

"Abigail wrote the letter that told me Montgomery was a bigamist," he choked out. "Did you know?"

Rhys recoiled in surprise at the news, and Nathan felt it was an honest reaction. Pippa, on the other hand, went pale, but did not seem surprised.

"Pippa," he said, his tone a warning.

Rhys pivoted to her. "Pippa?"

She folded her arms. "Yes. I knew."

"Good Lord," Rhys said, still shocked although he didn't seem angry. "And you never mentioned it?"

She sighed. "I sometimes wanted to talk to you about it, I promise you. But it was not my secret to tell. Abigail made it clear she never wanted anyone to know."

That confirmation sucked all the heat from Nathan's reaction, and he gripped the back of the settee with both hands as he willed himself not to go to his knees.

"She told you at last?" Pippa asked softly.

"No," Nathan said. "She wrote me a note. The handwriting seemed familiar to both Ophelia and me. We compared the two messages and came to this conclusion."

"Come sit," Pippa ordered, pointing to the settee.

As he did so, she marched over to the sideboard. Nathan was going to tell her he didn't want tea, but to his surprise she poured a whisky instead and brought it back to him.

He drank it in one gulp, welcoming the burn in his chest that briefly erased all the other feelings there. He stared at the empty glass perched in his trembling hands.

"She did this even though it risked herself. It...it destroyed her." He squeezed his eyes shut. "*I* destroyed her."

"No," Pippa snapped. "That is not correct. *Erasmus* destroyed her. She never wanted that to happen to another person. So when she realized your sister was in danger...yes, she did do this. And she never expected or wanted any credit for it."

"When I think that I all but accused her of being in league with the man the first time we met." He bent his head in shame.

Rhys sat down next to him. "But you two resolved that, didn't you? You knew very quickly that she could not have ever done such a thing."

"And she is too observant a person not to know that you were in pain when you said that. It was unfair, yes," Pippa said. "But not unforgiveable."

"I must talk to her," Nathan murmured. "I need to understand this. I should just go get her at the Gregorys' home and we'll hash it out."

"Gilmore," Pippa said, reaching over the back of the settee to catch his hand briefly. "I know you are a man of action, but this situation is more tenuous than that. You know it if you stop to *think*."

He stared up at her, desperate for an answer he couldn't find in his own addled, twisting mind. "Why?"

"Because she isn't trusting," Pippa said gently. "Love...scares her."

He flinched. "Love. So you know?"

Rhys drew back. "That you love her? I think we've all guessed. But I'm a little shocked *you* know, you've denied it for so long."

"I am the last one to realize it, it seems," Nathan said, and scrubbed a hand over his face. "So what do I do, Pippa? You and Celeste are closest to her. How do I manage to break past that armor?"

She sighed. "I'm not sure even the two of us have fully done it."

He wrinkled his brow. "But you're best friends."

"Her friendship is most important in my life, aside from Rhys's," Pippa mused softly. "And I adore her with every fiber of my being. Abigail is wonderfully loving and giving. She accepts others for exactly who they are, with no question. She would strip away her life for the chance to save someone else...just as she did for your sister."

"But," he encouraged gently, for he felt the word coming.

"*But* all that doesn't change the fact that she has walls. If you dig too deeply, she changes the subject or teases or backs away. And she'll do that with you, too."

"She does that with me, regularly," he huffed out. "She bends just the slightest fraction toward me and then snaps back as far as she can go. She is skittish as a colt."

"And how would you break a colt?" Rhys asked.

He drew back sharply. "I have no intention of *breaking* my wife."

Pippa pursed her lips. "Obviously not, but Rhys makes a good point. Not a colt then, not breaking her. But if you saw an animal that was injured, one that lashed out or ran away when it was afraid, would you stomp after it, demanding it understand that you were a friend?"

"No," he said softly. "I would go slowly. I would be gentle. I would earn their trust."

Rhys glanced up at Pippa with a smile. "Woo her," he said. "Win her heart and her confidence. You may have to face the past, yes. But in the end, it's all about the future that you could build together, no matter the cost."

Pippa's expression softened, and for a moment it was like Nathan wasn't even there. And while normally he would turn away from this display of intimacy, today he looked at it. Pippa and Rhys's love had been hard won, he knew. But seeing it flow between them, he could see that it was worth it.

And so was Abigail. He just had to teach her that he was also worth the risk. That he would never let her fall.

He cleared his throat. "Your husband is a smart man."

Pippa smiled at him. "The very smartest."

"Then hopefully between the two of you, you can help me chart a plan to do exactly as you say. When I go to find her, I want to start down this road right away."

Pippa nodded and came around to sit across from them again. "Then let us think on this."

"Do you think it will work?" He heard the crack in his voice. Felt the pain that accompanied the question.

Rhys nodded. "I hope so. No two people in the world deserve happiness more than you both."

CHAPTER 20

A bigail had thought to come to Celeste's house and clear her
mind, but the moment her friend had entered the parlor to
greet her, she burst into tears. Now she sat on the settee, Celeste's
arms around her.

"Oh, dearest," Celeste murmured as she rocked her gently, like she
was a child. "Come now, tell me. Tell me what it is and let me help
you."

"You can't," Abigail whispered, and sniffled as she tried to right
herself. She did not ever show this kind of vulnerability and she
needed to stop it now. She sat up and wiped her tears with the hand-
kerchief that Celeste produced.

"Is this about Gilmore?" Celeste asked gently.

Abigail considered denying it for a moment, but she needed
counsel and guidance in that moment. That eclipsed all self-protective
instincts.

"Yes," she whispered. "We had an argument and he left. I've ruined
everything, Celeste."

Celeste wrinkled her brow. "What did you argue about?"

"He doesn't like that I don't want to join him and Ophelia at Rhys
and Pippa's at the end of the summer. He thinks I don't want to

pretend to care for him at a ball he wants to hold. He doesn't like that I hold him at arm's length, even though it is what we agreed to do." She felt the tears welling back up and blinked to keep them at bay. "And now he *left* and I know everything is ruined."

"He left? How long has he been gone?" Celeste pressed.

"I don't know. He departed my study and then I c-came here."

Celeste stared at her. "Oh. So he left...he left the *room*, not the house? And this was *today*?"

Abigail nodded. "Y-Yes."

There was a moment's hesitation and then Celeste reached out to take her hands. "I don't disagree that these are serious issues, but...the argument doesn't sound like it was so horrible. You are navigating a new marriage, one you were thrown into suddenly. There were bound to be waves in the water. You can't believe that it would really cause such..." She trailed off and her eyes went wide. "Oh."

There was something about her tone that was almost pitying, and Abigail shook her head. "Oh?"

"That was what *he* did, isn't it? Erasmus."

Abigail bent her head, trying not to let all the memories come back. "Yes," she admitted once she had controlled her breathing. "If he left the room during an argument, then I didn't see him again for days. And when he came back, he was never sorry. He wanted my apology, but I don't think he ever gave one to me."

Celeste shook her head. "I'm so sorry. He and I weren't close. He never made me care for him or pretended to care for me, but I can imagine how painful and frightening that uncertainty must have been."

"Everything was the edge of the end," Abigail whispered. "Why shouldn't I believe it is the same now?"

Celeste caught her hands. "Because *Gilmore* is different. He isn't even close to being the same man."

"He is ten times the man," Abigail said immediately. Then she frowned. "Don't ever tell him I said that—he will be insufferable."

Celeste laughed softly and then leaned forward. She rested her forehead against Abigail's and whispered, "Erasmus Montgomery took *enough* from us. Don't let him take your future, too."

Abigail flinched. She might have come up with some pithy remark to diffuse the emotion of those words, but before she could, Owen's butler, Cookson, stepped into the room. "I'm sorry to disturb, Mrs. Gregory, Your Grace, but His Grace, the Duke of Gilmore, has arrived and is asking to see his wife."

Abigail jerked to her feet. "He is here?"

"Yes, madam."

She glanced down at Celeste. Her friend's expression was only one of support. She found a little strength in that and nodded. "You may bring him," she whispered.

The butler stepped away to do just that, and Abigail gripped the arm of the settee. Celeste covered her hand. "There now. He has come to find you—that does not sound like he doesn't care or he intends to disappear from your life."

"I have no idea what it means," Abigail said.

She said no more because Cookson returned with Nathan behind him. He motioned her husband into the room, and for a moment it felt like the world stopped. Nathan stared at her. She stared back, searching for anger in his dark eyes.

She saw none. How could that be true, considering they had quarreled? Was he just hiding it in mixed company?

"Gilmore," Celeste said, rushing to him. "Welcome."

"Celeste," he said softly, forcing his gaze to her. "I am sorry to interrupt your meeting. I just needed to see my...my wife."

Abigail tilted her head. There was something in his tone that she didn't understand. "Well, I am here," she said.

He nodded. "And are you ready to come home? My mount could be returned by a servant and we could ride together in your carriage. If you would join me."

Abigail glanced at Celeste and her friend nodded slightly, an encouragement to go with him. And she could think of no way to refuse, in truth. She worried her hands before her and then nodded.

"Of course." She reached for Celeste and the two women squeezed hands. "Thank you," she said softly.

Celeste smiled first at her, then at Gilmore, but did not insert herself as Abigail walked away to him. He didn't take her hand or offer her his arm, but he did walk beside her as they went from the foyer back to her waiting carriage. He motioned the footman away and opened the door for her himself. She stared at his outstretched hand. She had been so upset when she left that she wasn't wearing gloves. He had removed his, as well and so when she took that rough, strong hand, it was skin on skin.

She hissed at the sensation and released him as soon as she was in the vehicle. He joined her, sitting across from her. He did not speak until the carriage rolled from the drive and onto the street.

"You've been crying," he said softly.

She bent her head. "I...I would be a fool to deny it. I'm sure I look terrible."

"You are beautiful always, Abigail. But I'm sorry that you were in pain. That I caused it."

She glanced up at him. "You—you didn't. *I* caused it."

He arched a brow. "I pushed you when you were not ready to be pushed. And when I became frustrated, I walked away. I can own my part in this."

She blinked. Here she had been telling Celeste that Erasmus had never apologized to her for their quarrels. That she couldn't expect as much from Nathan. But he surprised her, as he was constantly surprising her. Even more significant was that he seemed like he meant the apology.

She cleared her throat. "I will also own my side. I have been... distant from you, as you said. I thought that when we married I would settle in and we would just know what to do. But my life has changed a great deal and perhaps I am not managing it as well as I could. I'm not a person who adapts easily, I suppose. A failing."

"Not a failing," he said.

She sat in the quiet for a moment, staring at him. "When you...

when you walked out of the room, I had this moment of panic that you might not...ever...walk back in again."

He tilted his head and his expression twisted as if that thought gave him a deep and abiding pain. "I will promise you that even if I walk away to gather myself, there will never be a time that I won't return. I—" He cut himself off and shook his head. "This was a small argument, Abigail, brought on by exhaustion on both our parts after the overwhelming circumstances of the past few weeks. It wasn't the end of the world."

Relief washed over her like a cool rain after a blistering heat, and she nearly melted in it, sagging against the carriage seat.

"Perhaps we can try to...to talk about where we go from here," she suggested softly. "And I will try to be a little more open minded about what it was you asked me earlier."

He smiled at her before he shifted to her side of the carriage. "Perhaps later. Later we can talk about all those things. For right now I would just like to..." He slid a finger along her jawline and she shivered at how close he was. How gentle he was.

He bent his head and his mouth found hers. The kiss was just as tender, a repair of a breach, a welcome back, a reminder that he was not the same as Montgomery. That he was a thousand times better, a million times.

And that she very much wanted him in her life, even if she never let him past the barriers that protected her.

He traced her lips with his tongue and she opened with a shuddering sigh, grasping at his biceps to hold herself steady as the kiss grew deeper and more passionate and more possessive.

He would have had her there on the carriage seat. She felt it in the desperation of his touch, but before they could move to that next wicked moment, the vehicle slowed as they turned down their own drive.

He pulled back. "Come upstairs with me?"

She nodded. In that moment, she wanted more than his touch. But she couldn't have that, so she shoved those desires aside and instead focused on the passion she would allow. It would bind them again, make things safe again. That was all she wanted. That was all she could ever hope to have.

~

Nathan had made a study of Abigail in the year they had been acquainted, but never had he seen her vulnerability so clearly as he did now as they entered his bedchamber and she crossed to the bed. It wasn't that her behavior was any different. Outwardly she was exactly the same. It was that he saw through her more now that he knew he loved her.

And what he saw gave him hope. She would not have cried over their argument if she truly didn't care. She wouldn't have seemed so small and heartbroken in the carriage. Now whether he could break down the barriers that kept her from sharing herself completely with him was another story.

He would try, and that was enough for now.

He moved toward her, and she stiffened as he reached her. It was evident she was still torn, fearful of losing the armor she'd built around herself for so long.

"Let me touch you?" he asked.

She didn't answer with words, but wound her arms around his neck and lifted her mouth to his. He took it eagerly, and for a few moments he lost himself in her taste, in her scent, in the feel of her warm body pressed to his. This was the first time he'd done so knowing he loved her, and it meant everything to him.

He drew back, watching her soft expression, brown eyes hazy with desire. He smiled at her as he let his fingers find the buttons along the back of her gown. He swiftly unfastened them, then drew her gown down around her waist.

He remembered the first time he'd done that. The first time he saw her naked and his entire world shifted. How had he not known he loved her then? It seemed so obvious now.

Then she had seemed nervous when he looked at her. Now she arched her back, just the tiniest movement, but one that showed herself off a little. He cupped her cheeks and kissed her again, this time harder, with more drive and force. She softened against him, giving where he took with a tiny groan that seemed to jolt its way through him like summer lightning.

He hooked his fingers around the straps of her chemise, loving when he brushed the soft skin of her shoulders. He let his fingertips drag along her body as he pulled the chemise down to join the gown and then pushed both off together. They pooled at her feet and he stepped back to enjoy his handiwork.

She was so utterly beautiful, so perfect in his eyes, that a lump formed in his throat. If he managed this correctly, if he was gentle and careful and persistent, he would get to love her like this for the rest of his life. He would feel her bend toward him, giving him the same love that he felt for her.

Which made the risk worthwhile.

"Will you please get in my bed?" he asked.

She giggled. "So polite all of a sudden, Your Grace."

He shrugged. "When I apologize, I do it wholeheartedly. So please, please, will you get in my bed? And take off the stockings and the slippers."

She shook her head, but she was smiling broadly as she climbed up on the high bed and then tossed her slippers and stockings over the edge with a clatter. He watched her as he began to undress. Once she was fully naked, she leaned up on her elbows to stare as he did so.

He took his time, exploring how her pupils dilated with each movement. It was a delicious thing, to be wanted by her. This woman who could have anyone, who could be loved by so many...wanted him in her arms. He never wanted to betray that trust. He only wished to multiply it. And also make her come and come and come until she was sated.

He shrugged out of his trousers at last and took his half-hard cock in hand, stroking it until it was at full attention. She licked her lips and he felt the movement like she had done so against him.

"Well, that was just too much," he grunted as he moved onto the bed beside her. He caught her lips once more and kissed her hard and fast, driving his tongue inside like he would soon do with his body. "And a good idea."

"What was a good idea?" she said as he began to kiss the side of her neck.

"Licking," he replied without moving his mouth from her skin, so the word was muffled.

"Mmmm. I've always enjoyed the way you lick," she breathed, and rested her head against the pillows with a shudder. Her body relaxed beneath him as he kissed lower, tasting the faintly salty flavor of her collarbone, her right breast. The nipple hardened beneath his tongue as he swirled it 'round and 'round. Tugged it gently with his teeth until she cried out softly in pleasure.

He moved to the opposite breast, watching her reaction to every little lick and bite and suck. Her head lolled and her hands fisted, one against the mattress, one against his back. The flexing of her fingers along his skin was like a drumbeat of passion, and his cock throbbed in time. He wanted to bury himself in her, drive until they were both panting and sweaty and weak.

But not yet. He could wait for that sweet explosion a little longer if it meant the pleasure of watching her writhe.

He inched lower, nuzzling the soft skin of her belly. He rubbed his cheek against her thigh, letting her feel the rough beginnings of stubble after a long day. She opened her legs wider with a faintly exhaled, "Yes, please."

He was nearly undone. Lost to her. And it was heaven. Almost as heavenly as when he used his thumbs to peel open her sex. She was slick already, and he scented the faint sweetness of her that was so uniquely hers. His mouth watered to taste it. Drown in it and her.

He licked her, watching again as she arched her back. Licked and licked, until he could only taste her on his tongue. He caught her hips, cradling her backside in his hands to hold her still as he dove into the work of shattering her. She ground against his tongue, making harsh sounds of pleasure, wriggling beneath him. He began to suck her clitoris, feeling it swell beneath his tongue and her legs begin to shake against his shoulders.

She was so close now. He felt the shift in her body, the flood of her pleasure. And then she keened and the world wound down to this one place in time. To her and the gorgeous experience of her orgasm.

He sucked her through it, forcing her to twitch long after the hard, heavy waves of the pleasure were gone. She dug her fingers into his hair, tugging against his scalp to drag him up her body. He complied willingly, enthusiastically, laughing as she pulled him to her mouth.

When she pushed at his shoulders, rolling him onto his back and straddling him, he also didn't resist. There was nothing like watching her as she aligned their bodies and took him inside, into warm, wet heat that fluttered around his cock.

She sat up, flexing her body over his. Her head dropped back, lips parted. He stared at her, mesmerized by how glorious she was in pleasure. She rolled over him in waves, driving them both toward release. He gripped her hips, guiding her, holding her for purchase as pleasure arced through his body, pulsed in his balls.

Her eyes came open at last and she met his gaze. He gripped her tighter, and she gasped, grinding even harder against him. Her hands lifted, covering her breasts, giving him a show as she rode harder and faster. When she came a second time, it was glorious. Her eyes never left his as she spasmed around him, pulling him, milking him. He lifted against her, and then it was all hot, streaking pleasure as he erupted deep within her.

She collapsed down against his chest, her mouth seeking his in one final hot kiss before she settled into his arms, half-sprawled across his body.

He had no idea how long they lay like that, her legs and arms tangled with his, her dark head cuddled into his chest. He combed his fingers into her hair, loving the silkiness against his skin. Her breathing became calmer, deeper, and for a brief, beautiful moment, he thought she might stay.

But then she lifted her head and looked at him. There was such a longing in her gaze, but he realized it wasn't something sexual. That desire had been sated, at least for a little while. It was a longing for something more. The same thing he wanted. And it gave him even more hope, because if even some small part of her desired to be more than merely lovers and friends in this marriage, then he could get there. He could earn her trust and her love.

She pressed a kiss to his mouth gently and then got out of the bed. He longed to grab her hand, ask her to stay, but he recalled Pippa's admonishment to go slowly. So he simply allowed her to gather up her things in an awkward pile. She smiled at him once more and then slipped from his room without further comment.

He rolled over on his side, breathing in the scent of her that had been left behind. This was going to be work, but it was worth it. She was worth it. And so was the future he was beginning to build in his mind.

CHAPTER 21

Abigail placed another book on her shelf and stepped back to enjoy her handiwork. The room was coming together. She had taken her time deciding how she wished to organize things, and now she had her books separated by subject and then alphabetical by the author. It was the first time they were so organized, and she thrilled that the next time she needed information, it would be easy to find.

She sighed as she moved to the window and looked out over the garden behind the house. Servants buzzed around, doing their duties and talking to each other. She knew it was the same all over the house. It had been three days since the argument with Nathan, and things had gone back to normal. Better, actually. They made love every night...and some long and lovely afternoons...and he often spoke to her about what she was working on.

They had even come to terms about the ball he desired to hold. A few more days and she would be hostess for the first time as Duchess of Gilmore.

Ophelia had become more kind, as well, though Abigail did sometimes catch her sister-in-law watching her with an odd expression. Still, she felt more comfortable in her role as duchess and in the vast and intimidating halls of this home.

There was a light knock on the open door behind her, and she turned to find Nathan standing there. Her breath caught, just as it seemed to always catch when he had been away from her for more than an hour. It was so very unfair that he was so handsome.

He smiled. "It looks marvelous, Abigail."

Her cheeks heated at his compliment and she looked around. "It does. It feels like my room now."

"I'm glad," he said softly. For a moment they just looked at each other, but then he shook his head. "I seem to be losing myself in thought. I have a surprise for you, which is why I came. Will you come with me?"

She blinked at the twinkle that had entered his eye. "A surprise? What is it?"

He laughed. "If I tell you, it won't be a surprise." He held out a hand. "Please."

The please was what got her, said in that rough tone he sometimes got. The one that seemed to dance up her spine. She took his hand and followed him down the hall to one of the many parlors. He opened the door and revealed a very pretty woman sitting on the settee. She rose as they entered, and smiled broadly at Abigail.

"Abigail, may I present the Duchess of Willowby. Your Grace, this is my wife, the Duchess of Gilmore."

Abigail was so shocked she couldn't move for a fraction of a moment. She had heard of the Duchess of Willowby before. She had married the mysterious Duke of Willowby a few years prior and it was well-known that she dabbled in the same healing arts as had caught Abigail's fancy. Abigail had always been fascinated by her, but had never felt comfortable reaching out to her. Their positions had always felt too disparate.

She rushed forward to take the hand the woman offered. "Your Grace," she gushed. "How lovely it is to meet you. I have heard so much about you."

The duchess smiled. "And I you, from my very good friend the

Duchess of Abernathe. When Emma speaks highly of someone, all of our group must listen."

Abigail's cheeks heated, for the Duchess of Abernathe had been one of the people who caught her and Nathan in this very parlor that night of his ball all those weeks ago. And while Emma had been very kind since, Abigail had to wonder if that fact had come up in whatever she said to her friends.

"She is a lovely woman," Abigail said as she motioned the duchess back to her seat. "And so kind to mention me to you. Will you have tea?"

Nathan held up a hand and waved her to her seat. "I will fetch it."

Abigail's eyes went wide. Nathan fetch her tea? That certainly wasn't what gentlemen usually did. And yet he did it without complaint so that her conversation with her guest did not have to be interrupted.

"Your Grace—" she and the duchess both began, and then they laughed together.

"Honestly, it is always impossible when you get more than one duchess in a room," the Duchess of Willowby said. "Why don't you just call me Diana? And I will call you Abigail, if it is not too forward."

"It isn't at all," Abigail said with a sigh of relief. "I admit, I am not entirely accustomed to the title. When people say Your Grace, I automatically look behind me to see what fine duchess has entered the room."

Nathan handed over a cup to Diana and the other to Abigail. Then he leaned down and squeezed her shoulder. It was like he deposited all his strength into her with that brief touch and she took it eagerly. "I will leave you two to get to know each other."

She glanced up and found him smiling down at her with such an expression of joy. As if her happiness and excitement gave him the same feeling. Her heart lurched at the sight, and she watched him go before she refocused on Diana, who was now observing her closely.

"He is besotted," she said with a smile. "Just as all the stories say."

Abigail caught her breath. Yes, the stories. All those stories of their great love that weren't true. Only they sometimes felt like they weren't a lie, either. It was confusing and a little terrifying.

She smiled nervously and changed the subject. "I admit I am so happy to meet you. I don't know if you knew that I share your interest in herbal remedy and progressive healing."

Diana nodded. "Gilmore said as much in his letter to me when he asked me here. I was thrilled to hear it. I adore my friends beyond reason, but none of them have the same obsession I do with such things. I am excited to be able to talk with a fellow healer."

Abigail smiled. She was bubbling with excitement as the two of them dove into a far deeper conversation on the topic. But even as she and Diana became fast friends, she couldn't help but think of Nathan and his expression when he left them alone.

The idea that he could be happy just by making her happy was... intoxicating. And she feared she could too easily be drunk on it and forget her senses if she was not careful.

～

Nathan was sitting at his desk a few hours after he had left Abigail with the Duchess of Willowby. A line of figures down his ledger was what he was supposed to be focusing on, but instead he kept thinking of Abigail and hoping she was having a good time.

As if conjured by his thoughts of her, the door to his study opened and she stepped into the room. Her face was lit up like a thousand candles and her eyes danced as she shut the door behind herself and leaned against it.

"Good afternoon," he said. "Has the Duchess of Willowby left us?"

Abigail nodded. "Just now."

"And did you have a good time?" he asked, even though he could see the answer written all over her face.

Her smile widened. "Oh, it was marvelous, Nathan!" she burst out as she came across the room toward him. "Diana is wonderful. She's so clever and she's been an actual practicing healer for years. She was so complimentary about my library, and then we walked the garden together and she helped me finally instruct the gardeners about what to plant and how. She also gave me some wonderful ideas about how to best utilize the greenhouse in Cornwall. I think she and the Duke of Willowby might come to visit us there. If that is agreeable to you."

He had leaned back in his chair as she spoke, and he couldn't help but grin. "Of course. I hoped you would get along and I'm so glad you did."

"We are going to meet regularly," Abigail continued. "And she has also invited me and your sister to a tea with the Duchesses, which is what everyone calls their group of friends."

"*That* is an exclusive invitation," he said. "I have never heard anything but wonderful things about their group, though. I am sure you will have a fine time and it will be good for Ophelia."

She nodded. "Perhaps I could even help you out with the dukes. Get you in their club."

He chuckled because it was clear she was teasing him. "A place in the famous 1797 Club. I might expire from excitement." He waved his hands around playfully and she giggled.

But as she took a step closer to him, close enough to run her fingers down the edge of his desk, her smile fell. "Why did you...why did you do that?"

He wrinkled his brow. "Do what?"

"Arrange the meeting," she clarified.

He held her stare as he reached out to catch her hand. He drew her closer, closer, into his lap. As she settled there, he lifted a hand to trace her cheek. "Why do you think?"

Recognition flared in her eyes, an understanding of what he was saying even if she darted her gaze away to avert it. Pretend it away. She cleared her throat. "Well, it was truly wonderful. Thank you."

"I will do everything in my power to make you happy, Abigail," he said. "For the rest of my life."

She stiffened against him, and now she did force herself to look down at him. "Nathan," she whispered. "We said that...I...I can't..."

198

He ignored the sting that accompanied that truncated refusal. He had tested the waters, and while they were certainly warmer than they'd ever been, she still wasn't ready. That was fine. He could wait.

"Don't tell me what you can't do," he said softly. "I wasn't asking for anything."

Her brow wrinkled. "How can you not?"

"Ask for anything?"

She nodded. "I've been thinking a great deal about our arrangement since the argument a few days ago. You could have married a woman with connections and a dowry to add to your coffers. Instead you ended up shackled to me, a woman who drags a scandal behind her big enough that you had to create an elaborate lie to make me palatable. A woman you likely considered your enemy until recently. You share your home, your connections, your money, your time and... what do I give in return?"

"You give so much," he said. "I like how you challenge me. Not just how we play, because we both know the wagers and the insults are all play. They're seduction. Perhaps they have been for a long time."

She caught her breath at that, but did not declare it untrue, so he continued, "I mean that you are so intelligent it makes me want to be more so. I mean that you are so kind and nonjudgmental, you make me want to be the same. I want to be clear: you make my life better."

Her breath was coming short now, her fingers clenched against her lap, tears gathered in her eyes. He could see she was on the edge of running because what he said was too meaningful, too intimate. So he switched tactics.

"Also, you are remarkable in bed."

That worked. She barked out a laugh of surprise, the tension gone from her face in a moment. Then she looked at him, playful sensuality on her face.

"Remarkable in bed, but what about not in bed?" she said. "Am I not remarkable in your study against the desk or on the settee in the parlor?"

"You were very remarkable on the settee in the parlor not that many weeks ago," he said, massaging her thigh through her gown. Her breath caught and she ground against him slightly. "Though I wouldn't want to try that one again until my nosy sister is out of the house."

"Good plan," Abigail whispered.

"However, if we lock the door, I think I would very much like to test just how remarkable you are against the desk. Or the wall. Or on the rug in front of the fire."

She bent her head and kissed him deeply. Her fingers slid into his hair, and he felt all the desire pulsing in her. It was all a way to distract him, of course. To make space from the emotional connection she so feared. But he didn't mind. After all, having her body was just another way he told her he loved her.

And one day, he would get to say those very words as he slid home inside of her. He knew it.

CHAPTER 22

Abigail smiled as her maid left the room, but the expression fell as she turned her attention back to her image in the mirror. Tonight she would host her first ball as Duchess of Gilmore. Tonight this house would fill with people who had once been her betters, people who wanted to see her fail. Of course, it would also fill with friends, old and new, but she couldn't help but be nervous.

She made a move toward the door to begin her day and all the final preparations there still were to manage when there was a knock. She halted and said, "Come in."

She was surprised when Ophelia stepped into the chamber. "Good morning."

"Good morning, Ophelia. Oh, your hair looks very pretty."

Ophelia turned her head so Abigail could see the back and the complicated twists and turns of her blonde locks. "Do you like it? I'm trying something to see if it would work for the ball tonight."

Abigail came closer and turned her head to look closer. "It's divine. I think it will be perfect for tonight."

"Good." Ophelia let out a sigh. "I admit, I'm nervous. Isn't that funny? After attending so many balls and parties. I still find myself standing in front of my wardrobe, fighting with myself over gowns and hair."

"You'll do wonderfully, as you always do," Abigail assured her. She wanted to take Ophelia's hand as she did it, but she held back. Although the waters between them had warmed considerably in the past few days, she didn't want to push too hard.

"Do you think you might...come look with me?" Ophelia asked. "You have a wonderful sense of style and I swear I've debated this until my poor maid, Laura, has started to block it all out to keep herself from going mad. I need a fresh set of eyes."

Abigail drew back. This was the first time Ophelia had reached out to her. She certainly wasn't going to waste the opportunity provided here. Not when their getting along meant so much to Nathan.

"Of course," Abigail said, motioning for Ophelia to lead them. They walked down the hall together in a not entirely comfortable silence, and then Ophelia led her into her chamber.

Abigail looked around briefly. Ophelia's bright, sometimes chaotic personality was reflected in how clothing and items were somewhat strewn across the chamber. Books were stacked on the end table, brushes and combs and jewelry were spread across the dressing table.

"Here are the options," Ophelia said, drawing Abigail's attention to two gowns that were hanging along the front of her wardrobe. One was a stunning green, with an intricately woven bodice in a darker shade than the flowing skirt. There was hand painting on the hem and gold threading throughout.

"This is beautiful," Abigail breathed as she lightly fingered the silk.

"Isn't it?" Ophelia said with a happy smile. "I adore it beyond reason. And yet, I'm not sure. What about the blue?"

Abigail shifted her attention to the other gown. This one was pale blue, almost an exact match to Ophelia's bright eyes. A white lace overlay gave the fall of the skirt marvelous depth and the dark satin sash at the high waistline was sewn with paste jewels that sparkled in the sunlight streaming in through the window.

"The blue," Abigail said. "The green is wonderful, but the blue will make your eyes pop. I think you should wear the blue."

Ophelia sighed as if this was a relief. "It was my same thought, but I couldn't talk myself into it. I needed your opinion."

Abigail tilted her head. "Well, I'm happy to give it, Ophelia."

"But you are surprised I've asked for it because of our distant relationship to this point," Ophelia said as she put the green gown back in the wardrobe and then laid the blue out on her bed for her maid to prepare later.

Abigail caught her breath. "We...I..."

"It's all right. We must speak of it sometime, mustn't we? I know I've been cool toward you."

Abigail shifted. "Perhaps. But it isn't as if there was no reason for it. You had your doubts. You are allowed them."

Ophelia wrinkled her brow. "You are almost too good. And I want you to know that I hope we can be better friends as we move forward. That we can truly become sisters over time. Not that I think I could ever replace what you lost."

Abigail stared at the young woman before her. "Not replace," she said softly. "But I would very much like to have you as a sister. In time."

Ophelia smiled. "And what about you? Are you nervous for tonight?"

"Yes," Abigail admitted, because she didn't have the strength to deny it. "I don't want to let your brother down."

Ophelia's smile fell a fraction and she stepped out. She took Abigail's hands between her own, squeezing gently. "You won't. You couldn't. But I want to thank you for caring about his happiness. And thank you for all you've done for me, as well."

Abigail wasn't certain what Ophelia meant by that, but she didn't pull away from it. "I hope over time I can do even more."

"Yes." Ophelia released her with a smile. "And now I am famished. Let's go see what Mrs. Smythe has whipped up for breakfast, shall we?"

Abigail nodded and the two left the chamber together. She wasn't certain what had brought on this shift, this final welcome, but she would take it. Tonight, she needed all the allies she could find.

~

A bigail smoothed her gown, a beautiful pink silk with a pale overlay stitched in flowers. Nathan had presented it to her earlier in the day, after he'd had it made by the same modiste who had made her bridal gown, so she'd had the most current measurements.

It was glorious and she adored it. At least she would look the part of a duchess. She hoped.

"You are...stunning."

She turned toward the door to the antechamber and found Nathan standing there, his jacket dangling from his fingers, his mouth agape as he stared at her in what could only be described as wonder. She bent her head, a blush of pure pleasure warming her cheeks.

"Thank you again for the beautiful gown. I love it." She glanced up at him. "And *you* are very handsome."

He slung the jacket back over his shoulder and did a small circle so she could see him better. Her heart stuttered. He really did look almost good enough to eat.

"I almost look like a duke," he said.

"You *always* look like a duke," she corrected.

He arched a brow. "Not always. Not earlier today after your gift arrived."

She shook her head, trying not to let her mind take her back to the way she'd thanked him on her knees in front of the fire.

"Do you want to just stay here and thank me again?" he asked, taking a step toward her.

"Don't tempt me." She attempted to laugh, but it didn't mask her worry.

His smile faded a fraction. "You're truly nervous about tonight, aren't you?"

She shrugged. "It is my first time to act as mistress of this house. With so many people coming, with so much at stake? There is a great deal that might go wrong."

He pondered that a moment. "What if we made a wager to ease your mind?"

She arched a brow. "You just love losing to me, don't you?"

He snorted out a laugh. "If you get too cocksure, I'm bound to catch you. Now, are you too cowardly to wager, Your Grace?"

"Never." She folded her arms. "What is the subject?"

He stroked a hand across his freshly shaven jaw absently, leaving her wanting to do the same thing with her cheek and then her lips. "Well, we are attending a ball, and my sister will be there—a center of attention, no doubt."

"No doubt," Abigail agreed freely. "I saw her dress today and it is beautiful. She will be admired by all who attend."

"Then why not wager on Ophelia and the number of her dance partners?"

"Interesting," Abigail said, and tried to keep her giddiness from her face. She and Ophelia had talked during breakfast, and Ophelia had confided that she did not intend to dance more than ten times that night. She wasn't going to fill her dance card. So Abigail had the advantage in this wager. "Do I get to choose the number first?"

"Yes. And whoever guesses closest to the correct number without going over will win."

She pretended to think about it. "Nine," she said.

"Nine?" he repeated. "Come, this is her first event since returning to London. She will be in great demand. I say fourteen. Her card will be full and only exhaustion will keep her from dancing all night long."

Once more Abigail tried to keep her excitement from her voice as she shrugged. "You know her best, so you are likely to win. But what are the stakes?"

He cocked his head. "What do you want, Abigail?"

He was toying with her, being seductive and playful and probably expecting her to ask for some sexual favor. And it was tempting, because she did love any time he touched her. And yet she wanted something more, foolish as it might be. Something she had been pondering a great deal in the last few days.

She shifted. "A while ago, you offered to tell me about your past. That deep, dark secret we both know you are carrying around."

"Ah yes, my secret room of portraits I've painted...badly," he said solemnly.

She shook her head at his teasing. "I lost the first wager where that secret was the prize, so I didn't get to know it. But I'd still like to."

He seemed surprised by her request, and for a moment she thought he might refuse her, but he nodded. "Very well. My secret is the prize if you win. And if I win...then after the ball, after I peel that pretty dress off with my teeth and make you shake with pleasure, after all of that...I want you to stay with me in my room. All night."

She swallowed hard. "You want me to sleep in your bed with you?"

"Yes." His voice grew rough. "Very much so, Abigail."

She worried her lip a moment. The reason she had avoided sleeping with him was that it felt so intimate. Even more so than sex, somehow. To sleep in the same bed was to fully trust a partner, to surrender the most vulnerable moments with them.

It was one of the last barriers she had left between them. And yet she could see how much it mattered to him and she wanted to give him this boon.

She nodded. "Yes."

He grinned. "Then may the best man...or woman...win," he said as he crossed the room, swept her into his arms and kissed her gently, as to not muss her. When he set her aside, he offered her his arm. "Shall we go, Your Grace?"

She drew in a deep breath and then took his arm. "Lead the way, Your Grace."

He did so, taking her from the room and leading her to the next step in their path together. The next step toward their future.

～

The ball was in full swing, and no one could have counted it as anything but a rousing success. Nathan had watched, swelling with pride, as Abigail embraced her role as duchess to the fullest. She was such a natural at making people feel comfortable, welcomed, no matter their station or income or title. He realized now that was one thing he had always admired about her, loved about her. Seeing it in action only made that love swell higher.

Now she had just entered the dance floor with Owen and the two began to waltz. Her movements were graceful and lovely, and all eyes seem to move to her.

He managed to pry his away and looked around the room for Celeste. He found her at the edge of the ballroom floor, watching them as he had been. He moved toward her with a smile.

"Care to join the fray?" he asked. "Since your husband and my wife are dancing together?"

She nodded. "Oh yes, I do love to dance." He led her to the floor and they fell into the steps with the others. "Owen would only dance with me," Celeste said with a laugh. "But I told him he must be freer with his favors." She blushed. "At least the dancing ones."

Nathan smiled with her. He did like Celeste so much. "He is very good at it. Though I can understand his desire to only dance with his wife."

Celeste glanced up at him. "You would only dance with Abigail, then."

He cocked his head as he pivoted her. "Are you going to pretend you don't know every single thing I confessed to Rhys and Pippa days ago? As if I don't know you all talk together about us?"

Her blush spread to her cheeks again but her eyes danced with playfulness as she said, "It would be polite of you to allow me to pretend that rather than calling me out right here on the floor."

"My wife would say I am never polite," he said.

Celeste shook her head. "You two do tease. It is very different from the rest of us. But there is something so lively in it. Like you're always having fun." She gazed across the floor toward Owen and Abigail again. "She is changing, Gilmore. We can all see it. Whatever you are doing, it does seem to be working."

Nathan swallowed, all the mischievous words fading from his mind. He looked at Abigail too. She did seem more relaxed now. And yet he knew she was still reluctant when it came to him. Fearful.

"I hope it's enough," he said softly. "It's a tightrope, you know. I try to give her space so that she knows her life is her own to control. But then I also must push those same boundaries, try to create some space where I can wiggle my way in closer to her heart. It's a bit like a battle. Attack and retreat, attack and retreat, hoping to make little gains each time."

"You've given her a great deal." Celeste squeezed his hand as they danced. "She went on and on about the garden she is planning when I saw her earlier tonight."

He nodded. "That is part of the plan. And my pleasure."

"But have you..." Celeste trailed off. "Perhaps I should not pry."

He wrinkled his brow. "I welcome any advice you might have, Celeste. Not only do you know my wife very well, but your own union seems very happy."

"Have you given her yourself?" she asked. "Because of what happened last year, so many of the worst moments in her life became public knowledge. We all know one of her greatest pains. She's a private person, and I'm certain that stings her."

He nodded. "Yes."

"It might make her feel less exposed if she also knew something about you."

Nathan thought of his wager with Abigail tonight. He had been trying to win the bet in order to keep her in his bed. But now he reconsidered. Celeste was right, after all. He knew about so much of Abigail's life: her heartbreak over her sister, her drive that had come out of that tragedy, her humiliation at the hands of Erasmus Montgomery. He even knew about her sacrifice to save his sister.

But he had not told her much about himself. Not because it was such a deep, dark secret as they often teased each other. But because he was so focused on her. But his past could be a gift. A way to offer vulnerability and perhaps show her that he could be trusted.

The music stopped, and Nathan executed a bow to Celeste as she curtseyed in return. As he led her from the dancefloor, he said, "You've given me something to think about. Thank you for that and for your support of our marriage."

She smiled. "You will always have it. I only wish you two the greatest happiness together."

He squeezed her hand. "I must see my sister before she dances too much tonight. Will you excuse me?"

Celeste seemed confused by that request, but she nodded regardless. He dashed away, seeking out Ophelia in the crowd. He found her at last, standing with some old friends, laughing at something they were saying. When he reached them, his expression must have spoken for itself, for her friends backed away.

"You look very driven," Ophelia said with a shake of her head. "What has you so intense, Nathan?"

"How many dances have you danced tonight?" he asked, almost breathless with hope.

She gave him an odd look, but removed her dance card from her reticule and fanned it out to look at it. "Er, it looks like I've danced six times tonight. You know, I had a dance with Louis Blankenship, the brother of the Earl of—"

Nathan shifted his weight in impatience. "Yes, but how many others have you promised?"

She pursed her lips and glanced at the card again. "It looks like two more spots are full at this point. I'm leaving my options open."

He sucked in a breath. That would put her total at eight by the end of the night. Close to the nine Abigail had guessed. "Will you do me the most enormous favor, and also not ask me why?"

"Are you well?" Ophelia asked. "Do you have a fever?"

"Please?" Nathan asked. "I will owe you the biggest boon."

"And I will collect it. What is the favor, then?" Ophelia sighed.

"Do not dance more than nine dances total."

She wrinkled her brow. "I want to ask why, but you've already told me I cannot." He nodded and held his breath as he awaited her answer. She shrugged. "I was already planning to limit my dances tonight so that I could appear mysterious. Very well, I will dance the other two I've promised and then save the remaining one for just the right man. If he ever bothers to show up."

Nathan leaned in and quickly kissed her cheek. "Thank you."

She shook her head. "You're as welcome as I am confused. And that is very."

He laughed, even as anxious excitement jolted through him. He did not often lose anything on purpose, but if he did this, perhaps it would have him on the road to win an even bigger prize: his wife's heart.

If he could do that, then nothing else in heaven or on earth mattered.

CHAPTER 23

The clock in the hall was chiming three when Abigail burst into the antechamber of their room, Nathan just at her heels. She was laughing, and she turned toward him. "Did you see the way Lady Fortescue was mooning over Mr. Barnes all night? Do you think that was to make her husband jealous, or was it a true connection?"

"I have no idea," he said, shutting the door behind himself. "But either way, they may create a scandal that will silence whatever is left of ours. Even Rhys and Pippa may benefit."

"Oh, I hope so," Abigail breathed. "Though I do have to say that it was a stroke of genius to invite the Duke and Duchess of Abernathe and of Willowby. They were so kind to Rhys and Pippa, almost protective. I think their fortunes were raised by the implied friendship."

Nathan tilted his head. "The fact that you care so much about everyone else's happiness is one of my favorite things about you."

She hesitated as the warmth of those words washed over her, but it was followed swiftly by a twinge of discomfort. He looked at her like he could see deep into her soul. She feared he could, and the last time she had allowed such a thing, it had ended so badly.

"Nathan—" she began softly.

He arched a brow. "I know exactly what you're going to say. You are going to crow."

"Crow?" she repeated with a shake of her head. "Over what?"

"Come now," he said, clucking his tongue as he slowly began to circle her. "Don't start being a good winner now. You bested me at our wager...again."

She worried her lip. She *had* been keeping track of Ophelia's number of dances throughout the night and she *was* very aware that she had won. And now it seemed he was willing to move on to that subject from the far more tender one.

She smiled. "Indeed, I have."

"And now I owe you a dark secret."

She moved a step toward him, growing more serious because she sensed real pain beneath the playfulness. "Nathan, I know we wagered this, but I do not hold you to it."

He wrinkled his brow. "You wouldn't dig into the grave?"

"Not if it will cause you pain."

He let his breath in a small laugh. "Of course you wouldn't." He took her hand. "Abigail, I have been privy to some of the worst moments of your life. Not because you wished me to be there, not because I was invited, but because of circumstance. I don't think it's so much to ask that you hear a little of my own history, painful as that exercise might be or not."

He motioned her toward his chamber, and she followed him. They took a place together in the chairs before the fire. He settled in, and she could see he was trying to exhibit all the signs that this didn't trouble him or move him. And yet she sensed the truth of it. She sensed a multiplication of the pain she'd felt in the antechamber.

Her hand trembled as she moved it to cover his. "Tell me," she said softly as she stroked her fingers along the top. "I'm here. I will be here."

And as she said those words, she realized how deeply she meant them. How much she wished to be this man's support, his steady north star. For the first time, that desire didn't frighten her, but it continued to mean the world to her. She would deal with the consequences of that realization later; for now she pushed it aside and put all her focus on him.

~

Nathan had spent the whole night telling himself how imperative this exercise was to winning Abigail. He'd focused on the outcome, that she would know him better, that she would see his vulnerability and perhaps learn to trust him more because of it.

All that remained true as he clung to her hand. And yet the reality of it hit him now. He had always been a private person. He didn't show the emotions that burned inside of him, for good or for bad, and yet he would strip down before this woman and show her every part of himself. Every pain.

He cleared this throat. "Not many people truly know me," he began. "Rhys is my friend, my brother, and I never troubled him with the most painful parts of my past. I think you and I are similar in that way. We self-protect."

She nodded slowly. "I learned the hard way. I suppose you must have, as well."

"Yes." His voice broke a fraction. "I watched my mother lay herself bare for my father every day she lived. She cut herself open for him, gave him everything…and it was not enough. And yes, I did learn that the kind of openness she showed was folly."

"He didn't love her in return?" she asked.

He held back a bark of humorless laughter. "No. They had an arranged marriage, almost from the moment my mother was born. But she fell in love with him, worshipped him. He? Not so much. When she chased him, he ran. When she bore his heir, then his daughter, he hardly came home long enough to look at either of us."

She flinched. "I am sorry. That must have broken her heart."

"It did, I know. I saw it. She would weep and gnash her teeth and tell me all the details of what he was doing wrong, what he was doing behind her back."

Abigail lifted her hand to her mouth. "To a child?" she gasped.

"At the time, I only wanted to comfort her. As I got older, as I became guardian to my sister and had to learn how to parent her, I could see what a burden my mother had laid on my shoulders. That she expected me to ride to her rescue when he wouldn't."

"What about your father?" she asked. "Was he kinder to you as he grew older?"

"No," he said, his tone flat as memories mobbed him. "My father was more interested in whoring and drinking and gambling his way around London. He was a rake and celebrated that with every action and word. His only attachment to me was that I was to inherit his title. He only ever ignored me or harshly corrected me."

"For what wrongs?" she asked.

"Whatever I did, it was never enough," he said. "What was worse was that my mother was so desperate to earn his affection that she would agree with whatever he did or said. As I got older, she began to blame me when he left for days on end. If only I was better, if only I was perfect, if only—"

He cut himself off because he realized his hands were shaking as he spoke these words he had never let be said out loud. His throat felt tight and his lungs burned. Abigail reached for him, taking his hands in both of hers as she scooted to the front of the chair and held his gaze.

And there was peace. He looked into her eyes and found peace there. Which only made him love her all the more, not that he had ever thought that possible.

"You were a child," she whispered. "It was unfair of her to place such a burden on your shoulders."

"Yes," he said. "But I took it. And I took it even more when she started to turn that sharpness onto Ophelia. I stepped in front of my sister, tried to be the shield between her and the failings of them both."

"How old were you?" she asked as her fingers traced gentle patterns on the top of his hand.

"Sixteen," he said. "Ophelia was five."

Her expression collapsed slightly. "Oh, Nathan."

He nodded. "I learned to be dependable out of self-preservation. For me, for my sister. And then, when I was twenty-two...they died."

"In an accident," she said softly. When he pulled back in surprise, she shrugged. "If you looked into my past, you cannot be angry that I did a little of the same with yours. The surface story is that they were in a carriage accident during bad weather in Scotland."

"They were both drunk," he muttered. "They'd taken some trip there to rekindle the flame. Occasionally she could convince him to do so. But they'd been seen arguing loudly at an inn. Whatever the truth of how that day ended, the only thing that mattered is that neither survived."

"You were so young to take on such responsibility."

"Yes," he agreed. "His title and his mistakes were slung around my neck. An albatross, if I let them be. Not to mention I was now guardian to an eleven-year-old girl who had been through a great deal in her short life. She'd already begun to go wild." He laughed softly. "Sometimes she still is."

That elicited a smile from Abigail. "Ophelia is charming and unfettered. She isn't *that* wild."

"Because she's on what is, regretfully, her best behavior as she's tried to defend me," he insisted with an arched brow. He shook his head. "So that is my great, terrible history. The secrets I never told anyone else. Perhaps because they weren't all that terrible after all."

She held his hands tighter. "You say that now, but I can tell how much these things pained you, Nathan. What happened wasn't fair. You didn't deserve to have such selfish, irresponsible parents."

Those words sank into him. Into his heart. Into the places where he had tried to shove away the fear and uncertainty of his growing up. "Thank you," he said softly. "I did what needed to be done to get through it all. But I hope knowing this helps you understand the worst parts of me. The parts I know you do not like."

She wrinkled her brow. "That I don't like?"

"If I am sometimes cold, if I sometimes reacted baldly to our shared past...it is because I abhor the kind of damage that kind of irresponsibility can create. I don't think that excuses what I've done, but I am trying to do...better, though. To be a better man in the future."

She stared at him for so long, he momentarily thought she hadn't understood him, but then she got up and sank down into his lap. She wrapped her arms around his neck.

"Let me explain something to you, Your Grace. If there is anything I know about you, Nathan, it is that you are dependable. That may not seem the most romantic notion on the surface, but it very much is if you've never expected it. I had bad parents, as well as a bounder of a first husband. So you are...you are a lovely dream after a terrible nightmare. And I don't dislike you for any of those things."

He gazed into her eyes for a moment, feeling her discomfort with this closeness, with these admissions, but also the deep truth of them. He gave a half smile. "Had I known that painful honesty was all it took to get you to compliment me, I would have done it months ago."

She laughed, her expression lighting up. "Oh don't worry, I do have a great, long list of your faults, too."

"I cannot wait to hear them," he said with false solemnity.

She sighed before she cupped his cheeks and then leaned in. Just before her lips found his, she whispered, "Thank you for telling me."

The kiss was feather-light at first. A gentle comfort, a quiet understanding. But as it went on, the tension it created began to grow. He flexed his fingers against her hip, she began to lightly grind down in his lap, she opened her mouth and allowed him to taste her.

They were both short of breath when she pulled away. "Now you promised to remove this gown with your teeth." She stood up and drew him to his feet. "So I expect you to deliver."

She backed toward the bed, eyes bright with desire, but also a need to connect with him. And as he caught her waist and drew her to him for another deep kiss, he hoped that they were inching closer to the moment where the barriers between them came down. Where he could love her openly and without frightening her away...and where maybe, just maybe, she could love him in return.

~

Abigail had doubted that one could remove such a beautiful gown with just teeth, and yet Nathan never failed to surprise her. He'd done it. But then he could surprise her with a look, with a touch or with the honesty with which he'd told her of his past. She understood so much more about him now.

And the parts of him that had been broken by the past called out to the parts of her that had endured something similar.

Right now, though, she didn't want to think about that. Right now she just wanted to touch him, especially since he'd removed all of his clothes after removing hers.

She crooked her finger and he joined her beside the bed, catching her by the waist, molding her naked body to his. When he kissed her, she relaxed against him. When he touched her, it was like coming home. She pressed her mouth to his shoulder, licking and nipping at his flesh. He hissed out a breath and cupped her backside, massaging there, grinding her pelvis to his and letting her feel the press of his hard cock against her belly.

She glided a hand between them and caught it, stroking it while she continued to nuzzle his shoulders, his collarbone, his throat.

"You are playing with fire," he rasped.

"Then burn me," she murmured in reply.

He jerked his head back and stared down at her. Then he lifted her to lean her against the edge of the bed. He pushed her legs apart and she trembled. He aligned their bodies and she moaned. Fast and hard, he thrust into her, but there was no resistance. She was ready for him. Always ready for him.

He thrust, digging his hand into her hair and tilting her head back so he could take her mouth as he took her body. She lifted against him, seeking pleasure, finding it so easily, like it was always there waiting for her.

He took her. That was the only way to describe it. He pounded hard into her, his groans and grunts increasing as she began to flutter with orgasm. The flutters turned to waves, the waves to clenching, overpowering pleasure. She keened against his skin, scraping her teeth over him like she could mark him as hers, and he swore as he came deep inside of her.

For a few moments they just stood there, foreheads pressed together, bodies entangled, their panting breaths slowing and matching.

"Too hard?" he asked at last.

She drew back. "God, no. That was remarkable."

He sighed as if relieved as well as satiated and then set her down so she could rest her feet on the ground again. They stared at each other. This was the point where she would normally gather her clothing and pad off to her own bedroom and its lonely bed.

But she didn't want to do that tonight. So much had been shared between them, she wasn't ready to let go.

"You know," she said softly. "It is possible we missed your sister dancing at some point."

He arched a brow. "You mean that she might have taken a turn around the dancefloor with ten gentlemen rather than nine?"

She nodded. "I was not always watching, you know. I assume you weren't either. So it might have been ten or eleven. And our agreement was that the person with the closest guess without going over would win. If we miscounted, that would mean I was the loser."

There was a tension to his face now. Almost an anticipation. "So you would owe me the boon."

"I wouldn't want to accidentally cheat my way out of paying the terms."

"Which are to sleep in my bed," he said.

"Yes. If you want me there."

He pulled the covers back with a flourish and smiled. "I do, Your Grace. Won't you join me?"

She shivered as she slipped into the sheets and he joined her. When he settled, she rolled against his side, placing her head on his shoulder. He wrapped his arms around her and held her there. It was warm and safe, or at least it felt that way in this charged moment.

But she still feared that if she let herself, she might never want to let him go. And the pure terror of that notion still ruined the perfect peace of whatever they were building.

She pushed all that away. It was just a night in a bed, nothing more. She wouldn't let it mean more than that...even if she desperately wanted to.

CHAPTER 24

"Abigail?"

Abigail jumped, her cheeks heating as she realized Ophelia was calling her name as she stared off into space. Her mind had wandered, as it had been wont to do these past few days. Where it took her? To Nathan.

It had been three days since the ball, and something had changed between them. Things were lighter when they spoke or touched or smiled at each other. And she had been sleeping in his bed each night, no longer running to hide in her own chamber to escape him.

But now Ophelia stared at her from the chair across from hers, brow wrinkled, and she was clearly expecting a response.

"I'm so sorry. I am woolgathering, it seems. Leagues away."

"It seems a more common experience for you lately," Ophelia said with a knowing smile. "I look and there you are, staring out a window or reading a book upside down."

"You are teasing me," Abigail said with a laugh.

"Am I?" Ophelia sat back and gave her a long look. "If I didn't know you better, I would say you are mooning."

"I'm not mooning!" Abigail burst out. But she felt very seen by these accusations. Too seen for comfort. "If I'm distracted, I'm just thinking of my garden and our plans for later this summer."

Ophelia arched a brow. "I see. Well, then I suppose I can do nothing but believe that. However, I wonder then, what do you think my brother is mooning about? He is suffering from the same affliction, and I do not think he cares as much about your garden as you do."

Abigail pursed her lips. Ophelia was treading in dangerous waters. "You would have to speak to him on that topic, I suppose. I could not speak to the inner workings of Nathan's mind."

Ophelia got up with a bark of laughter. "Well, perhaps I shall. I can ask him about why he's always got a secret little smile on his face now. Or perhaps I'll inquire about his new habit of playing faro with us every night after supper when I know he was never a fan of the game until you spoke of enjoying it."

Abigail blinked. Was that true?

"Or..." Ophelia laughed. "Perhaps I will finally get an answer from him about why he insisted I limit the number of partners I danced with at the ball a few nights ago."

Abigail sat up straighter. "Wait...what are you talking about?"

Ophelia's smile widened. "It was the oddest thing. Halfway through the night, he rushed over to me and begged me not to dance with more than nine partners in total. He refused to tell me why, but seemed willing to trade anything in order to get his way. One can only imagine it had something to do with you, because everything he does seems related to you now."

Abigail continued to stare at her sister-in-law, but her ears had begun to ring. Nathan had interfered in the outcome of their wager... in order to *lose*? Why would he do that? Unless he wished to tell her the story of the past...

But to what end? Was he trying to manipulate her? Trick her somehow?

She got up, hands shaking with all the questions. "I...I must excuse myself."

Ophelia's smile fell. "You have gone pale as paper. Did I say something wrong? I was only joking."

"No." Abigail caught her hands. "You did nothing wrong. I just...I must go speak to your brother about something."

She pivoted then, hurrying from the room with Ophelia's concerned voice calling out for her. She ignored it as she made her way toward Nathan's study. A few weeks ago, she might have simply ignored this issue. She would have seen it as proof he was behaving duplicitously and built an even higher wall between them.

But because of the last few days and nights, she found she couldn't dismiss him so easily. She wanted to know the truth. Even if it hurt.

She knocked and heard papers rustling. Nathan's tone was distracted as he called out, "Enter" from within.

She smoothed her dress and then did just that. He was focused on the ledger before him, the quill in his hand poised over the sheet before him. His jacket was draped across the chair behind him, his sleeves were rolled to the elbow. Her breath caught at the sight of him.

He glanced at her, and his expression lit up. "Well, this is a welcome surprise," he said, rising. "I thought you and Ophelia were having tea and then you were going to talk about the book you finished this morning."

She pursed her lips and tugged the door closed behind her. She stared at him, trying to find the words she wanted to say. Knowing that once she said them that everything would shift between them. Because it was inevitable. She'd known it for a long time.

"What is it?" he asked, his face growing concerned as he came around the desk toward her. "Abigail?"

"Why did you manipulate the outcome of our wager at the ball?" she asked in a rush of words.

But the jumbled way she asked the question didn't seem to impact his understanding. He came to a halt midway to her side.

"Ophelia told you that?" he asked after it felt like a lifetime had passed.

She nodded. "Yes. She said you asked her not to dance more than nine times. So that I would win, I assume. So that you could tell me about your past." She worried her hands before her. "Were you manipulating me, Nathan? Was this all part of some game?"

His eyes went wide. "No. Not a game. I suppose you could see it as a manipulation." Her heart sank and she gripped her hands at her sides. He shook his head at the reaction. "But not the way you think."

"Then explain it to me," she whispered. "I want you to explain."

"I *did* want to tell you about my past," he said. "For the very reasons I told you that night. Because I was privy to a great deal of your pain and wanted to even that score a fraction. I wanted to give you some piece of myself. And I thought you would more eagerly accept it if it was because you'd won the day."

She shook her head slowly. "But why, Nathan?"

He sucked in a long, slow breath. "It was always going to come to this," he said softly, almost as if more to himself than to her.

"What has come to what?" she asked, and hated how it felt like her throat was closing.

He shut his eyes and drew a deep breath. When he opened them, something in his expression had changed. He looked...peaceful. Certain. He reached for her, and she was too mesmerized to back away.

He took her hand and lifted it to press to his heart. "Abigail...I love you."

The world stopped spinning. It had to have stopped because it felt like everything had changed, not only this room or this man or her future. She stared at him, half-wondering if this was some dream and yet knowing it was real.

"You can't love me," she whispered because she didn't know what else to say. "You can't."

"But I do," he said, and smiled gently. "I felt the sharpness of it the first time I met you, even though we were contentious. It was why I kept coming back, poking my nose in, as you so often put it, during Owen's investigation."

Her mouth dropped open in shock. "No. No, you were stepping in because you wanted to protect Rhys. Because of the situation with your sister."

He shook his head. "I told myself that. I told you that. But the truth was, I wanted to protect *you*. Not only out of some guilt that I'd brought hell down on you. Out of a pure desire to see you happy."

She tried to tug her hand away, but he clung to her gently. "No, this cannot be true."

"And yet it is. What I felt for you didn't go away, even when the case was over. Even when you went into your official mourning period and we tried so hard to avoid each other. Do you know I used to ride past your house?"

"You did?"

He nodded. "Every few days, even though it wasn't on my way to anything. I wanted to catch a glimpse of you. When I did, I tried to explain the thrill I felt as some kind of adversarial emotion. But it wasn't. I know that now."

She stumbled away, and this time he let her go. She walked, not seeing anything before her, staggered to the window and pressed her hand to the cool glass as if the shock of it would pull her from this truth. From this man.

When she could form no words, he continued, "When I started seeing you again regularly, it was like a light came back on in my life. Before we were caught and forced to marry, dancing the dance was the highlight of any day."

She looked at him over her shoulder. "But you never said a word."

"I refused to admit my heart," he said. "I tried to pretend it wasn't happening until the day I realized that *you* were the one who wrote the letter that saved my sister from Montgomery."

Now she did spin around with a gasp. He nodded slowly. "Yes. I realized the truth."

"H-how?"

"You wrote me that note to say you were going to Celeste and Owen's after our argument. I recognized the handwriting."

She covered her burning cheeks with her cold fingers. "I didn't want you to know."

"I realize that," he said gently. "Because you didn't trust me. Because you didn't want to draw attention to what you'd done. Because you are selfless. Because *he* broke your heart and you are so afraid to let someone else hold it."

She hadn't realized she'd been holding her breath until that moment when she gasped it out. "Don't say that."

She turned away again, and he was quiet for a moment as she tried to gather herself.

"But it's true," he whispered. "All of it is true. And when I realized what you'd done, everything became crystal clear. I knew I loved you. And that I had to act. Look at me."

She hesitated, but then slowly turned to face him. She saw the truth of every word he was speaking in every line of him. Every emotion he was expressing was present in his eyes and his smile and the way he held himself.

"Every wager was an I love you, Abigail," he said softly. "Every little teasing gesture. Every time I touched you, I branded *I love you* into your skin. And every time you pushed me away, that feeling only got stronger, not weaker. I love you. Not because you saved my sister, not because you are such a good person that you risked yourself for someone else. I loved you before I knew that. And that only gave me the excuse to woo you as I should have done from the moment we met."

She blinked and thought back to the time that had passed since that argument. To the way he had taken care of her, pampered her, shared with her. To all those tiny declarations of the love he was expressing to her now. The love of action, the love of intention.

Of temptation.

He moved toward her, and she was too frozen by it all to step away. He touched her face, tracing her cheek with just his fingertip. "When we told the world we were in a great love story, I should have made that true immediately. Because I believe we are. If you trust me, if you allow yourself to love me, I promise you that we can be."

Her feelings burned inside of her as she held his gaze. The ones she had pushed aside for weeks, months. The thrill every time she saw him coming back to haunt her. To reveal her heart to her just as he had revealed his own.

"I cannot trust myself," she whispered.

"But you can trust me," he insisted. "And if you let yourself, come to love me, I hope."

She blinked. "Come to love you. No."

He flinched ever so slightly. "You think there is no chance?"

"No, I'm telling you that I already...I already love you, as well," she burst out.

The words hung between them, but to his credit, he didn't launch himself at her. He didn't celebrate. He lit up like a thousand candles, but he didn't force her into a position where she didn't wish to be.

"Nathan, some part of me was broken when all of Montgomery's lies came out. I promised myself I would never risk my heart again. And yet here I am, and the risk is even bigger because I have never felt the way I do when I'm with you. It is so much stronger and more beautiful and more abjectly terrifying than it was with him. There is so much more to lose if we fail. And I'm so afraid to fail."

"But what if we don't fail?" he said. "What if we work together, what if we promise to be honest, what if we only act with each other's best interest at heart from today until the world stops turning? Because I can promise you that, Abigail."

She leaned forward until her forehead rested against his chest. She could feel his heart thudding wildly, and she gripped his biceps to steady herself.

She considered this man she leaned on. The man who challenged her, who expected marvelous things from her, the man who encouraged her dreams. The man who could make her weak but never held it against her. The man who was always honest. Who understood the value of dedication and responsibility.

If she said no to him, if she pushed him away again and again, she had no doubt that at some point she could break him. She could make him stop loving her with enough time.

But what a loss that would be. What a tragedy to be so fearful of a past with another man, an entirely separate life, that she would throw away the future.

"I don't want to throw away the future," she whispered.

He cupped her chin and tilted her face up so that she looked at him. "Then *make* it with me."

She smiled, because there was nothing else to do but smile when she was staring into the face of the man she loved. The man who somehow loved her.

"Yes."

"Yes?" he repeated, eyes going wide.

"Yes," she said again, this time louder and stronger. "Yes, Nathan. I do love you, and I will fight for you and let you fight for me."

He tugged her closer, his arms coming around her, warm and comforting. When he claimed her mouth, she opened to him, this time fully and with no fear to stop her from truly feeling their connection.

And she knew with perfect certainty in that moment that nothing could ever tear them apart. Because she wouldn't let it.

EPILOGUE

Six Months Later

The parlor off the foyer in Abigail and Nathan's home in London was a cacophony of sound and laughter, but of course it would be. After a few months with everyone in their separate country homes, the three former Mrs. Montgomerys and their husbands had come together for a joyful reunion.

And there was so much to celebrate. Abigail rested a hand on Celeste's pregnant belly and laughed as her baby kicked in response. Owen wrapped an arm around his wife and beamed, the couple's pure joy and excitement about their impending arrival written all over their faces.

Rhys shifted his nephew to his hip and took Pippa's hand as they talked together at the fire. Much had changed for the couple, and all of it for the better. The steadfast loyalty of Nathan, and the welcome of the powerful dukes of the 1797 Club, had helped him find his way back into Society. Abigail was so proud of Nathan's unwavering affection for his friend.

Ophelia had also joined their happy little group. She'd spent some time traveling to see relatives and friends over the winter. Abigail thought she was trying to give her time with Nathan, and she appreciated it. At the isolated estate in Cornwall, their love had only blossomed further. She had come to fully trust him, because he proved again and again that he earned it. She had never been happier, she had never been more loved.

He caught her hand and drew her away from their friends for a moment. "I'd forgotten what it was like not to have you all to myself," he murmured close to her ear. "I think I'll spirit you away back to the estate and just keep you there."

She laughed. "I wouldn't argue. However, I have missed everyone." She slipped an arm around his waist. "Just think...a year and a half ago, Celeste, Pippa and I had only just found out about Erasmus's bigamy. We weren't friends yet, we were all lost and terrified about the future. And now we're close as sisters and all of us have found love and security."

He nodded. "I would not have wished such heartbreak on any of you, but it did bring you together. It brought all of you to the ones you were meant to love. It saved all of the men who are lucky enough to be loved by you."

She faced him. "Did I save you?" she asked.

She was teasing, but he didn't smile in return. He nodded, and it was a solemn thing. "You saved me, you *save* me and I am forever in your debt."

"Then I suppose we have no choice but to live happily ever after."

He bent to kiss her gently. "Happily. Ever. After."

The Regency Royals Series

This summer start a new adventure with Jess Michaels when her new series, Regency Royals launches! When the Royal Family of Athawick comes to London to join in the pleasures of the Season, they spark excitement, danger and maybe...just maybe...love. Here's the first look at *To Protect a Princess*, Book 1 of the series, out July 21.

Enjoy an Excerpt of
To Protect A Princess

❦

The Season of 1817 would become known for a great many things in the end, but at the beginning, all of Society was buzzing about one thing: the visit from the King and his family. But they weren't referring to their own king, gouty and mad in his tower. Or their future king, who flitted from brothel to brothel with his demands for champagne with breakfast. No, the buzz was about an entirely different monarch, the King of Athawick.

Such a tiny island for such a big stir, and yet Princess Ilaria, youngest sibling and only sister of the king, knew there would be stir. There was always stir when it came to her family. Their island's situation in the trade routes of the North Sea had always made them important...and precarious if she could believe her brother as he paced his study, that newly placed crown so heavy on his head and shoulders.

She leaned against the railing of the ship and closed her eyes as the salt air caressed her face. Every moment took them closer to England. Closer to a few months of madness. Her brother, of course, would not remain for that entire time, but their mother was insistent that Ilaria and her second oldest brother, Remington, take a Season in London. And their mother was not one to be denied.

"Your highness?"

Ilaria opened her eyes and squinted against the bright reflection of sunlight on the water before she turned. Her brother's steward, Stephen Blairford, was standing there, his lips pressed in a tight, irritated line, just as they always were. She had never liked the man, not when he served their father, not when he served Grantham.

"What is it?" she asked.

"The King and the Queen desire your presence in the family drawing room," he said. "Immediately."

The way he added the last made it sound like an order. And she supposed it was, though it chafed. Here she was supposed to take precedence, but courtiers carried power. And this one knew it.

"Very well." He motioned as if he would lead her and she jerked away from him. "I know where the drawing room is, Blairford. Thank you."

She walked away and to his credit, Blairford didn't follow. At least he knew his place that far. She made her way through the doors that led off the ship deck and through a narrow hallway to a large, ornately carved door. It was open at present and she could hear the voices of both her brothers and her mother drifting into the hallway.

"...how she will react..." came her mother's voice and Ilaria stiffened. That didn't sound positive.

She thrust her shoulders back and entered the room. "How who will react?" she asked as she pulled the door shut behind them for privacy.

Her brother, the new king of Athawick, stood ramrod straight in the middle of the room, every line of his clothing perfect, every hair in place. She could scarcely even recognize him as the brother who had ran with her through fields in Athawick a decade before, two decades. He looked stern and cross and...tired. She could see he was tired.

Her mother, Queen Giabella, sat on a settee in the middle of the room, a cup of tea perched in her fingertips. She was stunningly beautiful, no matter her years. Her thick, dark hair was only slightly touched by gray and her sharp brown eyes flitted over Ilaria from head to toe...judging, no doubt.

Her mother's secretary, Dashiell Talbot, sat at the escritoire on one side of the room, a quill poised over a thick sheet of vellum. Ilaria's heart sank. Unlike Grantham's man, she adored Dashiell. He'd been working for her mother for nearly a decade and was always wonderful. But when he was about to take notes, it meant something official was happening.

Last, but certainly not least because he wouldn't allow it, was Remington. Her second oldest brother leaned lazily against the mantel, a drink in his hand and a bored expression on his face. Remi did his best to play layabout prince, though Ilaria knew there was far more to him than just that. He arched a brow at her, held her stare.

God's teeth, something was going on and she dreaded it down to her toes.

"You know, before you answer my question," she said, crossing to the sideboard. "I need a drink."

Her mother pursed her lips. "I expect that sort of thing from Remi, but you really must be more proper, especially as we enter English Society, my dear."

Ilaria pursed her lips to keep from a sharp retort, but she still poured her drink and then crossed to stand beside Remi at the fireplace. He gave her a side glance that said multitudes.

"You called me here, Your Majesties," she said. "And clearly it isn't about family business in general, but about me. So what is it? How could I have possibly offended during the last day and a half on board a ship in the middle of the North Sea?"

Grantham took a step toward her. "You've offended no one, Ilaria. Mother and I simply believe it is…time to discuss…the…the…"

"The future," their mother finished with a quick side glance to Dashiell at the desk. He lifted his gaze as if sensing her stare and gave a tiny nod before he went back to madly scribbling.

"The future entails us disembarking on the shores of foggy, dirty London," Ilaria said. "And spending what will surely be a few boring months of balls and official events. I've agreed to attend them all in order to help you, Grantham, what else do you wish of me?"

Her mother rose from the settee and moved toward her, dark eyes locking with Ilaria's. Now her heartrate rose, fear fluttered.

"It is time for you to be married, Ilaria," the queen said softly, almost gently. "At twenty-five, some would say high past time and perhaps we would have pushed this issue sooner if not for your father's illness and death. But here we are and we have been granted an opportunity by the fact that your brother has been coronated at last and the world has some interest in our family's tour."

"England is not the world," Ilaria snapped.

Remi chuckled. "They believe they are. They're certainly trying to conquer enough of it."

"*That* is the material problem," Grantham said, his gaze growing sharp as it focused on Remi. "Yes, they are land mad and resource mad. And Athawick may not have much of one, but we have plenty of the other thanks to the trade route. Generations of our family have fought and occasionally died to remain out of the Empire's reach and I will not have that all fall apart during my watch. Ilaria, you are of an age to marry. And if you are linked to an important family of Britain, there is some thought that it will continue to protect Athawick."

She blinked. "You are going to barter me for freedom."

ALSO BY JESS MICHAELS

The Three Mrs

The Unexpected Wife

The Defiant Wife

The Duke's Wife

The Duke's By-Blows

The Love of a Libertine

The Heart of a Hellion

The Matter of a Marquess

The Redemption of a Rogue

The 1797 Club

The Daring Duke

Her Favorite Duke

The Broken Duke

The Silent Duke

The Duke of Nothing

The Undercover Duke

The Duke of Hearts

The Duke Who Lied

The Duke of Desire

The Last Duke

The Scandal Sheet

The Return of Lady Jane

Stealing the Duke

Lady No Says Yes

My Fair Viscount

Guarding the Countess

The House of Pleasure

Seasons

An Affair in Winter

A Spring Deception

One Summer of Surrender

Adored in Autumn

The Wicked Woodleys

Forbidden

Deceived

Tempted

Ruined

Seduced

Fascinated

The Notorious Flynns

The Other Duke

The Scoundrel's Lover

The Widow Wager

No Gentleman for Georgina

A Marquis for Mary

To see a complete listing of Jess Michaels' titles, please visit:
http://www.authorjessmichaels.com/books